She pushed him aside,
hiked up her skirt,
and took off running . . .

Narice ran track in both high school and college, but that had been over a decade ago. She also hadn't done it wearing three-hundred-dollar Italian pumps. But she had a head start and her old training kicked in. Moving like an athlete and not like the fancy CEO of Jordan Academy, her strides took her into the shadows of the buildings that made up the motel's complex.

Breathing hard from exertion and adrenaline, she ducked into an alley between two buildings that led to the main road. She could hear cars peeling out of the lot behind her, apparently in pursuit. She could also hear the pounding footsteps of her would-be captor.

He was gaining on her. Out of the corner of her eye, she spotted the cab. Waving her arms and shouting, she tried to flag it down, but a big, black SUV came out of nowhere, blocking the cab's way. Narice kept running.

Her goal now was the motel's office. Once there, she could call the police.

She never made it.

A blink later, he threw a powerful arm around her waist and swung her up and off her feet. He had the nerve to be laughing.

"I know you didn't really expect to get away in those shoes."

By Beverly Jenkins

THE EDGE OF DAWN
THE EDGE OF MIDNIGHT

ATTENTION: ORGANIZATIONS AND CORPORATIONS
Most HarperTorch paperbacks are available at special quantity discounts for bulk purchases for sales promotions, premiums, or fund-raising. For information, please call or write:

Special Markets Department, HarperCollins Publishers, Inc., 10 East 53rd Street, New York, N.Y. 10022-5299. Telephone: (212) 207-7528. Fax: (212) 207-7222.

BEVERLY JENKINS

THE EDGE OF DAWN

HarperTorch
An Imprint of HarperCollins*Publishers*

This is a work of fiction. Names, characters, places, and incidents are products of the author's imagination or are used fictitiously and are not to be construed as real. Any resemblance to actual events, locales, organizations, or persons, living or dead, is entirely coincidental.

HARPERTORCH
An Imprint of HarperCollins*Publishers*
10 East 53rd Street
New York, New York 10022-5299

Copyright © 2004 by Beverly Jenkins
ISBN: 0-06-054067-2

All rights reserved. No part of this book may be used or reproduced in any manner whatsoever without written permission, except in the case of brief quotations embodied in critical articles and reviews. For information address HarperTorch, an Imprint of HarperCollins Publishers.

First HarperTorch paperback printing: November 2004

HarperCollins®, HarperTorch™, and ™ are trademarks of HarperCollins Publishers Inc.

Printed in the United States of America

Visit HarperTorch on the World Wide Web at www.harpercollins.com

10 9 8 7 6 5 4 3 2 1

If you purchased this book without a cover, you should be aware that this book is stolen property. It was reported as "unsold and destroyed" to the publisher, and neither the author nor the publisher has received any payment for this "stripped book."

Woodson

To Karen Simpson, April Shipp,
and all their quilting sisters
for keeping the traditions alive

One

Arson. The word and its implications echoed inside thirty-seven-year-old Narice Jordan like remnants of a bad dream. *Arson.* No matter where she turned the word was there, laughing, taunting, reminding her that the fire responsible for her father's death had been deliberately set. According to the Detroit police a person or persons unknown had poured gasoline around the perimeter of Simon Jordan's home, then tossed in a match. The memorial celebrating his life had been held yesterday, and now a brokenhearted Narice stood waiting in her motel room for a cab to the Detroit airport for her pre-dawn flight back home to Baltimore.

She hadn't been able to sleep, so she was staring at a twenty-four-hour stretch with no rest. Both mind and spirit were exhausted. The cab company dispatcher promised the driver would arrive by three A.M. According to the gold watch on Narice's brown wrist, it was just about that time now.

As if cued, a knock sounded on the door. "Who is it?" she asked through the wood. A peek through the tiny spy hole showed a short, stocky brother dressed in an ill-fitting olive green suit.

"You called a cab?"

Narice undid the locks and opened up. "Yes, I did."

He showed her a smile. "You Ms. Jordan? Going to the airport?"

She nodded. "Let me get my bag." Narice had already settled her bill, courtesy of the check-out service on the TV, so she had no need to go down to the desk. She took a quick look around the room to make sure she hadn't left anything behind. Satisfied, she grabbed up her purse and the handle on the wheeled suitcase. Exiting, she closed the door softly behind her.

It was dark. The air was still close and sticky like it is sometimes in mid July. As she followed the driver down the stairs she could feel the heat building up inside her black suit, but she paid it little mind. She was too busy mentally blessing the cabbie for being early. She hated rushing through airports.

The yellow cab glowed eerily under the glare of the big lights ringing the parking lot. The heels of her pumps clicked loudly on the pavement. The driver opened the passenger door and took the suitcase from her. "I'll put it in the trunk. You get on in."

Before doing so, Narice fished around in her shoulder bag to make sure she had her ticket. After putting her hand on it, she bent to get into the back seat and froze at the sight of the well-dressed White man in the corner with the gun in his hand. "Come in, Ms. Jordan. I've been waiting for you."

Fear made her instinctively back up and away, but the stocky body of the driver firmly blocked her path.

"Get in," the cabbie ordered.

"No!" she yelled, but before she could tense her body for fight, the driver stuck a gun in her ribs. She stilled.

He whispered harshly. "Do you want your family to bury you, too?"

Narice's head snapped around. Did he know something about her father's death? Afraid, she said, "Who are you?"

He answered by forcing her into the cab. The door slammed shut beside her and her fear climbed. She stared at the man in the shadowy corner. He was smiling. "Put on your seat belt, Ms. Jordan. We wouldn't want anything to happen to you."

She eyed the man warily. "Where are you taking me?" Every horror imaginable played vividly through her mind.

"Just put on your belt."

Auto safety was not her concern. "Where are we going?"

"Relax. No one's going to hurt you."

Relaxing was impossible; she was scared to death.

As the cab pulled away, she prayed someone had seen her being pushed into the cab and that they would call the police, but she didn't hold much hope.

They left the motel lot without incident, turned onto Woodward and headed downtown. Narice could see a few other cars traveling the same route, but at this time of morning traffic was sparse. The cab stopped at a red light and a police car cruised up and stopped a lane over. Narice's hope soared. She had to let them know she needed help. She gave a quick look over at the man seated in the shadows. He had his gun pointed her way. "Sit back against the seat, Ms. Jordan. Slowly, please."

Her hope withered. Tight-lipped, she complied. A few seconds later she watched the light turn green. The police rode beside the cab through the next two lights, then the officers must have received a call because their car suddenly accelerated. Lights flashing, they roared away.

Narice felt very alone. Another look over at the shadowy man showed his slow, pleased smile. She was fighting to keep herself under control so she could think, but it was hard. *What is this about? Where am I being taken? Who are these men?* A million questions screamed for answers. "Where are you taking me?"

"The better question is *why*?"

Her reply was terse. "Okay, I'll bite. Why?"

"Because you hold the key to a long-lost treasure."

"What kind of treasure?"

"A beautiful blue diamond known as the Eye of Sheba."

Narice had no idea what he was talking about. "I

think you snatched the wrong person. I don't know anything about a diamond."

"But your father did."

Narice stilled. She studied him for a moment and wondered what was really going on here. She noted that he'd spoken about her father in the past tense. "You knew my father?"

"Once upon a time. Yes."

"He died in a house fire last week."

"I know."

"The police are calling it arson. Do you know who set the fire?"

"If I tell you too much now, you may not tell me what I wish to know later. Let's just enjoy the ride, shall we?"

"Who are you?"

"My name is Arthur Ridley and that is the last answer I intend to give."

Narice didn't know what to do or think. Her father had never mentioned a diamond. *Maybe this is all just a big mistake,* she thought, hoped, but the man named Ridley seemed convinced and that made her more afraid.

The cab was almost downtown now. Narice had been born and raised in Detroit. She was as pleased as all Detroiters over the revitalization of the city. Some pockets of blight still remained, however, and they were now cruising through one such strip. The light ahead was red, so the cabbie slowed to a stop.

Out of the darkness appeared three squeegee guys

dressed in black. Their faces were hidden behind ski masks and they immediately began spraying the windshield with clear liquid and wiping the glass clean with rags. Narice's hopes for rescue rose once more, but before she could come up with a way to get their attention, Ridley said softly, "One word or one move and I shoot you, Ms. Jordan."

She heard the driver up front shout angrily. "Get the hell out of here!" but the men ignored him and kept on spraying and wiping.

The driver hit the locks and threw open the door, "Dammit. I said—" He got out, intending to threaten them with his gun but one of the men had already drawn his own gun and had it in the cabby's surprised face. Narice drew in a frightened breath then jumped, startled as the door beside Ridley was yanked open and a big gun stuck in his face before he could react. It was all happening so fast, Narice didn't know where to look.

Ridley was told, "Give me the gun."

He handed it over.

"Now, get out."

"And if I refuse?"

"I shoot you right here."

For the first time, Ridley looked up into the masked face behind the gun. Narice saw Ridley smile. He said, "I recognize that voice. Fancy meeting you here, St. Martin."

The man in the mask didn't appear surprised that he'd been recognized. "The pleasure is all yours."

"You're on this hunt, too?"

"I am."

Ridley turned to the anxious-looking Narice and warned, "Don't trust a word this man says, Ms. Jordan. He'd torture his own mother."

That bit of advice got Ridley yanked out of the cab and thrown against the side of the vehicle. Hard.

The men out front were busy frisking the furious driver and the man with Ridley seemed occupied as well, so Narice slid over to her still-closed door and, trying not to draw attention to herself, slowly slipped off her pumps and tucked her shoulder bag close to her body. Taking a discreet look around to make sure no one was paying her any attention, she eased open the door and took off at a dead run. Narice had no idea where she was going but knew she needed to put as much distance as possible between herself and that cab. As she darted across the wide lanes, dodging cars and hearing horns blowing, she also heard a male voice holler with surprise, "Get her!" but by then she was in full stride.

Narice had run track in both high school and college, but that had been over a decade ago, and she hadn't done it wearing an expensive Italian suit with a straight skirt, but she had a head start on any pursuit, and after hiking up the skirt her old training kicked in. Running like an athlete and not like the fancy CEO of Jordan Academy that she was, her strides took her off the main drag and into the side streets. It was not the part of town anyone should be in at night and lord knew how much broken glass she might step on, but she had no choice.

She saw a car and she tried to wave it down but the driver, an old man, looked at her as if he were terrified and sped off. She ran on, hoping to spot a police car, a bus—anything or body that might save her from the man whose footsteps she could hear pounding the pavement behind her.

Saint, his long black coat flapping around him, wasn't happy about chasing this woman down. He snatched off his mask and crammed it into his pocket. He stuck his hand in his other pocket, found his shades and put them on. No one had anticipated she'd run. She was supposed to be a school principal, for heaven's sake, not Flo Jo, but she was hauling and he was doing well just to keep her in sight. When he saw her try and stop a car only to have the car roar off, he felt relief. The last thing he needed was for her to be rescued by some good Samaritan and have to hunt her down all over again. She darted between two old houses and he increased his speed.

Narice looked back. To her dismay he was gaining on her. A blink later, he ran her down, threw a powerful arm around her waist, and swung her up and off her feet.

"Let me go!" she screamed. He slapped a hand over her mouth to keep her from waking the neighborhood. She bit him.

He snatched his hand away and yelled, "Dammit!"

She immediately tried to take flight again, but he

had the presence of mind to grab her arm and yank her back. "You bit me?!"

She swung her purse but he ducked. She brought her nails up to claw his face, but his forearm blocked the attempt just in time. He grabbed her wrist and held, while she stood glaring back furiously.

Saint stared down. "Bite me again and I'll paddle your fancy little behind."

An unimpressed Narice pulled against his hold and snarled, "Let me go!"

He looked down at her as if she both amazed and amused him. "Didn't expect you to be this much trouble."

She opened her mouth to scream again, but he clamped his hand over her mouth so quickly she had no time to make a sound.

"I'm with the good guys, crazy woman. I'm not going to hurt you, but you're starting to get on my nerves. Do you understand?"

Narice's eyes flashed angrily.

"Now," he said menacingly, "I'm going to take my hand away and we are going to walk back. If you scream, I'm not going to be happy. You got that?"

She didn't give a care about his happiness. She wanted away from him, now.

He very slowly lifted his hand away from her lips, all the while holding her eyes prisoner with a gaze shrouded by dark glasses. Narice asked herself, *What kind of man wears shades at night?*

As he led the balking Narice back the way they'd

come, he kept a gentle but firm hold on her arm. He stopped next to a new-looking sports car, then reached down and pulled open the passenger-side door. "Get in."

Narice looked up at him and didn't move.

"Get in."

"No!" she declared.

He raised his eyes to heaven as if seeking divine strength or guidance, then placed his large hands on her waistline, and very slowly, and much too easily, raised Narice to eye level. She stared into the shades, and in spite of her show of bravado she was shaking.

"I'm through playing with you, now," he spat out in a deadly serious tone. "I've let you hit me and bite me. No more."

Just as easily, he set her down again. "Get in the damn car."

Enraged, she gave him a look, but obeyed.

Seconds later he got in on the driver's side. Her shoes were on the seat. He handed them to her. "Put on the seat belt."

Snarling, she stuffed her feet back into her pumps, fooled with the belt and strapped herself in. From somewhere in the car a phone rang. Narice looked on while he hit a button on the dash. A male voice came into the car asking, "Everything under control now, little brother?"

"Yes," Saint said, glancing over at Narice's sullen face. "Now, sign off so I can get the hell out of here."

"Keep her safe."

"I'm the one you should be praying for."

A laugh came in response to that quip, then the connection went silent. A second later, the powerful car barreled back out into the street.

He told her, "That was a stupid stunt you pulled back there."

"Trying to keep from being snatched off the street is not stupid," she countered testily. "Where are you taking me? What did he mean, keep me safe? No one's going to pay a ransom for me, you know."

He didn't reply.

"Kidnapping is a felony."

"So is biting a man."

Frustrated, she settled back against the seat while her mind feverishly searched for a plan that would free her from this mess. "Are you after this Eye of Sheba, too?"

No answer.

He drove out of the city and onto one of the state's major east-west highways, I-96. They were headed west.

She asked again, "Where are we going?"

"Make yourself useful and grab those CDs out of the glove box."

"Where are we going?"

"To meet a queen who's going to give you a million dollars. Now, put in a CD."

Narice didn't care for his sarcasm. "Do you do this sort of thing all the time? Snatching women off the streets, I mean?"

"Yes, and most of them are much better company."

"Then let me out at the corner and you can find somebody else."

"Sorry, Teach. Can't do it."

She stared at him across the darkness. "How do you know I'm a teacher?"

He replied easily, "Read your file. You didn't think Ridley picked you up at random, did you?"

"Are you working with him?"

"Not hardly."

"Then whom?"

"Friends."

"That's not an answer."

He glanced her way. "If I told you I was sent by the President would you believe me?"

Narice didn't hesitate. "No."

"Then maybe this will convince you. You're Narice Jordan. Thirty-seven. Divorced. Founder and principal of Jordan Academy, a ritzy private school in Maryland. You cater to the children of UN diplomats, D.C. power types and the occasional superstar athlete. How am I doing so far?"

She held his gaze but refused to acknowledge his accuracy or buy that he knew the President. Her silence didn't seem to bother him, though.

"Let's see. You have an MBA in finance and a doctorate in childhood education. That's quite a mix."

She didn't respond.

"You have a summer place in the Carolinas. Drive a

cobalt blue Z—six speed." He paused in his recital to say, "Not many ladies drive a stick. I'm impressed."

Silence.

He went on as if they were having the most pleasant of conversations. "You worked on Wall Street before you began your school, and according to the SEC you're rich as Cleopatra."

That was true too, but Narice didn't react, instead she said, "All that is public information. It doesn't prove anybody sent you, let alone the President."

He took his eyes off the road for a moment to say, "You know, you really should be nicer to me. I'm probably the only one who can get you out of this mess."

"And that's why the President sent you, I suppose, as opposed to the FBI."

"I work for them sometimes, too."

Narice sighed with frustration. She was in a car with a madman. This night was getting worse and worse. "And the Secret Service? Do you work for them, too?"

"Yep."

Narice shook her head. "Your nose should be breaking through the windshield any minute now, Pinocchio."

He chuckled. "Never thought a Wall Street principal would have jokes."

"You mean that wasn't in your file?" she asked in mock surprise.

"Nope. It didn't say you were so fast either. Where'd you run track?"

"MSU," she volunteered before remembering she wasn't supposed to be talking to this lunatic. He gave her a knowing smile that seemed to be magnified by the shades, but she ignored it, or tried to by asking him, "So who are you really?"

"Name's St. Martin. Most people call me, Saint."

She remembered Ridley calling him St. Martin, so she felt safe in assuming that was his true name. "And who do you work for, really?"

"I told you, the President."

Narice still didn't believe him, and she was too upset to find any humor in him or the situation. "Okay. Fine. Where are we going?"

"To Grand Rapids to see a queen."

Sheer disbelief made her blurt out, "What?"

"We're going to Grand Rapids to see a queen."

"I heard that part. Why?"

"She thinks you know where the Eye is."

"But I don't," she said throwing up her hands. "Why won't anybody believe me?"

He shrugged. "Well, you can tell her when you see her."

Narice tried reason. "Look I buried my father yesterday. All I want to do is catch my plane, go home, and grieve. I promise you on my daddy's memory, I will talk to this queen after I have a chance to pull my life back together."

"My condolences on your loss," he said in a sincere tone. "But I can't let you go. So, like I said, grab some CDs and relax. We'll be in Grand Rapids by sunup."

"Let me out of this car."

"No can do. President's orders."

Frustrated she slammed her fists on the seat. Her life was spinning out of control. No one seemed to care that she'd lost her daddy and that her grief was still fresh and real. All these men seemed to care about was a damn diamond she knew absolutely nothing about.

Soft jazz whispered melodically from the speakers. Apparently he'd inserted the CD himself. As the sleek black car cut through the darkness with only the green glow of the dash lights illuminating the interior, Narice felt cut off from the world. In another time and place she might have loved a late-night drive in a car as beautiful and powerful as this, but there was no pleasure in this ride, only uncertainty, fear, and the mysterious insane man behind the wheel.

A little over an hour later, they rolled past the city of East Lansing, home to Michigan State University, her alma mater. Memories of the good times she'd had on campus faded under the reality of her present situation. She hadn't lived in Michigan in over a decade but knew that Grand Rapids was a mere sixty miles west. She had to find a way to escape before then.

"Hungry?" he asked.

"No."

"I am. Time for breakfast." He exited the highway and pulled into the nearly empty lot of a fast-food joint. The sky was now pink, signaling the beginning of a new day.

When Narice spotted the police car parked near the

entrance of the restaurant, she felt hope rise again. Keeping her voice neutral, she stated, "I need to use the bathroom."

"All right, but no funny business."

She didn't make any promises.

They got out of the car, and when he escorted her inside, she got her first good look at him. He had on a long black canvas coat that fit him like an Old West duster. The heavy fabric was faded and frayed from wear. Under the coat, he wore black jeans, a black turtleneck, and dirty scuffed army boots. His skin tone was light, almost gold, but the color of his eyes were hidden behind the shades. Had Narice met him at a club or the bank she would have to say he was handsome in an unshaven, dangerous-looking sort of way. In fact, all he needed was a six-shooter and a wide brimmed hat and he could've auditioned for the male lead in a Hollywood western, but in reality, he was her kidnapper, and there was nothing handsome or cute about that.

The door to the ladies room was a few steps down the hall from the entrance. He walked her there and warned softly, "I'll be waiting here. In fact, hand me your purse."

Narice cast a discreet glance over to the two policemen seated by the windows, having coffee. "Why?"

"Just to make sure you don't go out of a window. There isn't a sister alive who'll run off and leave her purse behind."

Narice saw no problem with making him think she'd

given up on escaping. "Well, there's stuff in there that I need, so how about I let you keep my wallet. I'm not going to run off without my ID or my credit cards."

"I'll take the cell phone, too."

She slapped the items into his outstretched palm and walked away.

Inside the restroom, Narice surveyed herself in the mirror. She'd lost a button off the coat of her suit and her hair was a mess. There was a hole in her stockings as big as her fist, and her skirt was twisted and wrinkled. After righting herself as much as she could, and cursing the man responsible, she tried to come up with a plan that would get the attention of the officers at the table. She decided on a direct approach.

When she came out of the restroom, the man she knew as Saint was standing by the door just as he'd promised. She assumed the bag in his hand held the food he'd ordered but she didn't care. Stepping right past him, she quickly walked over to the seated officers. "Excuse me, but I need some assistance."

The cops, County Sheriffs, according to the patch on their brown and gold uniforms looked her over with her wrinkled suit and torn hose, and one of them asked, "What can we do for you?"

"I've been kidnapped."

By then her captor was standing beside her and asking, "You're not bothering these nice officers are you, angel?"

Narice turned around. *Angel?!* Then she noticed that his shades were gone. His eyes were the most arresting green she'd ever seen. The power in them was so unexpected, she lost sight of her role for a moment.

He took advantage and stepped into the breach. "My apologies, officers. My wife does this a lot—"

"I am not his wife," Narice stated now that she'd regrouped. "He kidnapped me in Detroit—"

"The hospital lets me take her home once or twice a month. She's under a doctor's supervision."

Narice stared. *What?!*

The next thing she knew, he was showing the police what appeared to be legal documents. "See," he said to them, "these are her papers. It gives me permission to take her off the grounds of the hospital where she usually stays. I had the doctors there type this up because every time I take her out, she gets people all freaked out claiming to be kidnapped and stuff."

Narice stood there stunned. Who in the world was this man?! She leaned down so the officers could see her clearly. "I am not crazy. This man is a kidnapper."

The officers studied the papers. After a few minutes they handed them back. One of the officers patted her on the hand, and said, kindly, "Ma'am, we can't arrest your husband. Why don't you let him take you on home. Okay?"

"He's not my husband!" she snarled.

By now, the restaurant's employees and customers were staring her way. "He isn't!!"

Her *husband* said gently, "Calm down, baby," then to the officers, "She's getting herself all worked up. I need to get her to the car so she can take her medication."

Narice threw up her hands. "I'm not crazy!"

"Come on, angel. Let's let these men finish their coffee."

"I am not crazy!!"

But she felt like it. How had he put her into this box so effortlessly? It was quite obvious that the police were buying his bogus story and weren't going to help her at all, so Narice shook off her captor's husbandly hold and stormed towards the door. She wiped at the angry tears threatening to brim from her eyes. He caught up with her before she could push through the wide glass doors. He opened it politely and she sailed through. He escorted her across the parking lot and had the nerve to be whistling confidently the whole way. Narice wondered if she could escape long enough to buy some rat poison for him to eat.

Once they were inside the car, he turned her way and asked, "So, what grade do I get for my performance back there, Teach?"

"Oh, you're conceited, too?" she drawled sarcastically. "Why did I already know that?"

He grinned at her.

"You get an A," she told him. "The papers were very clever. Hope I get the chance to return the favor someday."

"Hey, you might."

He fished a wrapped breakfast burger out of the bag. "Sure you don't want anything to eat."

"Real sure."

He seemed to sense how truly angry she was. "I really am with the good guys."

"Whatever you say."

"I'm not going to hurt you, rape you, put you in an underground dungeon, and make you eat mouse burgers—none of that. Okay?"

The part about the mouse burgers almost made Narice smile, but she simply answered, "Okay."

"Here's your stuff back."

She took her wallet. "My phone?"

"I'm going to hang on to it for now." Without another word he started the engine and drove back to the highway.

Saint was real sorry about having to put her through this. He'd been briefed about her father's death and assumed she was grieving, but sometimes circumstances were such that personal issues had to be set aside and this was one of those circumstances. Once they found the Eye, she could get back to her life but until then, her life would be tied to his and the search. "Our audience with the queen is this afternoon. We'll grab a room and hole up until then."

"I'm not sharing a room with you."

"Then I'll lock you in the car."

She shot him an ugly look.

"No? Guess it'll be the room then."

Narice turned away.

Saint chuckled softly.

When they reached the outskirts of Grand Rapids,

he pulled the car into the parking lot of an all-suites hotel and cut the engine. Narice's watch showed the time to be just past 6:30. She could see hotel guests loading luggage into their cars while others trooped over to the building for the chain's famous free breakfast buffet.

He turned to her and said, "Don't even think about reaching out to someone. The sooner we get this search underway the sooner you can have your life back."

Narice didn't respond. If he thought she was going to stop trying to escape he was crazy.

He got out. She knew if she ran, he'd catch her so she bided her time and watched him remove her suitcase from the trunk. She was surprised to see it. Last time she saw it Ridley's cabbie friend was placing it in the cab's trunk. She wondered if it had been put into this car by the same person who'd left her pumps on the seat after her foiled escape attempt.

The sight of him coming around to her side of the car brought her back to the situation at hand. He opened the door and she got out.

The all-suites hotel belonged to a national chain Narice often stayed in when she traveled. There were so many buildings on this particular site, the property resembled an apartment complex. Since her keeper didn't head towards the building housing the registration desk, she assumed check-in arrangements had already been made. Sure enough, he led her up a short flight of wooden stairs to one of the upstairs units and stuck a key in the door.

"Wait here," he told her, then added firmly, "and I do mean, wait."

Narice's chin rose. As of now, she'd been up a straight twenty-four hours and after all she'd been through since leaving her daddy's memorial, the fatigue had taken its toll. Her body felt like limp spaghetti. She wasn't giving up on escaping, but at this particular moment, she didn't have the strength to do anything but wait.

Inside, Saint drew his gun and searched the place from stem to stern, looking for intruders. The suite had two floors. The first level held a well-stocked kitchen, complete with stove, refrigerator, dishwasher, and microwave. To the right, lay the living room area with couch and chairs, and an intimate fireplace. The bed stood near the wall.

He stepped back outside. "Come on in. I'm going to put you upstairs."

The upper level held a big bed, a television, and a bathroom. He set her suitcase by the bed.

"Get some sleep."

Narice had one question to ask. "Did you have anything to do with my father's death?"

He looked her in the eyes and answered without hesitation. "No."

And he left.

Two

Narice awakened around noon to the smells of coffee and bacon. Turning over in the bed, she snuggled deeper, intending to sleep longer but the brief brush with consciousness made her remember where she was, and then it all came back—the encounter with Ridley, her kidnapping, her father's burial. She wondered if things could get any worse? Probably, said the cynic inside. Probably.

She got up and walked the short distance to the bathroom. On the way she saw that she'd slept in her suit and shrugged it off. She'd been so drained this morning the moment her head hit the pillow, she'd immediately fallen asleep. The six-hundred-dollar ensemble was a wrinkled mess, but she didn't care; she just wanted a shower.

Before stripping off her clothes, though, Narice made sure the lock on the bathroom door worked. Satisfied, she took care of her morning needs, then stepped into the glass stall. The spray was hot and powerful, a perfect combination for a woman trying to pull herself back together.

Dressed in a pair of jeans, a white silk Tee, and carrying the blue silk jacket she'd picked up in Barcelona last year, Narice came downstairs. Saint was at the stove tending bacon frying in a skillet.

"Hello," he called out. "Hope you don't mind having breakfast. I'm cooking enough for two if you want some."

A kidnapper who cooked breakfast at noon, and in sunglasses, no less. She noted that at least he'd taken off the High Noon coat. The navy turtleneck and the worn pair of jeans showed off the lean fitness of his six-foot-plus frame. The army boots were as dirty as they'd been earlier and he still hadn't shaved.

"Do you eat bread?" he asked, now standing by the toaster.

She found the question odd. "Yes, why?"

"Fashion types like you don't always eat bread. Didn't want to waste it."

"Fashion types?" she asked skeptically, coolly.

"Yeah." He dropped the bread into the slots, then went back to the skillet where the bacon was frying nicely.

Narice took a seat on one of the counter's stools and

drawled, "And here I thought I was just a kidnap victim."

He grinned a bit. "Just going by the way you dress."

"And if I judged you by the way you dress, what would you be, besides a kidnapper?"

"Ouch," he yelped. "You're hard on a brother." Using a long-handled fork he lifted the now-done bacon from the pan and laid it on a paper towel–covered plate. "My sister says I look like an outlaw."

"Does she know you kidnap women?"

He made an elaborate show of thinking that over, then said, "Nope." He added, "Did I mention that I'm with the good guys?"

"You did."

"You're not acting like you believe me."

"Maybe, because I don't."

"You think a bad guy would cook you this kind of breakfast, at this time of day?" he asked, stirring what appeared to be a small pot of grits. "Bad guys would feed you mouse burgers."

She couldn't help it. She smiled.

He paused for a moment to watch her. "I wondered if you knew how to do that."

"Do what?"

"Smile."

Narice tried to shrug it off. "Okay, so you're charming. Proves nothing."

"You think I'm charming?"

"I think you're fishing for compliments."

"Am I?"

He set a plate before her that had on it scrambled eggs, bacon, and a small steaming helping of grits. She looked into the dark glasses and did her best to ignore the pure male essence he exuded. "Yes, you are, but thanks for breakfast anyway."

"You're welcome," he replied, then went to fix his own plate.

The meal was surprisingly good.

He asked, "How's my cooking?"

"Not bad. They teach you this in kidnapper school?"

"Yep. First day."

She met his shaded eyes. "You get an A."

"Thanks."

"Why do you wear sunglasses indoors?"

"I'm nocturnal."

Her voice was skeptical. "Nocturnal."

"Yeah, sorta like a cheetah."

She shook her head. A *nocturnal* kidnapper.

He raised his cup of coffee to his lips. "Besides, Parliamentfunkadelic says you can't be cool without your shades."

Skepticism colored her tone once more. "Parliamentfunkadelic."

"You know, Sir Nose. George Clinton. The P-funk?"

She wondered how many women melted on the spot under his golden, unshaven good looks. He was insane, but gorgeous. "I know who they are."

"Good." He had the nerve to grin.

Her heart had the nerve to skip a beat. Angry at herself for softening to a man who'd snatched her off the street and was holding her against her will, she asked, "Is there any juice?"

He observed her for a long moment. "In the fridge. Stuff gives me hives, but help yourself."

Glad to put some distance between herself and him, even if for just a few seconds, Narice slid from the stool. Opening the fridge she took out the slim, still sealed carton and poured herself a small glass. She took a deep swallow. The orange juice was cold and refreshing; just what she needed to put herself back in control.

Saint ate his breakfast and silently watched her. Earlier, dressed in her expensive suit and shoes, she'd been the CEO headmistress. Now she looked a lot more regular dressed in the jeans and the blouse; if you ignored the little silk jacket draped over her chair. The short-heeled mules on her feet were probably as pricey as the jacket, but she seemed more approachable; less formal in spite of the flawless makeup, the perfectly arched eyebrows, and the laid, short-cut perm.

When she bent to put the juice back into the fridge, he found himself viewing her from another angle. She was well put together. The dossier on her said she was thirty-seven, but her body was still fit. It was a woman's body and had a curvy thing going on that definitely pleased a brother's eye. And the sister could run. He was going to have to keep a close eye on this one.

Narice returned to the counter with her glass of juice. "You know, when I don't show up in Baltimore in a few days, my friends are going to start to worry and then call the police." It was spring break for her school.

"And?"

"And people are going to start looking for me."

"Good for them."

"I'm serious."

"So am I. Good friends are hard to find."

Narice's lips tightened. She didn't like being patronized. "Well, since you think I'm such a fashion plate, I'll make sure I wear my best suit to your trial."

"You do that," he said, giving her another male grin. Getting to his feet, he picked up their plates and walked the short distance to the sink. "You should get your suitcase. Soon as I put this stuff in the dishwasher, we're outta here."

He then looked her way and said, "I know this has been hard—you just buried your father and now all this drama."

She didn't respond.

"I'm on your side. Believe that."

Narice wasn't convinced. "Put yourself in my place. Would you trust you?"

Saint didn't lie. "Probably not, so how can I prove it? Have I hurt you in any way?"

"No."

"Threatened you with a weapon?"

"No. Ridley did, though."

"Then, how about I show you my ID?"

"ID can be forged. I had two students who got in big

trouble last year for making fake five-dollar bills on their computers, but let me see it."

He went over to his coat and fished his wallet out of one of his many pockets. He handed it to her.

Narice compared the face in the photo to the man standing next to her. They were the same. When Narice first opened her school, the daughter of the then vice-president had been one of her students, so Narice had become very familiar with Secret Service ID and Saint's certainly looked real. She handed it back.

Saint waited for her to say something, and when she didn't, he asked, "So?"

"So, what?"

"Do you believe me now?" Saint found her to be an exasperating challenge of a woman.

She shrugged. "At this point, I don't know what to believe, but let's go and see this queen of yours."

Saint watched her head up the stairs to retrieve her suitcase and all he could think was *God, she is fine.* A woman with a body and face like that could make a man sell out his country. Under the circumstances, she appeared to be holding up well and he found that impressive. Even more impressive—no tears, no hysterics. He wished he could tell her more, though. She'd earned it.

A few minutes later, they left the room and he put her suitcase in the car's small trunk.

Narice said, "How much money would it take for you to let me walk away? You can just say I escaped."

He closed the trunk. "Nope."

"Why not?"

He chuckled, "And ruin my reputation. No thanks."

He opened the car door for her. She stared up. He lifted an eyebrow. Sighing aloud, the thwarted Narice got in.

The highway signs led them into downtown Grand Rapids, the state's second largest city. When he eased the car into the valet parking lane of a large stately hotel, she didn't know what to think. The red-coated doormen politely held open the door and the man she knew as Saint escorted her inside. The lobby had frescos painted on the high ceilings, ornate cherrywood furniture and a sedate air that exuded old money. He led her past the highly polished desk where smiling scrubbed faces greeted arriving and departing guests, and over to the bank of elevators. Narice had a thousand questions but kept them to herself because evidently hell would freeze over before he gave her any real answers.

They emerged onto the twelfth floor and stepped out into a carpeted hallway that was as hushed as it was elegant. Lush green plants in foot-high planters lined the hallway walls. The carpet was so thick she couldn't hear her own footsteps. At the far end of the hall were two burly men dressed in blue business suits, standing on either side of the last door. Both were brown-skinned men with foreign features that reminded Narice of the Ethiopian uncles of one of her students.

As Narice and Saint approached, one of the men smiled, showing beautiful white teeth, "Welcome back, Mr. St. Martin. Is this the lady?"

Her escort nodded. "The bad guys almost beat me to her, though."

"They are like cockroaches," the man answered with disdain, "but I'm sure The Majesty will be pleased that you played the role of champion."

The man then turned his attention to Narice. "Welcome."

"Thank you," she replied warily. She now had more questions than ever. It was obvious that English was not his native language, but he smiled at her as easily as if she were kin. What did this all mean? And who in the world was The Majesty? She thought the proper title for a ruler would be Her or His Majesty.

Once again she was ushered forward with her questions unanswered. The expansive suite had the rich exotic smell of incenses and perfumes. Amidst the hotel's conservative cherrywood furniture, pillows brocaded in striking ethnic patterns were spread about the carpeted floor like vivid desert flowers.

Areas of the room were shrouded behind gossamer-thin veils hemmed in silk. Bearded old men with brown skin and wearing sandals moved about silently. A few of them met her eyes but dropped them immediately and withdrew. Narice shot Saint a puzzled look, but the sound of a gong drew her attention away.

The deep note resonated in the air for a long moment before fading away. As the silence returned, a small group of men, also dressed in white, processed in.

Narice couldn't say if these were the same men she'd seen in the room earlier, but they certainly looked old enough. She'd be willing to bet a few of them had to be over a hundred.

When the procession halted, two younger men entered carrying a large gilded chair. It was opulently upholstered in bold purple velvet and embroidered with a large black griffin on the chair's back. The old men parted like the Red Sea so the chair could be placed between them. Then a man and a veiled woman entered. The woman had her hand resting gracefully upon her escort's arm. He was robed in white. Her robes were purple and underskirted with black. The purple and black scarf covering her hair flowed to her waist and had the sheen of polished silk. She looked old, but determining her true age was impossible. The veil revealed only that her skin was brown and her eyes, the color of gold.

The woman took a seat in the gilded chair, and the escort moved back to stand with the other men. Narice realized she'd been holding her breath and that her heart was pumping. Taking in a deep breath she calmed herself and prayed nobody could see her shaking.

At first, the woman didn't say anything at all, spending the moment studying Narice as if measuring her for something. Seemingly satisfied she turned away and focused her golden eyes on Saint. "It is good to see you again, Mr. St. Martin." Her voice radiated quiet power.

He responded by bowing solemnly. "It's good to see you again too, Majesty."

He'd removed the shades and Narice was mildly impressed by his show of respect.

He then settled his green eyes on Narice. "May I present, Narice Jordan. She is the daughter of the Keeper."

The queen inclined her head. "Ms. Jordan. I was saddened to learn of your father's death. My condolences."

Narice had no idea how this woman knew her father or why he was being referred to as the Keeper, but she responded genuinely, "Thank you."

"Let me also apologize for bringing you here under such mysterious circumstances. I'm sure you must be wondering what this is all about?"

Narice didn't lie. "Yes."

"Well, soon you will know all. For now, you are my guest. With your permission, my ladies will make you comfortable. I have some things I must discuss with Mr. St. Martin first and then you will join us. It will not be long."

Narice could see the old men assessing her. One man, the escort, had outright skepticism on his hawk-nosed face. Narice turned away from his burning gaze and refocused her attention on the woman in the chair. "Do I have a choice in any of this?"

Although Narice couldn't see beneath the veil, she sensed the woman smile. "Certainly you have a choice," she said. "You can stay and be my guest, or opt to leave, in which case you will be killed."

Narice stiffened. Her eyes flew to Saint, but his were trained on The Majesty.

The woman explained in a kind yet steel-edged voice, "We're not playing a child's game here, Ms. Jordan. The people who murdered your father are my enemies as well, and they will stop at nothing to attain their goals. If you leave here and fall into their hands, they can use you against me. If you are dead, they cannot."

It was if Narice had fallen down the rabbit hole and awakened in a North African version of Wonderland. On the throne sat the Red Queen, and Narice had the misfortune of being Alice. Narice had no idea what this *knowledge* The Majesty referred to consisted of, or the identities of the people responsible for her father's death, but in order to find out, Narice needed to be alive. "Then I will be honored to be your guest."

The Majesty nodded. "I knew you had the mettle for this journey, Ms. Jordan, though some around me had their doubts."

The last few words were obviously a jab at someone because it set off a lot of tight jaws amongst the men in white, especially the escort with the hawk's face. *This is not a sister to be messed with,* Narice thought.

The Majesty clapped her hands and a young woman wrapped in emerald green robes appeared from behind the thin curtains. She bowed respectfully to The Majesty, who said in return, "Fulani, take Ms. Jordan and make her comfortable. I will call for her in time." The Majesty spoke then to Narice. "You are in good hands."

Fulani, who appeared to be in her twenties, then turned and said to Narice. "Please follow me, Ms. Jordan."

Narice gave Saint a questioning look. He nodded almost imperceptibly, so she followed Fulani through the fluttering transparent draping and deeper into the suite.

Once there, she was shown into a bedroom that had a large adjoining bath complete with an onyx Jacuzzi tub.

Fulani said, "It is our custom to bathe before having an official audience with The Majesty, so I will draw you a bath."

Narice had showered this morning, but after her harrowing adventures, the prospect of a long soak in a Jacuzzi was just what the doctor ordered. Being the head of a school whose pupils came from all over the globe, Narice was very cognizant of custom and the value in respecting different cultures. If she had to bathe in order to get the information she needed about why her father was killed and to keep the Red Queen from screaming, "Off with her head!" then she would take a bath. "Why is your Queen called The Majesty and not Her Majesty," Narice asked Fulani.

"Our title has no gender. The ruler is The Supreme, The All, The Anointed. The Majesty," she said simply.

Narice thought she understood now. "How long have you been with the queen?"

"Fourteen years. I began service when I was six. The Majesty has made it possible for girls like me to attend school. At home, girls are forbidden."

"So, she has been good to you?"

"Yes, she has. Now, I must see to the bath."

And what a glorious bath it turned out to be. After sipping on a cup of herbal tea, Narice eased into the warm scented water and just knew she had died and gone to heaven. The temperature was perfect, the scents relaxing. She leaned her head back on the little terry pillow Fulani supplied and closed her eyes.

On the other side of the wall, Saint lay on his stomach on the bed. The towel over his butt was all he had on in order to facilitate the oiling and massaging of his now clean but tired body by two of The Majesty's female servants. The years of sneaking and hiding and running and skulking were starting to catch up with him physically. The leg he'd broken in Tibet ten years ago now ached every time the weather changed. His left shoulder, dislocated five years ago in a bar fight in Mexico, had been set, but was never the same since. On his thirty-six-year-old body were knife wounds from Jamaica, stitches from Portugal, and the remnants of a bullet he'd taken in Thailand to go along with an international collection of long-ago healed bruises and contusions. Saint was a mercenary. His specialty—intelligence. He began his career as member of the U.S. Army and had climbed the ranks to the top of his field by way of the many-acronymed clandestine agencies that operated under the official government radar. Eight years ago, he officially retired, taking with him his reputation for stealth, discretion, and success. He was now a highly paid freelancer; hired by governments, the U.S. included, multinational corporations, and private citizens for shadowy jobs big and small. It was a life Saint enjoyed and still got a rush from, even if he did sometimes feel like he was getting too old. Like now.

When the call came in about this job for The Majesty, he'd had been in the jungles of Belize tracking a band of grave robbers on behalf of the Belize Antiquities Ministry. The thieves had made off with the treasures found in a newly discovered Mayan temple, and the Ministry wanted them back. Saint and a small band of the country's soldiers found the men, but not before suffering through ten days of sleeping on the ground, eating bad food and fighting insects the size of pigeons.

Now, less than twenty-four hours later, he was here, the tiredness of the Belize jungles being stroked away by soft female hands and his body responding in typical male fashion. He shifted his position a little to accommodate his arousal. He'd given The Majesty the letter sent to her by the President, and afterwards, she'd made it clear that the women were at his disposal, but he'd have to take a rain check on the offer; the President and his advisors were sure The Majesty had a mole in her entourage reporting her every move back to the generals ruling her country, so he needed to be clearheaded in order to assess the players in this drama. Knocking boots with the two doe-eyed lovelies now working their hands slowly up and down the backs of his thighs and legs would leave his senses dulled and lazy.

He also had the curvy Ms. Jordan to keep an eye on. He wondered what it would be like to have her hands giving him this massage. He imagined her hands would be firm yet soft. In his mind's eye he could feel the way she'd knead, then stroke him. The arousal resulting from that fantasy made him adjust his position again. He had no intentions of turning the fantasy into reality, though. Had he met her under different circumstances he might not mind exploring the intricacies of Narice Jordan, but this was a job and he took his work seriously. She was hard not to think about, however. The question she'd asked The Majesty about choices hadn't really surprised him. He already knew that Narice Jordan was no shrinking violet. For a woman who'd been kidnapped twice last night, she'd shown steel beneath all that designer wear. On the other hand, The Majesty's answer to Narice's question hadn't been a surprise either. Of course, he wasn't going to allow anyone to take Narice's life, but The Majesty had been correct about the ruthlessness of the other side. If Narice were to fall into their hands, they'd get the information they were after, then kill her.

So, as tired as he was, Saint was about to embark on another adventure, this time with a curvy headmistress he had no business fantasizing about.

Dressed in a traditional dress that Narice thought looked very much like a sari, she followed Fulani to the room where the audience would be held. The dress was drab brown, but Narice could smell the rich scents of the oils and perfumes the women had worked into her skin. They'd covered her hair with a long cotton scarf the same shade of the dress. Fulani had even supplied Narice with a pair of soft black shoes. Narice looked like a wren on the outside but beneath her clothing, all the pampering and oiling made her feel like a Bird of Paradise.

Narice saw that The Majesty, and the hawk-faced escort were already seated on the brocaded pillows that covered the floor of the large room. Fulani exited silently. Beside The Majesty was a small table. On it sat a sparkling white china tea service. Saint was there too, wearing his dark glasses and dressed in a simple brown tunic and a matching pair of loose-fitting trousers. Narice noted his brown socks as she sat on one of the pillows near him. She wondered what he and The Majesty had talked about.

The Majesty said, "Ah, Ms. Jordan, you honor us by wearing the *cha* so elegantly."

Narice knew from talking with Fulani that *cha* was the name of the dress she had on. Fulani also told Narice that The Majesty never allowed herself to be upstaged by another woman in any way, thus the reason Narice had been given the simple brown gown. The Majesty on the other hand was grandly dressed in a *cha* of embroidered purple silk that on close inspection appeared shiny from age and wear.

The Majesty then introduced the man at her side.

"Ms. Jordan, this is my prime minister. He is named Farouk."

Narice inclined her head his way. She remembered the stormy look he'd given her earlier. "Pleased to meet you," she said.

He nodded back. "Welcome, Ms. Jordan."

The Majesty said, "Now, we will have tea and discuss our problem."

She had a servant pour everyone a cup and then she asked, "Ms. Jordan, let me begin by telling you about the Eye and how it ties to my country, Nagal. The Eye originally belonged to Makeda, the woman the Old Testament calls the Queen of Sheba."

Narice was surprised by that and wondered how The Majesty knew Sheba's given name.

The Majesty was continuing, "When Makeda journeyed to King Solomon's court, she brought him many gifts. One of which was a brilliant blue diamond we now call the Eye of Sheba."

The Majesty paused and her golden eyes turned on Narice. "How well do you know your Bible, Ms. Jordan."

"Probably not as well as I should."

She smiled softly. "Makeda returned home carrying Solomon's child. She bore him a son and she named him Ibn-al-Hakim, which means *son of the wise man.* In the Bible he is called Melenek, and is said to have stolen the Ark of the Covenant."

Narice knew the Ark had been given to the Israelites by God. Her only other reference to the icon was the movie *Raiders of the Lost Ark.* She shook herself and settled her attention back on the queen.

"Our legends say Melenek took something else, too. The Eye. Through time and marriage it found its way into my family. It became the symbol of the Nagal monarchy, and our tie to the great queen Makeda."

Narice found the story fascinating. "So how does my father figure into all of this?"

"When Rommel and his Nazis overran Nagal during WWII, my grandfather, the king, gave the Eye to your father to keep it out of the hands of the Germans."

Narice knew that her father had served in northern Africa during the war, but he'd never mentioned meeting a royal family.

"Your father promised to smuggle the Eye out of the country and to keep it safe until my grandfather sent for it, but after the war, generals in our army staged a coup. My grandfather was killed in the fighting. His heir, my father, was executed shortly thereafter. My grandmother, mother and I were forced to flee our home or suffer the same fate."

Narice asked, "Where did you go?"

"Paris, where my mother had relatives." She quieted for a moment as if thinking back, then said, "I am the last of the Nagal royal line. Over the years the old generals were replaced by new ones, but they all cared more about power than the people."

"Why do you need the Eye?"

"Because according to the prophecy, when the Eye is returned to its home prosperity will return as well."

"And you believe my father has had it all this time?"

"We believe so, yes."

Farouk leaned across the table and stated bluntly, "And now, we want it returned."

Narice held his glare. "Fine. Just tell me where it is."

Saint weighed in for the first time. "Nobody knows. Everybody assumes your father hid it somewhere for safekeeping."

Narice wasn't convinced. "He never mentioned anything to me."

"Are you certain?" The Majesty asked.

"Very."

Farouk asked tightly, "If he did hide it, where might it be?"

Narice shrugged. "I have no idea."

The prime minister's face said he didn't believe her, but Narice had no control over what he believed.

Saint asked, "What about his acquaintances, friends, would they be of any help?"

Narice shrugged again. "Uncle Willie might know."

"Where's he live?"

"Toledo."

The Majesty asked, "This Uncle Willie is your blood?"

Narice shook her head. "No, but he was my father's best friend. If Daddy told anyone about this it would be Willie. They served in the army together?"

"Then we start the search there," Saint declared.

The Majesty seemed pleased. "A starting point."

Narice wasn't sure, but she kept it to herself. "So, who is Ridley, and how is he involved?" Narice remembered how terrified she'd been in the cab.

Farouk's pale brown face twisted with distaste. "He serves the generals as their prime minister. He is after the Eye, too."

Narice hoped to not run into him again. "Ridley recognized your voice, Saint. He must know you well."

"He does," was all he said.

Narice studied him and wondered what he'd meant, but his tone let her know she'd get no further explanation, at least not now, so she didn't press him. She did have another question, though, and hoped someone had an answer. "What about my father's death. Do you know who set the fire?"

Farouk answered, "All roads lead to the generals and their agents. If you help us the killers will be brought to justice."

Having the arsonist convicted was a priority for Narice, but did she really want to get involved in all this? The sane parts of herself said no, but Simon Jordan had been an honorable man and would have wanted the Eye returned to its rightful owners. As his daughter she had a familial responsibility to pick up where he left off so that that his pledge to The Majesty's family could be kept. She knew in her heart that he would want her to help these people and to find his killers.

Farouk asked, "Will you help?"

Narice nodded. "If finding the Eye will help put the people who murdered my father behind bars, I'm all yours."

The Majesty smiled. "Good. Now, we have less than two weeks."

"This has a timetable, too?"

"Yes, in about thirty days, your state department will be proposing a treaty that will give your government access to a very strategic strip of land in my country that is on the Red Sea. With all the turmoil in the Middle East, they've been after the port for years. The U.S. wants the generals to hold an open election, but the generals know that without the Eye the people will not vote for their candidate. Without the Eye the generals are nothing more than armed squatters on my family's throne."

"Why did you wait so long to return to your country?" Narice asked

"The political climate was not right, and the rebels were not strong enough. Until now. If I can return home with the Eye, the country will vote for the monarchy and throw the generals out."

"What's to keep the generals from taking power anyway?"

Saint answered, "The U.S. wants that port, but not if world opinion says they are supporting an illegitimate regime. If the generals don't have the Eye, the U.S. won't back them."

"And if the generals do get their hands on it, then what?"

"It's a toss up. Some in our government and a few fat-cat corporations want to run their own candidate."

Narice was almost afraid to ask, "So are they looking for the Eye, too?"

"Probably."

She shook her head. There were an awful lot of dogs in this hunt, but she'd made up her mind. She wanted in.

The Majesty took a sip of her tea. After setting the cup down, she declared, "It is decided then. Mr. St. Martin and Ms. Jordan will begin the search with the Keeper's Toledo friend. From there we will see where it leads."

She stood. "I will see you both soon. May the Eye shine on your quest."

Then she exited with her hand on Farouk's arm.

Three

After the audience, Fulani escorted Narice back to the bedroom where Narice removed the *cha* and replaced it with her own clothing. As she positioned her gold hoops in her ears, she thanked Fulani for her help.

Fulani bowed. "You are very welcome." She handed Narice her purse. "Are you truly going to help The Majesty retrieve the Eye?"

Narice saw no harm in responding. "Yes. I'm hoping it will lead the police to my father's killers."

Fulani nodded as if she understood. "Well, my countrymen will be pleased to have the Eye home, and I hope the killers get what they deserve, too. Good luck, Ms. Jordan. May the Eye shine on you."

Narice smiled, and said again, "Thank you."

Saint was waiting when Narice was escorted back to the main room.

"You ready?" he asked.

"Yep." Suddenly Narice noticed the silence in the room. Unlike earlier, there was no one moving about. No servants. No old men in sandals. No gilded chairs. "Where'd everybody go?" she asked, looking around.

"Off to place their bets on the winner, probably," Saint cracked.

Narice was confused, "What?"

"Never mind. Come on."

Confused still, Narice followed him out into the hallway—which was by the way just as quiet and as empty as the suite. The burly guards who'd greeted her arrival were gone.

"What happened to the guards?"

"The Majesty has flown the coop."

"Why?"

They were now at the elevator. He hit the triangle-shaped call button. "So she'll be alive to claim the Eye when the time comes."

Narice didn't understand.

He explained, "There have been two attempts on her life in the past month. Because of that, she's keeping her movements fluid."

Now Narice got it. "Where will she go?"

He shrugged. "Don't know. When she needs to contact us, she will."

"And in the meantime?"

"In the meantime, we try and stay alive, too."

Narice wasn't sure how to take his words. "Are you trying to scare me?"

"Hope so."

"Why?"

"Because the other side wants us dead. Fear will keep you alive."

Narice suppressed the shiver that ran up her spine and waited silently for the elevator to arrive.

When the elevator doors opened, Narice and Saint stepped in. Admittedly, Narice was having second thoughts about this little adventure. A sister in her right mind would admit that she'd made a mistake signing on, plead my bad, and go back to her safe life in Baltimore, but her life wasn't safe anymore; according to what she'd heard, she was not only Alice, but the fox in this bizarre hunt as well. The only way she could get out of this was to go forward and pray.

When he hit the button on the panel labeled *Garage*, she asked him, "Did you forget we valet parked?"

"Nope."

"Then why are we going to the garage?"

He looked her way and asked, "Did you ask a lot of questions growing up?"

"Yes."

"You haven't changed."

Narice reached over and hit the elevator's emergency stop.

The car lurched and halted so violently, it threw

Saint and his bad shoulder painfully against the wood-paneled wall. He grabbed at the ache and barked, "What the hell's the matter with you?"

"Just trying to get your attention."

He evaluated her malevolently from behind his glasses. "Okay, you got it. Now what?"

"You are going to stop patronizing me, do you understand?"

"Or, you're going to do what?"

"Make this trip a living hell."

"You're already way ahead of yourself," Saint cracked, while he rubbed his shoulder and studied her face. Her chin was raised defiantly and challenge sparkled in her dark eyes. He'd be the first to admit that he had a real thing for strong women, but this fancy schoolteacher appeared to be stronger than most. "Okay, I apologize. So, what do you want me to do?"

"Answer my questions as if I'm an adult."

He eyed her, making a vow to never cut up in her classroom. "What's the question again?"

Her narrowed eyes met his shaded ones. "My question was, why are we going to the garage?"

"So I can check out the car before it's brought around."

"Why?"

"To make sure the bad guys didn't fix it to go boom when we drive off."

Narice's eyes widened. "A bomb?"

"A bomb. So hit the button and let's go."

She just stood there with her mouth open.

He reached over and did it himself. "You wanted an answer."

While Narice continued to be frozen in place, the elevator resumed its descent.

A shaken Narice followed him out of the elevator and into the shadow-filled lower levels of the garage. As in most big cities, parking was at a premium so some hotels rented a section of a nearby municipal lot for its valet guests. This garage was vast and every space was filled. She wondered how he'd find his car in this sea of vehicles.

Saint stood there a moment and looked around for the black sports car. Because he didn't spot it right off, and he didn't have the time or the inclination to spend the next hour hunting it down, he reached into his pocket and took out the handheld computer he never left home without. Ignoring the curiosity on the curvy Ms. Jordan's beautiful face, he punched in a few codes then waited for the screen he needed. When it came up, he punched in another code and a new screen appeared. He finally looked her way. Pointing with the handheld, he said, "That way."

An amazed Narice fell in beside him. Although she couldn't make out all the details on the handheld, she could see a cursor blinking in the middle of what appeared to be a blueprint grid. She had questions, of course, but she let him concentrate on what he was doing.

The car was up on the second level. They saw no one as they walked the thirty or so yards it took to reach it.

Narice chalked it up to her imagination but the silence felt alive—sinister.

He reached into another coat pocket and took out a piece of paper and a pen. He scribbled some numbers on the paper, then handed it to her. "If anything happens to me, you call that number and friends of mine will come and get you. Okay?"

Narice glanced at the number, then put the paper in her purse. "Okay."

"Good. Now go over there and stand behind that van for a minute. No sense in both of us being blown up."

Concern etched her face, but she didn't argue. She moved quickly to the blue van he'd indicated and waited silently to see what would happen next. He reached into his coat and drew out a small penlight. After flicking it on and being careful not to make contact with the car's body he directed the light through the window on the driver's side and into the dark interior. She watched silently, her heart pounding while he slowly circled the car and peered into each of the windows.

Only after he'd flicked off the light and put it back into his coat, did she exhale and ask, "Anything?"

"Not so far."

He went back into his pockets and took out a small round device that fit easily into his palm. He pointed the object towards the car and once again began a slow walk around the perimeter. This time, when he scanned the passenger side, Narice heard a series of soft beeps.

"Bingo," he said with soft triumph and smiled.

Narice couldn't help it. She smiled, too. "You do know what you're doing, don't you?"

"Yes, Teach. I do."

"Are you going to disarm it?"

"No time."

"But my suitcase is in there."

"Sorry."

"But—"

"You can buy more soon as we get a chance, okay?"

Her chin went up. "Okay. So, what do we do now?"

He went back to the handheld. Punching more buttons, he said, "If I know my brother, there should be another car around here somewhere for us to use."

"Your brother?"

But his attention was on the computer that seemed to be leading them deeper into the garage. A few rows to the left he stopped, then directed her attention to a big SUV with black tinted windows. "That one."

By now, she had so many questions eddying in her head, she didn't know which one to ask first.

When she came back to herself he was already seated behind the wheel and buckled in. The passenger-side door was open, and he was asking, "You coming?"

An embarrassed Narice shook herself and quickly got in.

Once she was in, and her belt secured, he hit the stick and backed up. Heading forward now, he steered through the half shadows while he reached up into the visor and pulled out a garage ticket. "This should get us out. Look in that glove box. There should be an envelope. Take out a ten so we can pay the attendant."

A rattled Narice found the envelope. There was a fat stack of bills lying inside. The denominations on some were small but many were one-hundred-dollar bills. She was about to ask him where all this came from, but out of her window, she spotted what appeared to be a thin female figure slide quickly back into the shadows as they passed. For some reason, Narice thought it was Fulani. Wondering if her eyes and the shadows were playing tricks on her, Narice turned back for confirmation but saw no one. "Did you see that?"

"What?"

"I thought I saw Fulani."

"Where?"

"Back there."

"I need a ten, Narice. Come on, we're here."

She hurriedly pulled out a ten from the stuffed envelope, and handed it over.

"Thanks."

While she mulled over why Fulani might have been in the parking lot, he handed the attendant the ticket and the ten, took the change and roared out of the garage and into the sunshine.

"You sure it was Fulani?" he asked as he merged into the traffic.

"Pretty sure."

"Okay, we'll check it out later. Maybe The Majesty just sent her down to check on us."

Narice didn't feel that to be the case; the figure

seemed to be hiding, but she let the matter go. "Where to now?" she asked.

He turned a corner and followed the signs directing them to the highway. While they sat at a light, he reached down and flipped up the console. Inside were buttons, a small GPS screen and a bunch of other electronic bells and whistles Narice could only stare at.

Saint looked over at her awestruck face and chuckled.

Her eyes narrowed in response but he chuckled again, then hit a switch and said, "Big brother. You there?"

Silence. Then the male voice Narice remembered hearing after her failed escape attempt came on and said, "Hey, little brother. I'm here."

Saint replied, "Your buggy has bugs, so me and the lady took your gift."

Big brother said, "Aw, man. I loved that buggy."

Saint laughed. "Hey, not my fault. The cockroaches got to it first. We need you to call the exterminator."

The voice gushed with anguish. "I knew I shouldn't have let you drive it."

Narice asked, "Why's he sound so crushed?"

Saint's voice was laced with amusement. "That sports car we were driving was his."

Big brother came back on the line. "All right. We thought you might need the SUV, so exterminators are on site. You get yourself out of there."

"Will do."

"Little Touissant sends love."

Saint nodded. Little Touissant was his sister Sarita's

nickname. "Sending love back." He closed the panel and eased the big truck away from the light.

A few moments later, Narice heard a loud explosion that seemed to rock the very air. She quickly turned in her seat and looked back towards the direction they'd come. Through the truck's tinted rear window she could see smoke pouring out of the garage. "Was it the car?"

He nodded. "Better to blow it now than to have it accidentally tripped by some poor citizen."

As the sound of wailing sirens came out of the distance, Narice faced forward, prayed no one had been hurt, and fixed her eyes on the road.

They drove for a long time in silence. Saint looked her way a few times but didn't say anything. He figured she'd talk soon enough.

A few minutes later, she did. "How did you know the car had a bomb?"

"I didn't, but I thought about what I'd do if I were the bad guys and wanted to make sure the Eye wasn't found."

"Eliminate the people looking for it?"

"First thing."

She shuddered again. "This is real, isn't it?"

" 'Fraid so, angel."

Narice watched the scenery through the window beside her seat.

Saint asked, "You going to be okay?"

She chuckled softly, "When this is over, yes. Right now, I'm still adjusting. I'm okay."

"You sure?"

"Don't have much of a choice, do I?"

He shook his head. "Nope."

Needing to think about something else beside the potential of her immediate demise, Narice asked, "Where are we headed?"

"Toledo to see Uncle Willie."

"Should we call him?"

"No, cell phones aren't secure. We'll talk to him face-to-face."

"Do you think he might be in danger?"

"More than likely, yes."

Narice didn't like the sound of that. "Well, they may be in for a surprise. Uncle Willie's a retired cop. He can probably still handle his business, even at his age."

Less than three hours after leaving Grand Rapids, the big black SUV cruised into Toledo, Ohio. Narice's back and behind were stiff from the long ride, so when he stopped to get gas, she stepped out so she could stretch.

His hand on the pump, he asked her, "How you doing?"

Saint watched her stretch her arms above her head, innocently teasing him with the rise of her soft breasts. He turned away smoothly, so he wouldn't be caught staring at the way the white silk tautened over her nipples.

She finally responded to his question, "I'm a little stiff, but otherwise okay. I'm also hungry, but I want to make sure Uncle Willie is okay."

Pierced by the sharp arrow of lust, Saint had a sudden hunger too, but he ignored it; or at least attempted to. "We can eat after."

Narice agreed. Right now, making sure Willie was okay took precedence over her empty stomach.

She waited and watched Saint do the windows and found herself studying his hands. They were capable hands; the fingers long, the skin scarred in a few places. He wore a carved silver band on the ring finger of his right hand. The ring's exotic make made her curious about its origin. She wondered about his origins as well. Who was he really, and what kind of life prepares a man to be so wary he looks for bombs wired to his car? It was quite obvious he was not your everyday, run-of-the-mill brother. He'd mentioned having a sister and she'd heard the voice of his brother. Did he have other family members as well—a wife, children? Where had he trained to be who he was?

Saint looked up from tossing the dirty towel into the waiting trash can to find her watching him. It was impossible to know what she might be thinking, but he was thinking that she'd be a sister worth pursuing if this job weren't so important and she weren't so classy. Saint knew a dessert fork from a salad fork, and over the years had attended his share of state dinners and embassy balls, but he didn't like the high life. His two half-brothers, Mykal and Drake, both powerful and wealthy men were accustomed to life's finer things and enjoyed them. For Saint, the good life meant having a bed to sleep in and enough food in your stomach; growing up in foster care gave him an appreciation for simpler things. So, no, he wasn't going to get mixed up with the elegant Narice Jordan no matter how sweet her nipples looked. He didn't wear suits and he didn't shave; women like her expected both.

Narice continued to be haunted by Ridley. Who knew where she might have ended up had Saint and his squeegee partners not shown up. She wondered if he would now volunteer more details. "How did you know I was with Ridley?"

"Friends of mine have had him under surveillance. They figured he'd make a move on you after the funeral, and he did."

"What will happen to him?"

"Deported, maybe. He's a Canadian citizen, but there's no guarantee he'll stay put because he's as slippery as he is deadly."

"So, we'll probably see him again."

"More than likely."

Narice added one more worry to her growing list.

Uncle Willie's name was really William White. He wasn't blood, but because he'd been her father's best friend he'd become an uncle of the heart. Narice directed St. Martin to the small blue-and-white bungalow without trouble. Uncle Willie lived within hollering distance of the Toledo Zoo. When she was growing up, the frequent trips to see him had always coincided with a trip to see the animals, so by the time Narice was nine years old, she could find his house with her eyes closed.

Saint parked by the curb and took a moment to survey the place. Two windows upstairs facing the street. Probably bedrooms. One big picture window downstairs. Living room, more than likely. He opened his door and stepped out. Taking a moment to scan the layout of the block, he noted that it looked like most urban sides of town. There were a few vacant lots and a boarded-up home two doors down, but there were also freshly painted fences, flowers in pots and in window boxes. All the homes had their lawns cut and he saw kids riding bikes near the convenience store on the corner. He checked the street for parked cars that might hold men watching Uncle Willie's house but saw none.

A white wire fence encased Uncle Willie's well-kept flower-filled front yard. Guests had to come through the gate in order to access the stone walk that led up to the wide, old-fashioned porch. Narice put her hand on the gate and wondered how many times she'd done this before in her life? A modest estimate placed the count somewhere in the hundreds, she'd bet. Uncle Willie and her daddy fished together, went to regiment reunions together, played cards, drank brown liquor, and always, always told lies together. The memories brought tears of grief to her eyes. Her father hadn't deserved such a terrible death. She wiped the water away and opened the gate.

William White, all six foot two and three hundred

pounds of him, stepped out of the house and onto the porch. When he saw Narice, his eyes lit up like the Fourth. "Baby girl!"

Saint watched Narice hurry up the steps and be hugged fiercely by the big man with the gray hair. White held her like his life depended upon it, and Narice hugged him back tightly. Saint could see she was crying and his heart began to pound in sympathy. Tears ran down the retired cop's cheeks as he rocked her and crooned comfort.

Narice let herself cry. Since leaving her father's grave site, her greatest desire had been to be held and salved this way. She'd wanted someone to hold her who'd loved Simon Jordan as much as she, and who'd understand her tremendous heartache. William White was that someone because his pain and grief equaled her own.

Narice finally stepped back. She ran her fingertips over her eyes and knew she probably looked a mess, but she didn't care. Out of the blue, a hand appeared offering her some tissues. She took them from St. Martin with thanks, blew her nose and said, "William White, this is St. Martin."

Uncle Willie looked the sunglasses-wearing Saint up and down, then asked, "What's he trying out for, Cyclops in *X-Men 5—The Black Mutants*?"

Narice coughed and laughed. She couldn't see Saint's eyes, but she sensed he was not amused. "I don't think so, but let's go inside."

Saint followed them to the door, but paused a moment to look up and down the street for cockroaches before going in.

Inside, Uncle Willie was asking, "You all want something to eat? I just did some chops on the grill. Always cook too much so I won't have to cook later in the week. You're welcome to join me."

"Thanks, I'm starving," Narice gushed appreciatively.

Willie looked at the silent St. Martin. "What about you, Cyclops? You hungry?"

Saint gave up. He smiled. "Yes, sir."

Willie smiled back. "Then come and get it."

The grilled chops had been brushed with a sweet dark barbecue sauce that got all over Narice's hands and lips. It had been a long time since she'd tasted 'que this good, and just being around Wild Willie, as her daddy called him, lifted her spirit.

While they ate the chops, cole slaw and baked beans, they talked about Simon's death.

Willie said to Narice softly, "Sorry I didn't come to the funeral."

"That's okay. I understood your reasons."

"Hate to have the last memory of someone I love be of them lying there all stiff and still—funeral home paint all over their face." He shuddered. "Hate funerals." He went silent for a moment, then turned her way and asked, "Was it a good turnout?"

"Yes."

He nodded. "Good. Knew it would be. Everybody loved him."

In light of all that had happened, Narice thought he needed to know the truth about the death of his best friend. "Not everyone, Uncle Willie. The police said it wasn't just a fire. It was arson."

Willie stared. Visibly shaken he set down the jar holding his green Kool-Aid. His dark eyes radiated anger and emotion. "Arson? You didn't tell me the fire was set."

"I know, but it was bad enough that *I* knew."

Willie stared at Narice, then at the silent watching Saint. "Lord, have mercy. Glad you didn't tell me. I'd be in Detroit right now, busting heads. Nobody deserves to die like that. Nobody." His gray mustached lips tightened. "Damn," he whispered. Tears ran down his face again. He wiped them away and asked, "So what are the cops up there doing? Are they looking for the arsonist?"

"Yes, buy they weren't sure how long it might take. They said they'd get in touch when they had something." She then asked, "Do you know anything about the Eye of Sheba?"

His head turned sharply. "Why?"

His abrupt and wary answer made Narice pause and observe him for a moment. She picked her words carefully, "Because it might be the reason daddy died."

Willie looked at Narice, then at Saint before sighing heavily. "I told him bringing that thing back to the States was a bad idea. I told him."

Saint asked, "What do you mean?"

"He wanted to help the king, but I thought smuggling it out of the country and then hiding it would be more trouble than the damn thing was worth."

"Do you know where he hid it?"

Willie shook his head, saying, "No, but he did hide it. That much I know. Somebody after it?"

Narice nodded. "And after me because they think I know where it is."

"The king's family?"

"Yes, but she's with the good guys, I hope."

Willie turned on Saint. "You look like military. You in on this, too?"

"Yes, sir."

"Whose side?"

Saint nodded towards Narice. "Hers."

Willie seemed to relax. "Good. I got something I want to show you."

While he was gone, Narice looked over at Saint. His statement that he was on her side had done funny things to her insides. She'd always gone through life under her own steam; she'd never wanted a man to declare himself on *her* side. Brandon, her ex, could certainly attest to that.

Uncle Willie returned carrying a large box. Saint hurried over to help relieve the elderly man of the heavy burden, but Willie glared. "Back off, Cyclops. I'm all right."

Saint stepped back.

Willie placed the box on an empty kitchen chair and Willie said, "Six weeks ago, Simon drove down here so we could go to Atlantic City. He had this box in the car.

Told me if anything happened to him, I was to give the box to you."

Narice's face creased with puzzlement. She walked over to it. "Did he say anything else?"

"Nope. I tried to give him the third degree, but he said it was personal, so I left it alone. You think the folks wanting the diamond were already after him?"

Narice nodded. After meeting with The Majesty, Narice was fairly certain that had been the case. More than likely agents of the opposition had contacted him and demanded the return of the Eye. When he refused, they'd set the house on fire. Farouk did say all roads led to those opposing The Majesty. "Well, let's see what's in here."

Inside were old notebooks, letters, and newspapers. In the middle of the pile she found an old address book. She slowly turned the pages. The familiar scrawl of her father's handwriting brought grief to the surface once more, but she was determined to find out what else the box held, so set her emotions aside and dug deeper. More letters; his high school yearbook. There were a few pictures, too. One, a black-and-white picture of a twelve-year-old Narice at the beach on Belle Isle. She looked at the skinny, grinning kid that was herself and smiled. She set it aside. The last photo pulled at her heart painfully and the resulting tears flowed unchecked down her brown cheeks. Hands shaking, she lifted it out of the box. It was framed and had been taken on her parents' wedding day. Her daddy looked solemn in his fancy suit; her mother, dressed in yards and yards of white silk and lace, looked beautifully dignified. Their young faces stared at Narice across time. She ran a slow finger over the faces and felt the knot of grief grow in her throat. When her mother died, Narice and her father had gone through the rest of their lives without her. Once again, Narice's pain echoed; he hadn't deserved to die alone among the flames. She put the photo aside and picked out the last item. It was cylindrical, wrapped in brown paper and tied closed with string.

A curious Narice set it on the table and carefully opened the paper. Inside, lay the most beautiful quilt she'd ever seen.

Four

The quilt wasn't very large; its size would barely cover the top of a small coffee table. Midnight blue and black were the dominant colors, but the threading and the appliquéd symbols were done in gleaming golds, greens, and reds. Squares of soft purple velvet framed the two vertical edges. Each corner had a penny stitched to the fabric. Narice had never seen anything like it. Moved by its beauty, she turned to Willie. "Do you know where this came from?"

"Nope," he confessed.

Both he and Saint came closer in order to get a better look. Narice draped the quilt over the top of the box and held up the edges so everyone could see the intricate design. She ran her hands lightly over the textured surface, then using her fingers pinched her way around the outside edges.

Willie asked, "Hoping he hid something inside?"

She nodded, then felt something. Turning to St. Martin, she whispered, "Bingo!"

He grinned back. "You're learning." He reached into his coat and handed her a small closed pocketknife. "Use this."

Narice shook her head with amusement. Forget Cyclops. St. Martin was really Inspector Gadget.

Narice very carefully slit a few of the threads on the edge then handed the knife back to Saint. Using the red tips of her manicured fingers, she slowly withdrew a folded piece of paper. Unfolded, it read: *Narice. If Willie has given this to you, I'm probably dead. To find the Eye use this quilt first, then go Home.*

The idea that he knew he wouldn't be around when she retrieved the quilt made Narice's anger at the unknown killers flare again. She handed the note over to the men to read. Once they had, Saint reached into his coat and took out a butane charcoal lighter. He flicked on the flame. Holding the note, he carefully set it afire, then walked the small flaming note to the sink Seconds later, it was ash.

Willie looked on with surprise. Narice now accustomed to Saint and his magic tricks, directed her attention back to the quilt. It was certainly gorgeous. Last summer, she and a few of her sorors had attended an Underground Railroad lecture at the Smithsonian Institute. On display were dozens of old quilts used by escaped slaves to find their way North to freedom. Her daddy's quilt bore a startling resemblance to those displayed. She only wished she could remember the meanings behind the symbols.

Saint eyed the quilt and confessed, "If this is our map, we're in trouble."

Narice was more optimistic. "We have to go to a bookstore."

"Why?"

"There's a book I need. If this quilt *is* our map, we have to learn to read it."

She saw his eyebrow rise.

He said with an impressed tone, "You are getting good at this, aren't you?"

"Just trying to keep up with you," she tossed back easily.

He grinned beneath the glasses and she turned away because her heart was beating fast and she didn't want him to know he'd affected her.

Willie was still peering at the symbols. "That looks like water there."

Narice agreed. There were three wavy lines beneath what appeared to be a box within a larger box. "And a sun. This is a monkey wrench," she stated proudly. She recognized the four-sided square with its signature half-triangle points on each corner. According to what she could remember from the lecture, the monkey wrench signaled potential runaways to gather their tools—escape would be soon. She explained this to Willie and Saint, then confessed, "But does daddy mean to literally gather tools?"

They didn't know.

Saint had a suggestion. "Let's do it this way. I'd think your daddy would try and keep this as simple as possible."

Narice agreed.

"So, why does he want us to gather tools? What would we need them for?"

Willie shrugged and offered, "To tear something down—dig something up?"

Saint replied, "That's as good a guess as any. We'll stop at a hardware store and pick up some basic tools. Shovel, pickaxe—whatever else we think may come in handy."

Narice wondered if her father had done the quilt himself? Her gut said, yes. During the Jim Crow years of the forties and fifties, Simon Jordan had been a very successful tailor. Not until segregation was broken did he get the chance to pursue his lifelong dream of becoming a medical doctor. He'd always loved puzzles and rubrics and reading about ancient objects of mystery like the Rosetta Stone. It would be just like him to leave his behind. She smiled and looked up to heaven where she could just see him seated in a comfortable chair, kicked back with his feet up, watching and wondering if she'd be clever enough to figure it out. *I'll figure it out, daddy, just wait. And I'm going to find the arsonist, too,* she pledged silently.

Narice rolled the quilt back up in the thick brown paper and retied the strings. "That's enough drama for now. Uncle Willie, you go and watch your 'Wheel of Fortune.' Cyclops and I will clean up the dishes."

Saint nodded.

Willie who loved Vanna White, grinned. "You'll get no argument here. I love a good mystery, but I have to see my Vanna."

He left the kitchen and Narice and Saint were alone. Narice suddenly felt very self-conscious. Truthfully, she knew the reason—it was the over six-foot-tall man with the dark glasses watching her so silently. Reminding herself she was way past the age of being turned inside out by a bearded stranger, she took a deep breath to regain control. Then she put the stopper in the large stainless-steel sink and turned on the faucet. I'll wash."

"I'll dry." He shrugged out of his trench coat and laid it over one of the kitchen chairs while she found the dish soap and put a few squeezes into the running water. She put the silverware in the water and washed them first.

"I always do the plates first," Saint, said drying a bunch of the now-clean forks and knives with the blue stripped dish towel in his hand.

Narice glanced up at him and countered, "Well, when the silverware goes in my mouth, I want it clean."

Saint guessed that made sense. "Never thought about it like that. Guess I'll be washing the silverware first, from now on."

She smiled then moved on to the plates and glasses. Very conscious of his silent presence, Narice rinsed the sudsy plates in the companion sink and put them one by one in the green plastic dish drain on the counter. He reached for a wet plate just as she was putting the last plate in the drain. Their hands bumped. The sizzle of the contact made them quickly draw back.

"Sorry," he murmured.

"That's okay."

Their eyes met. She hastily looked away.

Saint could feel the heat rising between them; he was pretty sure she could feel it, too. He didn't push it, however. He'd already told himself he wasn't going to get involved, but he could still feel the electricity of her touch.

The rest of the dishes were finished without incident, and by the time "Wheel of Fortune" was done, so were they.

Narice dried her hands and took off the apron. Fending off Saint's growing nearness made her want air. Maybe a walk in Aunt Pearl's garden would help. Aunt Pearl was Uncle Willie's late wife. She died a few months after the death of Narice's mother. The double passings hit both husbands hard; each had lost their loves at an early age, but that mutual grief made them blood brothers forever.

Before Aunt Pearl died however, she'd had the mother of all gardens. Narice said to St. Martin, "I want to see if Aunt Pearl's garden is still here."

Saint didn't know why that was important to her, but he didn't want her going anywhere alone, so he followed.

Outside, Narice felt like she'd stepped into paradise. She hadn't been to visit in over a decade. In her absence the garden had grown and spread like a tropical forest. Narice had been nine years old when she helped Aunt Pearl put in eight Rose of Sharon plantings along the yard's left fence. Now those plants looked to be twelve feet high and were covered with glossy green leaves and blooms of white, red, and pink. Crowding the remaining three fences were more Rose of Sharons, towering lilacs, and stands of green forsythia bobbing in the evening breeze. There were red and white daisies, purple coneflowers and in the back of the yard, a stand of milkweed in full bloom. To her delight, orange and black monarchs were fluttering around the milkweed's blossoms, searching out the nectar.

Saint couldn't remember the last time he'd seen a monarch butterfly in the States. He'd grown accustomed to seeing them on his visits to Central and South America, but here—he hadn't seen one in an urban neighborhood for years. He could tell the sight made Narice happy. She was smiling. That was a good thing. The last couple days couldn't have been easy for her; she'd earned these few hours of peace.

Narice took Saint on a tour of the garden, pointing out different species of flowers, clueing him to the fact that monarchs rarely fed on the milkweed plants they were born on.

"How do you know so much about monarchs?"

She answered easily, "Aunt Pearl and Uncle Willie have always had milkweed in the yard, and I learned from them. Aunt Pearl was a science teacher."

"She and Willie divorced?"

"No, she died when I was young. A drunk driver hit her on her way to church one Sunday morning."

Narice watched a robin land on the edge of the bird-bath, dip his beak to drink, and fly away. The peace and quiet was a sharp contrast to all she'd been through; she didn't want to leave. Thinking about Aunt Pearl made Narice realize that Uncle Willie was the only person in her life now with a direct link to her past and to her parents. She turned to ask Saint about his past, when the silence exploded with what sounded like a cannon fire going off in the house, followed by Uncle Willie bellowing, "Cyclops! Get in here! Now!"

But Saint was already running towards the patio—gun drawn, coat flying behind him. "Hide!" he barked back at Narice.

He vanished into the house and Narice took off for the far end of the yard. Shaking and scared, she fought the mosquitoes for a hiding place amongst the tall, wide-leafed milkweed. Slapping at the bloodthirsty insects, she huddled and waited.

After what seemed like an eternity, she saw Saint step out onto the patio. The sunglass covered eyes swept the yard for her. "Narice!" he yelled.

She heard the anxiety in his voice, but it took her a moment to beat back the insects. "Down here."

When she stood, he seemed to visibly relax. "You okay?" he asked walking to meet her.

"I've been bitten a million times, but I'm all right. What's going on?"

"Come on in. Uncle Willie caught some cockroaches."

Inside, the two foreign born men seated in the front room on the blue sofa looked scared to death. Narice didn't blame them; the huge gun Uncle Willie had leveled on them had a barrel large enough for her to crawl in and go to sleep. She'd be scared, too. Only then did she see the dead man on the floor in the foyer. She quickly averted her eyes from the disturbing sight. "What happened?" Narice whispered.

"You okay, baby girl?"

"Yes, Unc."

"Wanted to make sure. These two, well three, came to my door posing as Jehovah's Witnesses, only they weren't carrying Bibles."

The men's heads dropped in what appeared to be both embarrassment and shame. "They asked if they could come in for water. I told them no. I went to sit back down and they slit my screen, reached in, and unlocked the door. I calmly pulled *Arnold* here out of the grandfather clock, and when the first one crossed my threshold, I blew him away. These two I invited in for tea."

Narice knew this was a serious matter, but . . . "The gun is named *Arnold*?"

"Yeah," Willie replied with pride. "After the Terminator." He never took his eyes off of his guests. "Minute I saw it in the catalogue—knew I had to have it. Knew what I was going to name it, too."

Narice shook her head and scanned the big gun. "Is that thing even legal?"

Uncle Willie said, "Cyclops, what do they teach you in the military?"

Saint didn't miss a beat. "Don't ask. Don't tell, sir."

"Exactly."

Narice smiled. "Never mind. What are you going to do with, them?"

"Already had Cyclops call the cops. My buddies should be here momentarily. In the meantime, Cyclops, search 'em. Let's see who they are."

Saint said, "I think we already know," but he had the two men stand up one at a time. From the anger in their eyes, it was plain they didn't like it, but with *Arnold* still trained on them they had no choice but to cooperate.

The two men and their dead friend had on them passports verifying that they were indeed from The Majesty's country of Nagal. Saint also found enough fake ID in their wallets and suit-coat pockets to supply the entire senior class at a local high school. Saint laid the passports in a line on the carpet. While Narice looked on, he produced a camera from the recesses of his magic coat and photographed the faces and information on each one. "Get me an envelope, angel, if you would please?"

"Look in the desk in my bedroom," Willie told her helpfully.

Narice returned and Saint stuffed the passports, the fake social security cards, and driver's licenses into the large manila envelope. He licked the top and sealed it. He then asked the visitors, "You guys ever been to Guantanamo Bay? The U.S. government has a five-star bed-and-breakfast you'll really like."

One of the men spit at Saint.

Uncle Willie warned ominously, "Do that again, and you're going to join your boy over there by the door."

The man's eyes blazed, and he sneered. "There are more where we came from. Thousands more. We will not rest until the Eye is found."

Saint cracked, "Glad to hear it. Just tell your buddies not to forget their Bibles."

Uncle Willie's booming laugh filled the room.

Ten minutes later the authorities descended on the house with siren screaming police cars, helicopters, ambulances, and swat teams. The neighbors lined the streets trying to see what they could see; TV people were running up and down the block, microphones in hand, attempting to find and interview someone who'd seen something—anything so the station could be first with the breaking news.

Narice was in one of Willie's upstairs bedrooms watching the circus through the curtain-framed window. Now that the police knew Uncle Willie had everything under control, they were trying to clear the street.

She turned away and flopped down on the bed on her back. The bedroom was the smaller of the two guest bedrooms in the house. It was the room she'd always slept in whenever her parents spent the night. Back then, the young Narice would never have imagined that in this house there would be a day like today. Never. The dead man's tarp-covered body had been taken out on a stretcher by the EMS and driven to the morgue. It would take a while for her to forget how he'd looked lying there on the floor. She shuddered involuntarily and turned over. She was tired. A heartbeat later, her eyelids closed.

Downstairs, Saint and Uncle Willie were finishing up their statements to the police. Uncle Willie took great delight in telling his former colleagues how he'd personally thwarted the band of foreigners who'd he said, targeted him as just another helpless senior citizen. Uncle Willie told the detectives he was convinced the foreign thugs had intended to rob him, "But I put a stop to that!" he boasted proudly.

In the end, the police believed the men were robbers, too.

Saint didn't say a word.

When the police were gone, Willie got himself a Molson out of the fridge, then gestured for Saint to sit, so they could talk.

Willie's first words were, "Man-oh-man. Haven't had that much fun in a while." He then asked, "How do you think they found you?"

"Tracking device maybe. Probably planted somewhere on Narice."

Willie took a draw on his beer and nodded. "You have a way of checking?"

Saint nodded.

"This is turning out to be pretty nasty. You'll keep her safe, won't you?"

"And have you coming after me with Arnold if I don't? I'll keep her safe, don't worry."

"And keep your hands off her?"

Saint assessed the old cop for a long moment, before saying, "That's between me and Narice."

Willie smiled, "Good answer. I respect a man who'll tell an old man to butt out. Break her heart, though, and it'll be me, you, and Arnold."

Saint didn't doubt that for a minute. "I'm going up and see if I can't find the tracking device."

Saint entered the room quietly when he saw her asleep on the bed. He didn't want to wake her but he needed to check out the contents of her purse.

He crossed over to the bed and stood over her for a moment to watch her sleep. Inside of himself, something was up. Earlier, after he'd run into the house to answer Uncle Willie's call then come back out to the patio to tell her the coast was clear, not finding her where he'd left her had scared him to death. In the space of those brief seconds while he visually and frantically scanned the yard, all kinds of bad scenarios concerning her whereabouts raced through his head.

Finally when he saw her stand and fight her way out of the milkweed, no words could describe the flood of relief he'd experienced. That's when he knew something was up. Although he'd only been around her a few days, he'd never been so concerned about a woman before. Sarita, his foster sister, yes, but not anyone else. Saint figured he could deny everything and chalk it all up to reactions to the drama surrounding the Eye, but that wouldn't be the truth. The truth—Narice Jordan was getting to him and he didn't know how to make it stop.

The shadows of dusk were creeping into the bedroom. Saint checked his watch. In less than an hour it would be dark. Willie had graciously offered them a bed for the night, but the cheetah in Saint was restless; he wanted to get on the road and drive. They'd hole up for the night in Detroit with family. They'd be safe there, and in the morning see about deciphering the quilt.

To Narice it seemed like a mere second had passed when she heard a soft male voice, "Hey, angel, wake up. We need to go."

Narice really wanted to sleep. "Five minutes," she croaked.

She heard him laugh gently, "Come on, baby doll. Time to roll."

Narice opened her eyes to see Saint seated on the bed beside her. Dark glasses on. Beard on. *Lord he is gorgeous*. She scanned the faded green coat. "Do you ever go anywhere without that tacky coat?" she asked, humor lacing her groggy tone.

He drew back in mock offense. "No dissing the coat, woman. We could live on a deserted island for years with the stuff I carry around in this so-called tacky coat."

The still sleepy Narice pondered living on a deserted island with him. He'd keep her safe, that she knew. She also knew that without him, this adventure would be a whole lot scarier. She slowly sat up. "I'm ready."

Their faces were only a few inches apart. Time slowed. He ran his eyes lingeringly over her face, her mouth.

Seeing him, feeling him, Narice trembled with anticipation.

Saint had to call upon every discipline he'd ever learned to keep from reaching out and tracing his finger over the sultry shape of her mouth. He vowed to leave this woman alone, and he thought he'd meant it. Now he wasn't so sure.

Before getting her degree in childhood education, Narice's job on Wall Street had put her in contact with some pretty powerful men, yet none of them exuded the intensity and purpose pulsating from inside this shade-wearing man. Just being near him made her dizzy. He was dangerous in so many ways. Grabbing hold of herself she scooted away and off the bed. Standing now, she croaked, "I'm ready when you are." Feeling self-conscious, she cleared her throat.

Saint smiled to himself. She was shaking like a virgin at a Thai whorehouse. He found that surprising.

Since hooking up with him, she'd been all business. He was now even more curious about the woman lurking beneath the iron maiden exterior. "I think you may be bugged. Let me see your purse a minute."

"Really?"

"Yeah, that might be how the cockroaches tracked us here."

"Where might it be?"

He smiled.

Confused, she asked, "What's wrong?"

"Nothing. Just love the way you speak. 'Where might it be?' "

She put her hand on her hip. "Sorry. Didn't mean to offend you with my *perfect* speech."

He help up his hands. "Whoa, whoa, baby. I wasn't mocking you. It was a compliment. Really."

Narice retracted her claws. "Sorry. Too sensitive."

He eyed her. "No kidding. You always so defensive?"

"Depends on the situation. Now, what were we saying?"

Saint noted that she'd gone icy like that on him before, but sitting next to her on the bed just now, and the heat he'd experienced down in the kitchen, let him know that the glacier wasn't as rock-hard he'd first believed. "We were talking about where the bug on you, *might be*."

She cut him a look. His shot her a teasing grin in reply.

Narice turned away to hide her smile.

"Where's your purse?" he asked with a chuckle.

Narice walked over to the old upholstered chair in the corner of the room. Her purse was on the seat.

After she turned on a lamp, he dumped the contents of her handbag onto the bedspread. Out of his coat pocket he withdrew a device that was about the size of a lipstick.

Narice asked, "What's that?"

"Bug finder. It's a prototype. The German company that made it wanted me to field test it for them."

"So, what, you're the Consumer's Reports for the spy industry?"

He grinned. "She's got jokes, folks."

Saint scanned everything; the contents of her small makeup bag, her wallet, keys, comb, brush. Nothing. He looked her way. "Zip."

She'd moved closer to him so she could watch what he was doing. When he turned the little scanner her way, she instinctively took a step back.

"Hold still," he told her easily. "It might be in your clothing."

He waved it up and down, then began slowly circling her. "Did anybody else handle your things besides Fulani?" Stepping closer he moved the detector up and down her legs, then across her waist.

"I don't know. There were two other women with her."

He was circling her now, silently teasing her with his nearness and making the butterflies she'd had while sitting on the bed beside him return. For a woman who prided herself on her control, her reaction to him was all new. Logically she knew it didn't make sense to be attracted to him, but she was and she didn't know how to proceed other than to try and pretend it away.

He continued his scan. "I think we may need to check Fulani out."

A beep sounded.

He waved the scanner across her chest and the beep sounded again. "Might be your bra. I need to take a look."

Narice responded with a sisterly I-don't-think-so look.

Saint dropped his head to hide his smile. "Sorry. How about I step out in the hall. You take off the bra and hand it out to me. Will that work?"

"That's better."

He grinned and left the room, closing the door behind him.

The idea that someone may have planted a tracking device in her brassiere made Narice angry, feel violated and embarrassed. She quickly removed the Tee and then her black silk bra. Shrugging back into the blouse, she then walked over to the door and opened it. Ignoring the mischief emanating from behind the shades, she dropped the lacy garment in his outstretched hand.

Saint slowly scanned the bit of silk and tried not to imagine how she'd looked removing it but he couldn't. It held her scent and the warmth of her skin. He could feel himself hardening and forced himself to pay attention to what he was supposed to be doing instead of wondering what a schoolteacher was doing wearing undies sexy enough for a lingerie supermodel.

The bug was in the bra strap. It was made of a lightweight metal and so small that it might never have been discovered without the scanner. He'd have to remember to tell the Germans their prototype worked well. Now, though, he had to scan her again to make sure there weren't more. "You can have it back. But let's make sure that was the only one."

Narice stood silently while he moved around her again. Truthfully, he'd handled the situation with her bra as respectfully as she could have wanted, so there was really no reason for her nipples to tighten the way they had at the sight of her bra in his hand. They had, though, and she hoped he hadn't noticed.

Saint couldn't help but see the points of her bare breasts through the thin white silk, nor could he ignore how the sight affected him. The more he tried to resist the siren call of the curvy Ms. Jordan the stronger he heard it. He pocketed the scanner. "You're clean."

"Thanks," she said. "We're having enough of a cockroach problem without me leading them straight to us."

He agreed and tried not to look at the tempting buds of her breasts. "We need to get rolling, so get dressed and I'll meet you downstairs."

"Okay."

Downstairs, the time had come to say good-bye to Uncle Willie. Narice didn't want to leave; he didn't want her to leave. She had to go, though, and so gave him a great big hug.

He hugged her back just as emotionally. "You let me know how you're doing, okay?"

Her tears were wetting his shirt. "Will do."

"If you need me just call. Me and Arnold will jump in the Buick and be there faster than Jackie Robinson."

She hadn't heard that old saying in a long time. It made her smile, and then she stepped back. "Okay."

Uncle Willie put an arm around her waist and walked her outside to the porch. "If you didn't have Cyclops with you I'd worry, but he's a good one. He could watch my back anytime."

"I'll tell him."

Saint was already in and running the SUV, waiting for her to finish her good-bye. Narice asked Willie, "Are you going to be okay?"

"With Arnold here? Silly question."

She supposed it was. She gave him one last kiss on the cheek. "Bye Unc."

"Bye, baby girl. Send me an invitation to the wedding."

She laughed. "You'd better get back in the house. I'll see you when this is done."

He grinned.

Seconds later, Narice was in her seat next to Saint. He eased the truck away from the curb. Uncle Willie waved and Narice waved back until he was out of sight.

Five

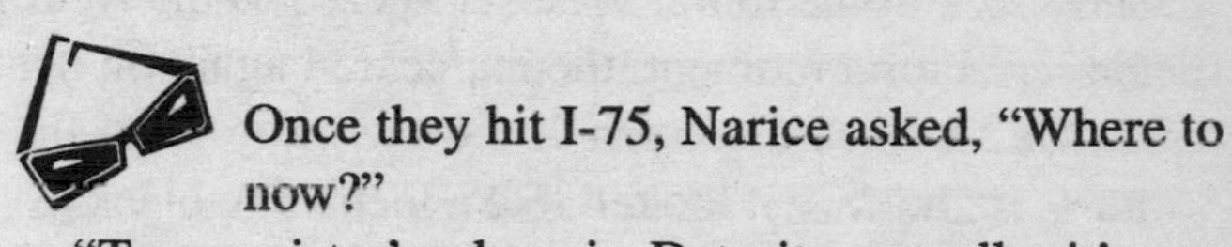

Once they hit I-75, Narice asked, "Where to now?"

"To my sister's place in Detroit—actually, it's my brother's house. We'll catch some sleep and in the morning go after that book you say we needed."

Narice peered at him through the darkness filling the interior. "Your family won't mind us showing up on their doorstep in the middle of the night?"

He shrugged, "Probably not, but let's ask." Reaching down, he flipped up the console face, hit a button, and said, "Big brother, you there?"

A cheery female voice responded, "Hey, Outlaw Man. Little Touissant here. How are you?"

Narice saw his smile by the green light of the dials. He opened his mouth to speak when out of nowhere, big bright lights flooded the car, blinding them. Then came a sound so loud Narice had to cover her ears. Panicked, she turned to look out of the rear window and her eyes widened. There was a helicopter on their tail, hovering no more than ten feet above the highway!

Saint checked it out in the rearview mirror. Cursing, he stepped down hard on the accelerator and the SUV's big engine leapt up to speed.

Little Touissant came over the speaker. "What's that noise?"

"A chopper. I'll talk to you later!" He hit the button and cut off communications.

Narice pulled her seat belt tight. She kept sneaking glances back at the thing. When it veered to the right, disappeared for a moment, then appeared again on her right, she bit back a scream and drew away from the window. In the dark it looked like a menacing black insect. When it swung closer and tried to run them off the road, she yelled out, "Saint!!"

Cursing again, Saint swerved sharply. The copter swung closer, repeating the attempt, making him swerve again.

The SUV was now rumbling at 110 mph. Saint did his best to drive, keep his eyes on the dark road, and stay ahead of the chopper. When the bird came around to the front and tried to intersect him on the road, he took it up to 120. The big truck was shaking, but rolling. "Hold on, angel!"

In spite of the warning, Narice was unprepared for the hard right he took as he left the highway and headed into the trees lining the road. The truck bounced across the bumpy terrain with such force Narice swore her head hit the ceiling more than once. The copter had been unprepared also. With its prey now off road and in the trees, all it could do was climb above the tree line and follow.

Saint was driving through the night like a bat out of hell. The body and tires of the big Chevy were taking hits and jabs from unseen objects that banged and pinged, but he didn't slow down. Narice could hear the chopper droning ominously above but she was too busy trying to keep body and soul together to worry about what it might be doing. She called out, "More cockroaches?"

He hollered back, "Yeah, but my gut says government kind."

"The U.S. government?"

"Yeah."

"Why? I thought you worked for the President?"

"I do. Remember me saying parts of the government want to get the Eye and run their own candidate?"

"Yes."

"Well, this might be them. Hold on!"

He did a doughnut on the edge of a field and Narice's head whipped around in concert. They were plowing forward again, heading back the way they'd come. The helicopter swung to follow.

With the tires squealing and the engine booming, he steered the truck back onto the highway. Up ahead Narice could see faint flashes of light off in the distance. Seconds later, tiny raindrops began to appear on the windshield. The chopper was nowhere to be seen and she hoped the rain had sent them home. She almost relaxed, only to be scared to death by the chopper now hanging directly in front of them.

To her surprise, Saint growled, "Oh, they want to play chicken, huh? Well, let's see what their balls are made of!"

Narice couldn't believe her ears. Was he really going to challenge them?

He stepped down on the accelerator once more. The rain had picked up, coating the glass with a sheen of rain. Through the swing of the wipers a terrified Narice could see the watery lights of the waiting copter. She could feel her heart pounding loud in her ears. The SUV was going at full throttle and the chopper hadn't moved. Her fear increased and she dug her nails into the leather handrests. They were now close enough to see the pilot, and the recognition in his eyes when he realized the truck was not going to stop. The bird rose up seconds before the truck intersected and Saint sped below it, screaming like a triumphant banshee. Mother Nature then threw a lightning bolt beside the highway that lit the night like day.

Narice fell back against her seat. Her heart—what was left of it—was beating like a drum. "Don't ever do that again!"

He grinned. "You didn't like that?"

She stared at him. "No. You scared me to death. How did you know they'd blink first?"

"I didn't."

Had Narice been in a cheesy romance novel, she would have fainted dead away. Instead, she said, "Not funny. You're not the only one in this car you know. What if they hadn't moved. "We could have been killed."

Saint didn't like being fussed at. Danger and risks went with the job, and sometimes you had to deal with both to stay alive.

When he didn't reply, she asked, "Doesn't that bother you?"

"Sure. I like living as much as the next guy, so next time I'll just pull over and say, 'Okay, we give.' "

Narice didn't care for the sarcasm, but she got the point. "You just scared me, that's all."

"Not my intent. Just trying to be around to see tomorrow."

The storm was upon them with full force. Rain, lightning, and thunder. She looked back, but the copter was nowhere in sight. "It's gone." She'd never been so glad to be in a thunderstorm in her life.

"Good. Let's slow our roll here. Don't want to escape then die in a crash because we spun out on wet pavement."

Narice agreed. Only now was her adrenaline starting to slow.

Little Touissant came on again. "You two okay out there?"

Saint answered, "Bogey's gone. We're a little shook up, but in one piece."

Narice cracked, "Speak for yourself."

He chuckled. "I don't think the angel's going to want to date me again after this."

Narice drawled, "You got that right."

The female voice laughed, "Well, are you two heading this way?"

"Yep. She wanted me to ask and make sure its okay."

"Of course, but I appreciate her manners. Your angel need anything?"

Narice called out, "Yes, clothes and some insect cream." As if being chased by helicopter wasn't bad enough, the anxiety of the last few minutes seemed to have awakened all the bites she'd received while hiding in Uncle Willie's milkweed. She scratched at her arms through her silk jacket. "I've got bites all over me."

The voice sounded concerned. "Bites?"

"Mosquitoes."

"Oh, okay. We'll fix you up."

"Thanks," Narice said, trying not to scratch but wanting to very badly.

Saint said, "Thanks, general. See you in about an hour."

"All righty. Stay safe."

"We will." He hit a button and closed the console.

"Is that your sister?"

He looked her way and nodded.

"She sounds nice."

"Yep."

"Why do you call her the general?"

Saint laughed. "Because she's always in charge."

"I see," Narice replied, even though she didn't see at all. She was looking forward to meeting the family of the mysterious St. Martin, though, then to a long hot shower and a good night's sleep. She scratched at the bites on her arms.

"They got you pretty good, didn't they?"

She scratched some more. "Remind me to choose a different hiding place next time."

"I was worried when I came back out and didn't see you."

She paused and looked his way. "I know. I could hear it in your voice."

Saint held her eyes for a moment, then redirected his attention to the dark highway. "We'll go shopping tomorrow so you can get some new things."

"That'll be great."

Narice studied his bearded profile in the dark. She sensed that he too felt the attraction rising between them, but then again, he'd probably been attracting women since birth; being attracted to her was probably just another day at the office for him. With that in mind, Narice reminded herself that when this adventure was over, he'd go back to his life, and she to hers. It made no sense to even think about forming an attachment.

They arrived in Detroit about an hour later. Saint pulled into the driveway and cut the engine. Narice was sleep; had been for the last thirty miles. Once again, he hated to wake her up, but he was sure she didn't want to spend the night in the truck.

He reached over and put his hand on her shoulder, then shook her gently, "Wake up, Narice."

Narice swam up to consciousness. Still half asleep, she mumbled, "Are we here?"

He smiled, "Yeah, babe. We're here. Want me to carry you?"

She sat up straight, and said groggily but firmly, "No. I can walk."

Saint chuckled at her refusal to be pampered. "Okay."

He went around to her side and opened the door for her. The half-asleep Narice grabbed the rolled up quilt, stumbled out the vehicle, and followed Saint to the front door of the large house.

His sister met them there. She was short, brown-skinned, and wore her natural hair cut very short. Dressed in a Detroit Lions T-shirt, a pair of shorts, and some Scooby-Do slippers, she greeted her brother with a long welcoming hug, then wrinkled her nose. "God, Saint. When are you going to burn that coat?"

He backed up and said in mock offense, "Hey. Lay off the coat."

Narice liked her right away.

Sarita smiled at Narice. "Come on in. I'm Sarita Chandler."

Narice smiled back and stuck out her hand, "Narice Jordan."

"Glad to meet you, Narice. Welcome."

As they were led into the house, Narice scanned the beautiful furnishings and artwork on the walls. She wondered if the Chandlers had personally picked the pieces or if the interior had been done by a professional designer. Either way the rooms were stunning.

Sarita looked at Narice's dirty clothes, wrecked hair, and no longer perfect makeup and said, "I'm guessing you want a shower first."

A grateful Narice gushed, "Oh yes."

Sarita told her, "Then come on with me. Afterwards, we'll get you some clean clothes and you can relax."

She then looked to her brother. "Myk's in his office. He said come up when you get the chance."

"Okay."

The women headed off.

Saint climbed the stairs to find his brother. Technically, Sarita was Saint's foster sister. Her grandmother had taken him in during his preteen years, and he and Sarita were raised together. Last year, Saint discovered that he had two half-brothers, Mykal Chandler and Drake Randolph, Detroit's mayor. Saint and Myk still weren't as close as Myk and Drake; those two spent their childhood summers together. Saint still wasn't sure just how close he wanted to be. He'd been a loner most of his life. Sarita's family had been his only family; word was still out on whether he needed more.

Myk turned from his chair and greeted his brother with a smile. "Glad you made it."

"Me too."

Saint took a seat in one of the leather recliners, laid his weary head back against the head rest and closed his eyes. "Sorry about your car."

Myk shrugged. "Couldn't be helped. The SUV was a better idea, anyway. Just like you said."

Saint didn't open his eyes. "Just like I said."

"I figured we needed speed."

"Well, I wanted bulk. If the bomb hadn't got us, that chopper certainly would have had we been in that small car. Remind me to send General Motors a fan letter."

Myk laughed. "We got a make on the chopper from the rear camera."

Saint turned his head. "What camera?"

Myk said slyly, "You're not the only one with prototypes, my brother. There's a camera mounted in the taillights and the headlights. Here are the pics."

The photos were black-and-white shots of the helicopter. Saint's jaw tightened grimly. It wasn't possible to know whether the clowns flying the chopper were intent upon murder, but it sure seemed like it. "Do you know who they were?"

"I ran the make of the copter through some channels and all I got back was—it's government issue. Could be Justice, Defense, could be stolen for all we know."

Mykal Chandler was head operative for a clandestine government group called Nia. In Swahili the word meant *purpose,* and the purpose of Myk's organization was to rid the city of crime and drugs by any means necessary. Myk and Sarita met during one of Nia's stings. "Well, the pilot was a good one. Flew that bird like he ran folks off the road for a living."

"That might be an angle to check out."

"Maybe, but don't spend too much time on it. I know your plate's full."

"Never too full to help if you need it."

Saint was unaccustomed to asking for help; he usually operated on his own, using his own people, contacts, and resources. He knew his brother was being sincere and that Myk in his own way was offering the help to strengthen their bond, but Saint's personal issues kept him from wholly accepting the friendship and familial ties his brother wanted him to embrace.

"How's the lady holding up?" Myk asked.

Saint smiled almost wistfully. "Real well, considering there have been three attempts to stop her in the last twelve hours."

"Three? I know about the bomb and Sarita told me about the chopper. What else happened?"

Saint spent the next few minutes telling the story of Uncle Willie, Arnold, and the fake Jehovah's Witnesses.

Myk chuckled, "Guess you won't have to worry about him taking care of himself in a pinch."

"Oh, no. Arnold was a serious piece of fire power. Serious."

They then talked about the quilt.

Myk was impressed. "Hell of a way to hide a map."

"No kidding. Can we decipher it is the question, though. Narice knows of a book that might help. We'll check it out in the morning."

Silence crept up between them for a few long moments. Myk finally said, "Well, welcome home."

Saint held his brother's eyes. "Thanks. How's Sarita doing?"

"Running everything as always. We're well, too."

Saint cracked, "Sorry to hear that second part."

His brother answered with sparkling eyes. "Don't hate."

Saint grinned. Sarita was the only woman Saint had ever loved. In his youth, he'd imagined growing up and asking her to marry him. Little did he know he'd be the one to introduce Sarita to Myk and that they'd fall in love. Sarita knew nothing about Saint's feelings for her, but Myk did. In a way that knowledge made the brothers closer, but it had also added another edge to their relationship, before Saint saw how happy Sarita was with her marriage and with Myk. In the end, Saint came to accept the fact that although Sarita loved him, she loved him like a brother and would never love him the way she did her husband. "Is there coffee?"

"In the kitchen."

"Well, I'm going to grab a cup, and clean up. We'll talk more later." Saint left the office.

Sarita showed Narice into a spacious bedroom that had its own attached bathroom. The room's furnishings were done in varying shades of green. "You can bunk here for the night."

Narice always prided herself on her good taste and her ability to arrange a room, but the furniture and appointments in here left Narice in awe. Everything from the lamps to the drapes to the huge bed were elegant and stylish.

"How are you and my brother getting along?"

Because Narice had no idea how much Sarita knew about her brother's role in the search for the Eye, she chose a simple answer, "We're doing fine."

"Saint's unique."

"That he is."

Sarita looked about to say something else, but apparently changed her mind. "Well, let me get you some clean clothes. You're taller than I am, but we should be able to find you something to put on. You go ahead and relax, and I'll be back later."

Sarita walked to the door then turned back to say, "Oh, I left some insect-bite cream in the bathroom on the counter. Hope it helps."

Narice smiled. "I hope so, too."

Then Narice was alone. She opted for the shower instead of a bath. As tired as she was, she was sure that if she got into the huge black tub, it would feel so good, she'd doze off, slide under the water, and drown.

After the shower, Narice wrapped herself in one of the huge towels in the cabinet Sarita pointed out before her exit, then stepped back into the bedroom. On the bed was a fluffy white robe with the tags still on it, a nightgown, also new, and a pair of blue footies, also new. Narice wondered if Sarita had a department store hidden in the house? Putting that silly thought out of her head, Narice got dressed.

Later, downstairs in the kitchen, Narice and Saint sat with Sarita and Myk around the table. Narice saw that Mykal Chandler was dark to Saint's light. Sarita's handsome husband had dark skin, a mustache, and dark eyes. Although he and Saint were about the same height, Myk was more muscular. Saint's body looked as powerful, but was leaner. The cut of their jaw and the slope of their cheeks showed their shared parentage.

As the conversation flowed, Narice learned that Sarita ran a neighborhood center in the inner city and that her husband was a big-time architect and philanthropist. The talk then turned to the Eye. To Narice's surprise the Chandlers were pretty much up to speed on all that had occurred, even the discovery of the quilt.

Mykal said, "I never knew anything about slave quilts. I'll be going on the net later to see what I can find. Fascinating when you think about it."

Narice then told them about the lecture she'd attended and how beautiful and moving the quilts were. "Many of the symbols are African-based. Some were from secret societies. Different colors meant different things and some quilts even carried symbols designed to protect the quilt itself."

Saint raised an eyebrow. "Like magic?"

"I suppose you could call it that, yes. That book I told you we needed should help us figure what our quilt means, at least I hope."

The clock on the wall showed it was nearly midnight. Sarita yawned behind her hand, then said, "You all will have to forgive me, but its been a long day. There's a health fair going on at the center that kicks off at eight A.M., so I need to go to bed."

Mykal Chandler ran a sympathetic hand up his wife's back. "You do too much."

She preened under the slow back massage he was now giving her. "That's because there's a lot to do, Mykal."

He leaned forward and whispered something in her ear, and she giggled, "You are so bad."

She took him by the hand. He was smiling down at her with such love in his eyes, Narice made herself look elsewhere. Before her own marriage fell apart, she wondered if Brandon, her ex, had ever looked at her that way, but she couldn't remember. Back then she'd been so focused on scaling the corporate mountain, everything else became secondary. Everything. Including her marriage.

Narice turned to Saint. Because of the sunglasses, she couldn't see his eyes but he seemed to be enjoying the interaction between his sister and brother. Once Narice and Saint were alone, she said, "They seem like a very happy couple."

"They are, but when they first got married, I hoped they wouldn't be."

Narice cocked her head his way. "Why?"

"Come on outside with me. I need to stretch my legs after all that driving."

Narice tossed back. "Is this a date?"

He grinned, then said, "Maybe."

Narice could feel herself succumbing to him again, and for this moment in time decided not to fight it but to enjoy it.

The moment they stepped out of the doors, she felt the cool night breeze and smelled the water of the Detroit River. Because she'd been half asleep when they first arrived here, she'd had no idea until now just how close the Chandler home was to the river. To her right she could see the Christmas-like lights of the Ambassador Bridge that connected Detroit to its Canadian neighbor, Windsor, Ontario. The darkness kept Narice from seeing the landscaping around the deck where she stood, but the solar lights in the ground lined a wood-plank walk that sloped down to a dock on the river's edge. "It's peaceful out here."

"Yeah, it is."

"Why were you mad about your sister being in love?"

He looked at her.

"Or is it supposed to be a secret?"

He dropped his head in what appeared to be amusement, then asked, "You're Miss Cleo now?"

"Being psychic has nothing to do with it. You brought this up. How long have they been married?"

"It'll be a year in February."

"She's obviously happy."

"I take full blame. I introduced them."

"What's wrong with that?"

"She was supposed to marry me."

Narice was confused. "You can't marry your sister. That's illegal and strange."

"She's my foster sister. We aren't blood."

"Oh."

Admittedly, a small part of Narice was disappointed knowing he loved someone else, but the thinking parts of herself were convinced it was good news. Now, nursing an attraction for him was entirely out of the question. "Why didn't you tell her how you felt before she got married?"

"She sees me as blood. Telling her would have made her real uncomfortable around me, and that's not what I want." Saint then studied her in the dark. "Why am I telling you this?"

Narice shrugged. "No idea, but talking sometimes helps clarify things." She then added, "I won't tell anyone, if that's what you're worried about. Does anyone else know?"

"Yeah, Myk."

Narice went still. "He knows that you're in love with his wife?"

"Was. I'm not anymore. It's a long story but to make it short, when Sarita wound up in the hospital last year, I told him. He took it well, I thought."

He then turned to Narice and explained, "Sarita is unique, no other woman in the world has her fire or her strength. Before she married Myk, she ran that neighborhood center of hers on no money—none, but she still managed to do after-school tutoring, meals for the shut-ins, and Christmas trees and Christmas dinners for families unable to afford their own."

Narice was glad she'd met Sarita and come to like her before hearing Saint's evaluation. To hear him talk, the woman was Mary McLeod Bethune and Dorothy Height wrapped up in one. No sister liked being compared to a saint knowing she'd fall short. "Do they have any children?"

"No—not yet."

They let the silence rise again and Narice could hear the wind in the trees. She thought about the rainstorm they'd encountered down by the state line. "Do you think that weather's coming this way?"

He lifted his head and looked around. The wind was rising. "Maybe."

Narice let the breeze bathe her face. Out here, she didn't have to think about choppers, or quilts, or dead men lying in Uncle Willie's doorway. The blustery gusts seemed to blow away all of her tension and anxiety. "I could stay out here all night."

"So could I."

Narice smiled, "That's right, you are nocturnal, aren't you?"

He grinned in the darkness.

"Well, I'm kinda nocturnal myself, truth be told. I enjoy the quiet and the relaxation after a hard day, especially on a stormy, windy night like this. Makes you want to curl up with a good book."

"*Or a good woman,* Saint thought.

Narice met his eyes then looked away. She was glad for the darkness.

Saint then said, "You've been a trooper through all of this. I know it can't be easy."

"No, it isn't, but I have a feeling it's going to be harder the closer we get to finding the Eye."

"You're right, but I'm going to do everything I can to keep you safe."

The genuine feeling in his words touched her. "I know."

Silence again.

Narice could feel the tiredness of the day catching up with her. In another time and place she could have stayed out here with him all night, but tomorrow was coming and maybe so were the cockroaches. "I need to go to bed. If I can find my way back to the room your sister gave me." She laughed.

"It is a big place. Come on. I'll show you."

Upstairs outside of Narice's door they stood facing each other as if this were indeed the end of a date, and she felt as nervous as a sixteen-year-old. "I'll see you in the morning."

"You, too. Get some sleep."

"Thanks."

While he watched, she slipped into her bedroom and softly closed the door.

After she was gone, Saint stood in the hallway, thinking about her, and wondering what it was about her that had made him open up to her the way he had.

Other than Myk, no one knew how he felt about Sarita, why in the world had he told her?

Unable to answer the question, Saint shook himself free, then headed off to his own bed.

Six

Narice awakened the next morning to the sound of knocking. Turning over in bed, she peered around blearily then remembered where she was. "Yes?"

"Are you awake?" Saint called through the door.

"Yes," she groused sleepily. Narice had never been a morning person, and doubted she ever would be.

"Come downstairs a minute. Something I want you to see."

Narice raised up wearily. "It's not more cockroaches, is it?" *Lord, don't let it be cockroaches. Not at this time of the morning.*

Saint laughed. "No cockroaches. This is something you'll like."

Narice didn't believe him, but got out of bed anyway.

After attending to her morning needs and brushing her teeth, Narice, still wearing her robe, left her borrowed bedroom. Unfamiliarity with the layout of the big house sent her in the wrong direction again at first, but she finally came across the staircase. It led down to the large, well-furnished sitting room she'd been so impressed with last night. This morning, the big wooden door was ajar and Saint stuck his head around it. "Mornin.' We're in here."

But when Narice walked in she couldn't see the *we* he'd referred to because she was too busy staring at the racks and racks of women's clothing; all hanging on hangers, all brand-new and bearing price tags. She saw blouses, slacks, dresses, suits, so much merchandise, in fact, she couldn't see the furniture.

Out of the racks stepped Myk Chandler. "Morning, Narice."

"Morning," she replied, still looking around at the mini department store.

"Sarita said you needed some clothes, so I had a friend bring some things over. Pick out what you need and I'll send the rest back."

Narice stared at him as if he'd grown another head. She turned to Saint. He was wearing his signature coat and leaning casually against the fireplace mantel. Covering his eyes were the shades, so lord knew what he was thinking, but he was smiling. "Pretty scary, isn't it?" he asked, gesturing to the clothes. "He does this to Sarita all the time. She's trying to find him a twelve-step program, but so far, no luck."

Amused, Narice began to slowly move through the clothes, looking at blouses, fingering skirts. There was a small stack of boxes on one of the coffee tables. Some of the boxes were pale blue, others gold, a few were ivory but all bore the names of the city's finest stores: Nordstrom's, Lord & Taylor, Marshall Fields. She gave Myk a questioning look.

He responded, "Those, too."

A curious Narice picked one up. A peek inside revealed a beautiful indigo nightgown trimmed with lace. The sensual gown lay in the box delicately layered between folds of scented tissue paper. Just looking at it let Narice know it would slide over her body like a caress. Her eyes strayed to Saint and found shaded eyes watching her with a powerful intensity she could feel. Swallowing in her suddenly dry throat, she closed the box and moved on.

She snaked her way through shorts, swimsuits, sundresses and skirts. There were capris and jeans; bathrobes and packages of fine pantyhose. She shook her head. "There's so much here."

Saint pushed himself away from the mantel. "Need help deciding?"

Narice eyed him, and said, "Maybe," then added dubiously, "but not from you."

He placed his hand over his heart as if she'd wounded him, "Why not?"

She laughed. "Look at how you're dressed?"

He studied himself for a moment.

Myk interjected drolly, "She does have a point."

Ignoring them, Saint strode over to a rack holding a bunch of blouses. After a few silent moments of hunting he held up an ivory silk number that made Narice's mouth water. He asked, "So, you wouldn't wear this?"

Narice knew the blouse would be an asset in any woman's closet. "Well, yes."

He moved over to another rack and held up two long-sleeved cotton sweaters—one red, one black. "How about these?"

"I'd wear those, too," she confessed. Both would be perfect for the chilly summer nights of August. She asked, "So, should I apologize and say, you have great taste, even if you dress like the hero in a spaghetti western?"

Myk's laugh filled the room.

Saint ignored him. "Yes."

She smiled. "I apologize. You do have great taste."

Myk said proudly, "Runs in our genes."

Narice looked from one brother to the other. "You two do favor."

"No, we don't," the brothers replied in unison.

"Yes, you do. You have the same cheeks, the—"

"No, we don't," they said again, firmer this time.

She shook her head. "Never mind. Myk, let me go and get my purse so I can give you my credit card number."

He asked, "What for?"

"So I can pay for what I'm going to choose."

"Your credit isn't good here—your money either. Just pick out what you need. Me, I have to get to work."

"But—"

"No buts. It's the least Sarita and I can do."

"But—"

He smiled, then turned to his brother. "Are you going to stick around?"

"Depends on whether we can find the book or not."

"Okay, but don't leave town without letting me know. I'm on my way to pick up something you'll probably need."

Saint looked confused.

Myk waved him off. "I'll see you later. Narice, there's a suitcase you can use in the hall closet."

She nodded. "Thanks, thanks for everything."

He left without a further word.

In the silence that followed his exit, Narice took a slower stroll through the clothing; picking out pieces here and there, holding items against her torso in an attempt to gauge how the garment might look once she had it on. Through it all, Saint waited and watched silently. Narice was very conscious of his presence. "You know, you're going to go blind wearing sunglasses inside all the time."

"I'm already blind, that's why I wear them."

Her eyes swung to his. "They're prescription?"

"Yep."

"Why didn't you tell me?"

"You never asked."

She gave him an embarrassed smile. "I didn't did I?"

He shook his head. "No."

Narice's guilt stung her. She'd had no business being so judgmental, but he was so unlike the men she was accustomed to being around. "How long do you think we'll be on the road, that way I can figure out how much stuff I'll need to take."

He shrugged. "No idea."

"A week's worth maybe?"

"Sounds good."

So she spent the next few minutes gathering jeans, tops, sweatshirts, T-shirts, and other practical wear. Choosing those garments made much better sense than trying to run from the bad guys in Bandolinos and Dior suits with tight skirts. Speaking of Bandolinos, the Chandlers had also provided a slew of shoes: sandals, hikers, running shoes, and dress flats. Narice stuck her left foot into a sandal and the right into a running shoe. Both fit well, so she put them with their mates and set them in her keeper pile.

Narice was pleased with her choices; she didn't need to take much with her, she had tons of clothes at home. The only thing she hadn't spotted yet, and she prayed they were here somewhere, was underwear. She shot a quick look at Saint. She really didn't want to ask him, but she needed more underwear than the single change she possessed now. "Is there underwear here, somewhere, I hope?"

"Try checking the rest of those boxes on the coffee table."

Sure enough, one of the gold boxes held three sexy brassieres and matching panties. The jewel-tone colors and the lace trim were just her style. A quick search through the other boxes turned up more underwear, a couple of camisoles, pajamas, and a robe. She walked the boxes over to her keeper pile. "Does your brother really bring clothes in like this for his wife?"

"Clothes, jewelers, furriers. He bought so many clothes for her when they first got married, lots are still in bags and boxes in her closet. She has enough stuff for *three* women."

"Does he do it to impress her?"

"Nope. Does it because he loves her."

"I see," Narice replied. Most women never got that kind of love. Narice thought it best to change the subject. "I'm going to take all this upstairs and get dressed."

After breakfast, Narice and Saint went out to the van. Last night, the darkness kept them from fully assessing the SUV's damage, but now that it was morning, the big dent on the passenger-side front wheel well was quite apparent. The paint had been badly scratched on the driver's side. There were bumps and bruises on the doors, and a headlight was broken. "Considering what we went through, it looks pretty good," he said pleased. "Gives it some character."

Narice wasn't sure if character was the word, but as long as it could outrun a helicopter, she didn't care how it looked. "So where do we go first?"

He looked at his watch. "I need to get a headlight, then we can find a bookstore.

Wearing a short-sleeved blue blouse, matching shorts, and her new running shoes Narice climbed into the passenger seat and clicked in her belt. "You know," she said as he got in on his side, "I've been thinking about the clue daddy left in the quilt."

He stuck the key in the ignition and turned on the engine. "What about it."

"It said, *'then go Home'*. I'm wondering if he meant our home, the house I grew up in?"

"Is it the same house where the fire was set?"

"Yes."

"Well, let's swing by there after I get the headlight and see what we can see."

She nodded her agreement, but in reality Narice dreaded the prospect of revisiting the scene of her father's death.

Saint made a few calls and found an auto shop that could replace the light. An hour later, the work was done and he was driving down Forest Avenue on the city's east side en route to Narice's home. She'd been pretty quiet most of the morning. He didn't press, figuring if his childhood home had been torched and someone he loved had died in the fire, he'd be pretty silent, too.

Per her directions, Saint took a left onto Sheridan Street and drove halfway down the block. On their left was a large city playground filled with kids on swings, in the sandbox, and shooting hoop. On the right, the charred remains of Simon Jordan's house. Saint eased the SUV to the curb and cut the engine.

For a moment, Narice didn't move to get out. She sat there looking up and down the street at the familiar houses. The memories of playing in the park when she was young rose to mind as clearly as the happy sounds of the children playing there now. Her eyes finally settled on the blackened wood and bricks that had once been her home and the grief filled her throat. Pushing it aside, she took hold of the door's handle and swung the heavy door open.

Saint could feel her pain. "Are you sure you want to do this, now?"

"Now or later, it's all the same."

She got out and he followed.

The roof was gone. Yellow police tape cordoned off the perimeter. A sign nailed onto the temporary plywood door declared the place condemned and warned trespassers to stay out.

Narice held the yellow tape up so she could duck under it, then she and Saint stood there for a moment scanning the hulk.

Narice said softly, "Well, daddy, we're here. Now what?"

Saint asked, "You don't think the Eye's in there somewhere, do you?"

"I doubt it, that would be too obvious, but it's too dangerous to go inside and look." She studied the house again. "I wonder why he wanted me to come here? He said, *home,* and this is home."

She turned to Saint hoping he had a theory.

He shrugged. "I have no idea."

Narice walked slowly around the burned perimeter, stepping over wood and around scorched furniture and other debris. Her first trip here had been the day before the funeral. In her pain and sorrow all she could do was stand in front of the remains and weep for her father and for herself. Coming here today, she'd hoped the purpose behind the visit would give her the strength and distance she'd need to look for whatever clues might be contained in the ashes, but grief still had the upper hand.

When Saint looked up and saw the tears standing in her eyes, his heart went out to her. "How about we go to the bookstore? I don't think we're going to find what we're looking for here."

She discreetly wiped her eyes. "You're probably right. If there was anything valuable it's long gone."

A woman's voice interrupted them. "Well, good morning, Narice."

Thelma McNeal had been the Jordans' next door neighbor for thirty years. Narice took in a deep breath and looked over to where the woman stood on her back porch. "Good morning, Mrs. McNeal."

Once upon a time, Thelma McNeal had been hot. With her dark brown skin, beautiful full figure, and jet black hair, she drove the neighborhood's husbands and widowers wild. She drove their wives wild too, because Thelma had many of those husbands sneaking in her back door at night. Now, the years of alcohol abuse and fly-by-night sugar daddies had drained her beauty and aged her well beyond her sixty years. Her skin was now mottled and creased, the eyes bleary. One of the reasons was easy to see. It was barely 10:30 in the morning and Thelma was already buzzed; probably from the brown liquor in the glass she had in her hand. Her platinum-blond wig was on slightly crooked and the once traffic-stopping curves were now just bulk beneath a flowered muumuu that should have been turned into a dust rag years ago. Her other hand held her current yap dog against her formidable chest. Like all little yap dogs, it had the nerve to growl and bare its teeth.

Mrs. McNeal ignored the dog and said to Narice, "Sorry about your daddy's passing. I was in North Carolina burying my sister the day the fire broke out."

Narice said sincerely, "Thank you, and my condolences to you and your family, too."

Mrs. McNeal smiled sadly. "She was a good sister and a good friend. I'm the only one left now out of the six girls my mama had." She bent to kiss the dog, "Aren't I sweetums. The last of the Welch girls. Yes I am, yes I am."

Narice looked at Saint. He tossed back a raised eyebrow.

Thelma's eyes went to the burned-down house. "Police said it was arson."

"Yes, that's what they told me, too. Did Daddy ever mention anything to you about being threatened by anyone?"

Mrs. McNeal shook her head. "No, but some government men came by here yesterday afternoon and asked me the same thing."

Saint asked, "What did they look like?"

"One Black. One White. The White man had red hair. Black guy had a patch on his eye."

"The one with the patch sounds like Gus Green," Saint said.

"Friend?" Narice asked.

He shook his head. "Foe."

"What did you tell them?" Narice asked.

"Nothing. Once the government gets in your business, you can't get them out. They're like a cranberry stain on your best Thanksgiving tablecloth. Besides, I had nothing to tell."

Narice looked back to the house. *What had daddy meant? Where would a clue be?*

Mrs. McNeal's voice broke into Narice's thoughts. "He your new husband?"

"No. A friend."

"Your daddy said your husband got married again. Two little girls."

Narice's body and voice stiffened. "Yes."

"Pity you all couldn't make it."

"Yes, it was."

"First time I ever heard of a woman having to pay her man alimony."

Narice didn't reply.

Saint saw the tightness in Narice's jaw and realized there was more going on here than just pleasant conversation between neighbors. Mrs. McNeal's eyes were gleaming with dislike as she asked, "What was your husband's name again?"

"Brandon."

"That's right. I remember that time you both came home for Thanksgiving. That was right after the wedding, wasn't it?"

Narice decided this interview was over. "Yes, it was. It was nice seeing you again."

"Do you want me to tell Larry you said hello?"

Narice's manners kicked in and she stopped. "Please do."

"Larry's my son," Mrs. McNeal told Saint. "Married to a doctor down in Atlanta. She gave up doctoring for a while so she could stay home and raise their son. He's almost three now."

"That's nice."

Narice began to walk back to the tape.

Mrs. McNeal's caustic voice followed them, "My Larry was sweet on Narice growing up, but he wasn't never good enough. She was college bound," she added sarcastically, then cracked bitterly, "No staying home and being a wife and raising babies for Narice."

The dog was barking his two cents also, but by now, Narice was striding to the truck. The heat of her anger competed with the sun beaming down. No, she hadn't wanted to stay home, go to the local college, and marry dumb, dull Larry McNeal. Her father raised her with the belief that her life lay beyond the confines of the city of Detroit and he'd been right.

Inside the van now, Saint looked over at the silent Narice as he started the engine. "You okay?"

"No. I want to snatch that blond wig off of her head

and beat her with it," she tossed back between gritted teeth. "If I was Larry, I'd live in Atlanta, too. Crazy old heifer."

Saint's eyes were wide as saucers. "Narice?"

She shot him a look, "What?"

He chuckled. "I didn't know you had it in you."

"You can take the girl out of Detroit, but you can't take the Detroit out of the girl."

Saint grinned. "I'm glad to know you, Ms. Thang."

She cut him an amused glance. "Just drive, Cyclops."

Once they were underway, he headed up Sheridan to Gratiot and took a right. At Van Dyke they took another left and Narice couldn't help but notice the changes in the area. A Sears store had been on the corner of Van Dyke and Gratiot during her childhood. During the seventies and eighties it and other big-name department stores fled the inner city for suburbia. As a result this corner remained a vacant lot for many years. Now, to her surprise and delight, there was a big, fabulous senior citizen high-rise on the spot. With its well-manicured grass and stands of multicolored lilies and black-eyed Susans, the complex stood at the intersection like a beacon of hope and progress.

When the traffic light turned green, Saint didn't turn. Instead, as horns honked behind him, he pretended to fiddle with the radio. Just as the yellow slipped to red, he slid through the light.

Narice was confused. "What are you doing?"

"Trying to see if we were being followed."

She said skeptically, "Okay."

"If someone was tailing us, the light's caught them."

Pleased by the ploy, she said approvingly, "You are definitely smarter than the average bear."

"And you're much prettier than BooBoo or Ranger Smith."

She laughed.

Their eyes held and she could feel the call of their mutual attraction filling the space like sensual music. She turned away so he couldn't see her response. "Do you think we were followed?"

"If not now, we will be. Gus being in the neighborhood is not good news, but it's not a surprise."

"Who is he?"

"He used to work for the State Department but lost his job for selling state secrets. I thought he was in jail."

"Have you run up against him before?"

"Yes, and he's a killer. Period."

"Where'd you first meet him?"

"South Africa."

"What were you doing in South Africa?"

"A little fieldwork for the UN."

Not sure what that meant, Narice studied him closely. "Why was Gus there?"

"To be a mole for the South African government."

Narice's confusion must have shown on her face because he explained further. "Gus's job was to infiltrate

Woodson

the African National Congress and report back to the government."

"And he did that?"

"For money, some people will do anything."

Narice was stunned. "How did he sleep at night?"

"Knowing Gus, probably very well. If you don't have any loyalties you don't need a conscience."

Narice supposed he was right; history was filled with Benedict Arnolds of all races, but she made a mental note not to trust Gus Green under any circumstances.

Once they reached the entrance to the highway, they merged onto the eastbound Ford Freeway.

Saint kept his eyes out for tails. If Gus and his cronies were in town, they were bound to show up sooner or later, and Saint put his bet on sooner. As he passed the Alter Road entrance a black car sped down the ramp and merged into traffic. Saint smiled. There they were, right on time. He didn't have to see the plate or registration to know who they were. The black no-frills sedan screamed federal issue. "We're being followed."

Narice twisted around in her seat.

Saint said, "See that big black box a few cars back?"

She did. It looked like your standard everyday government car. Back home in Maryland, they were everywhere. "Are you sure it's them?"

"Pretty sure, but let's find out." Traffic was fairly light, so he moved into the far-left lane and eased the speed up to eighty.

Narice kept her eyes glued on the mirror next to her

window and waited to see what the black car would do. It sped up and began jockeying through the traffic in an attempt to keep up. "Too bad we can't lead them to some place like Moscow."

Saint chuckled. "I vote for Rio—better food."

"Are we still going to the bookstore?"

"I don't see why not."

"What if they put a bomb in the car while we're gone? Won't it be hard to keep an eye on the car if we're inside?"

"Yep, but I've got it covered."

Narice had no idea what that meant, but she'd learned to let him handle the technicalities of keeping them a step ahead of the bad guys. A few moments later, he parked and cut the engine.

The mall had grown in size since Narice shopped here last. There were a lot more stores and the parking lot was huge. Narice got out. He did the same, then pointed the clicker on his keys at the SUV to lock it and she assumed to arm the alarm. A quick look around the immediate area showed no black sedan, so Narice followed him to the mall door.

This being a workday, it was fairly quiet inside. She spotted a few seniors walking the mall for exercise, young women pushing infants in baby strollers, and a couple of teenagers who looked like they should have been in school with the rest of the kids their age.

The bookstore was down by the food court.

When they got there, Saint told her, "You go on inside. I want to grab a cup of coffee."

Narice wasn't sure she wanted to be on her own. With so many cockroaches sniffing around, she didn't want to wind up being snatched again, but since the food court was in shouting distance, she nodded her agreement and walked into the store.

The young male employee behind the counter verified that the book Narice wanted was indeed on the shelves and then pointed her in the right direction.

Narice walked to the back of the store and when she saw it, she snapped it up like the day's winning lotto ticket. A heartbeat later she had it opened and was browsing through to make sure it was the same book recommended by the Smithsonian lecturer. Happily, it was indeed. In the front were the symbols used by the slaves, and Narice scanned them with a rising excitement. There was the Monkey Wrench. She couldn't wait to sit down with both the book and the quilt. She looked up to see if Saint had come in yet, but he hadn't, so she closed the book and browsed through the section to see if there were any more quilt books that might aid them in the search.

"Do you like quilts?"

The male voice caused Narice to turn. He was tall, black, and wearing a green leather eye patch. She was surprised to find him standing beside her because moments earlier she'd had the store to herself. He smiled, showing her two gold incisors that seemed to gleam under the store's light and Narice could feel her fear rising. Even though she'd never set eyes on him before, she knew by the eye patch that this was the man, Gus Green. The man Saint accused of spying on the ANC for the South African government. "Yes, I do like quilts," she said, hoping her voice didn't betray how scared she was. Her book in hand, she nodded politely. "I need to go pay for this. Excuse me."

She moved to step by him but he reached out and grabbed her arm. "Why are you running off, Ms. Jordan? We've only just met."

"Let go of me."

He grinned that gold at her again, then looked at the book clutched in her hand.

"Let go!" she snarled louder.

He didn't. Instead he asked in a calm voice, "Now, with all that is swirling around you, why are you here buying that particular book?"

"I will scream," she promised angrily.

Only then did he raise his other hand and allow her to see the loaded syringe it held, and her eyes widened with fright. "And it will be the last sound you'll make for quite some time," he promised. His voice hardened, "Now, tell me about the book."

Keeping a frightened eye on the needle, Narice lied. "It's for a friend. I promised I'd buy her a copy when I ran across one."

She couldn't tell whether he believed her or not. Trying to keep her fear under control so she could think, she cast another hasty glance around for Saint.

Green seemed to have read her mind. "If you're

looking for St. Martin, he's occupied with some friends of mine. He won't be back anytime soon, if at all. So, let's go."

Hearing that Saint wouldn't be around to offer his unique brand of assistance made her knees go rubbery for a moment, but she forced herself to hold it together. As he tried to make her walk towards the door at the back of the store, the Detroit in Narice surfaced and she shouted indignantly at the top of her voice, "Get your hands off of me!"

She swung her purse. He blocked it, giving her the blink of an eye she needed to knee him in the groin as hard as she could.

He yelled and immediately grabbed his fire-filled genitals. Eyes bulging with pain and surprise, he dropped to his knees. Moaning, he toppled sideways like ice cream falling out of a cone.

A breathing hard and angry Narice wondered if she should let him know he'd dropped his syringe.

Seven

Saint nursed his coffee at a seat in the back of the food court so he could keep one eye on the bookstore and the other on the lookout for the folks in the black sedan. He knew they were in the mall somewhere; he could smell them. Sure enough, a minute or so later they strolled into view. Wearing dark suits and shades, they looked like refugees from a Blues Brothers convention. Saint wondered if they were too dumb to realize they stood out like Klansmen at an NAACP fundraiser, or if they just didn't care.

To draw attention to himself, he madc a show of knocking over his cup, then jumped up from his seat to keep the coffee from flowing down onto his coat. Pretending not to see the agents, he quickly snatched a handful of napkins out of the table dispenser to sop up the mess. When he was done, he tossed the napkins in the trash, paused a moment to assess his coffee-damp hands, and strolled to the restroom situated a few steps away. A discreet look back showed them following him like rats behind the pied piper. Saint simply shook his head. He enjoyed tangling with arrogant government types because their egos made his job easier.

Once inside the restroom, Saint quickly positioned himself behind the door, then reached into his coat and took out his hinged nightstick reinforced with lead inserts to give it an extra kick. He snapped it out to its full length then held it high like Sammy Sosa waiting on a pitch.

The first cockroach to enter was just drawing his gun when Saint hit a home run across the bridge of the Black man's nose. Blood gushed, the man screamed and fell to his knees. A blow to the back of the head rendered him instantly unconscious. Contestant number two's blue eyes went wide seeing his companion go down, but before he could react, Saint whirled and cracked him across the knees. Number Two groaned then buckled. A lightning fast crack on his back made the man cry out. A second rap across the jaw dropped him like a sack of potatoes and he joined his partner in dreamland on the brown tiled restroom floor.

It had taken the adrenaline-charged Saint less than ten seconds to put both men out. Breathing harshly, Saint exhaled slowly and willed his heartbeat to slow. He picked up their guns, pocketed them, then quickly rifled through their suit coats for ID. He stuffed those into his coat as well. He'd check them out later. Still breathing harshly, he folded the baton, put it back into its hiding place in his coat, and then washed his hands at the sink. Moments later, he stepped over the unconscious cockroaches and left the restroom to go check on Narice.

Saint hurried into the bookstore just in time to hear Narice shouting. The kid behind the counter looked up in response to the sounds of what was obviously a Black woman going off, and met Saint's eyes with a questioning look. Saint told him, "That's my wife, I'll handle whatever it is."

Saint kept walking, but reached into the deep outside pocket of his coat and placed his hand on his gun.

He found her at the back of the store in the kids' section. Saint was so surprised to see Green lying on the floor, he stopped confused. Narice for her part was standing off to the side. Her tear filled eyes were furious.

Saint asked quickly, "Are you okay?"

"Now I am."

She handed him the syringe. "Here."

Saint's eyebrow rose. "Where'd you get this?"

"It's his. He was going to use it on me."

Saint turned startled eyes on Green who was obviously in great distress, "So what happened to him?"

"I kneed him in the nuts."

Saint's surprise etched his face, then he began to chuckle.

Green, who had managed to drag himself to his

knees, but was still bent over from Narice's attack, glowered at Saint and growled, "I thought she was a lady," and he cast a malevolent glare at Narice.

Narice shot him a go-to-hell look, then asked Saint, "Where were you?"

"In the bathroom stepping on some cockroaches."

That pleased her. "Good. Can we leave now?"

He grinned. "Sure. Give me a minute, though. I want to talk to my man here."

Saint pulled out his gun and walked over to where Gus was still struggling to breathe. Green appeared pale and ashen, but Saint knew that a knee in the nuts will do that to you. He reached into the man's coat and pulled out his gun. "The next time you put your hands on her, a knee is going to be heaven compared to what I'm going to do to you."

"How was that Thailand prison, Ridley sent you to?" Green threw back. "When did you get out?"

Saint snatched Green up so quickly and with such force Green didn't see the large, exotically sculpted knife in Saint's hand until the glittering point was pressed against his shuddering throat. "I should cut your traitor's throat right here," Saint gritted out.

Though Green was sweating profusely, he tossed back boldy, "But you won't."

Saint's responding smile was filled such hate it seemed to shine as bright as the knife. "Won't I?"

Even though Narice wanted these cockroaches out of her life, she didn't think this was the place to be gutting anyone. They were in the children's section at the back of the store and it was pretty shielded but, they were in the mall for heaven's sake. "Saint—"

He didn't seem to hear her. Instead he told Green, "While I was in that prison I used to dream about all the many ways I was going to kill Ridley when I got out, and you're this close to helping me practice making my dreams come true."

Green smiled dismissively, but when the blade pricked him just enough to make him bleed, his features registered horror.

"Saint!" Narice whispered harshly. His anger was so real he was scaring her. *What had Ridley done to him?*

"Stay out of this," he snapped coldly.

Narice's hand went to her hip in offense.

Green was now visibly shaking.

Saint said softly and firmly, "The only reason you're not dead right now is Narice." He then showed Green the syringe. "You were going to use this on her. What's in it?"

Gus seemed real scared now. "Just something to put her to sleep."

"For how long?"

"Three, four hours. That's all. I swear."

Saint said to Narice. "Angel, go pay for your book. I'll meet you up front. Tell Ms. Jordan, 'night night', Gus."

Gus could see the syringe in Saint's left hand and he began to shake even more.

"Say it!" Saint demanded in a cold emotionless voice.

Gus shot a terror filled eye to Narice. "Night-night," he said in a high-pitched voice.

Narice left.

At the counter the young male employee said, "I see you found the book."

She nodded and gave him a twenty and a ten to pay for the book. While she waited for him to make change and place the book in a bag, she noticed the crowd of people standing near the food court. "What's going on over there?"

"Security found two guys beat up in the bathroom."

Saint walked up then, and Narice searched his face to see if it held a clue as to what transpired between him and Green after she left them alone, but the shades made his true expression unreadable. A few seconds later, Narice left the book store escorted by a silent, jaws tight Saint.

Once they got back to the Caddy, Narice assessed him silently as he took out his keys and clicked off the alarm. He then used the small sensor from his pocket to check the vehicle for explosives. While he slowly walked the device around the perimeter, she realized she still knew very little about him. Yes, they'd been together for a couple of days now and had been through some stuff, but who was he really? Who was this man who'd talked about gathering info for the UN, walked around with hi-tech prototypes in his pockets, and carried a knife large enough to carve a Thanksgiving turkey? She felt a shiver go through her bones and hoped it wasn't someone walking over her grave.

Inside the SUV now, Saint sat a moment before turning on the engine. He needed to calm down. He'd almost lost it back there when Green taunted him about the prison. Saint had issues when it came to Ridley and the issues ran deep. Were it not for Ridley, Saint would never have been thrown into a Thailand prison to be beaten and degraded; would never have been snake bit or had to fight rats for food. Just thinking about that hell hole enraged him all over again.

He then heard Narice say coolly, "Thanks for riding to the rescue, sheriff, but the schoolmarm doesn't like having her head snapped off when she's just trying to help."

Saint met her eyes. She was mad. He could tell. Tight-lipped, he dropped his head onto the steering wheel for a moment, then looked her way. "You're right. You didn't deserve that. I was just so mad—"

"I thought you were going to geld the man right there. Clifford the Big Red Dog and Dora the Explorer would not have been happy."

"Who?"

She waved him off. "Never mind. What happened between you and Ridley?"

"It was a long time ago." And that's all he said.

As he started the engine and backed the SUV out of the parking space, Narice stared unfocused out of the window. She had no idea where they were going next, and for now, she didn't care. All she really wanted was off this merry-go-round. She thought back to the first night she met him and how frightened she'd been. For the last two days, she'd been able to set that fear aside because she and Saint seemed to be an okay dynamic duo. Now came the reminder that this was the most serious mess she'd ever had the misfortune of being involved in. She truly was Alice, only the characters in this Wonderland were car bombs, dead men, sinister helicopters, and cockroaches. It was way more drama than she needed. She just wanted to find the people responsible for killing her father and let the authorities take it from there.

He merged onto the Ford Freeway and headed west towards the heart of the city. Narice didn't bother looking in her mirror for black sedans; that was his job. Hers was to figure out the markings on her daddy's quilt, so, while he drove she took the book out of the bag and opened it.

The table of contents listed various topics, but one in particular focused on the secret signs in slave quilts. She flipped through the pages to that chapter and began to read.

When Narice came up for air, the SUV was parked and the engine was off. She looked up and saw water. Startled, she realized with pleasure that they were on Belle Isle. She looked his way and saw him sitting behind the wheel, his emotions hidden behind his shades. "I haven't been here in years."

Belle Isle was a 704-acre island in the Detroit River. In the 1700s the French called it Hog Island because of all the wild pigs. In the early 1880s, Frederick Law

Olmstead, the man who designed New York's Central Park, was commissioned by the city fathers to design a plan for the undeveloped island. Under his vision it became a park.

When Narice was young, her father would bring her here on summer Saturday mornings and they would swim at the beach, fish, ride their bikes, and rent canoes. Back then there had been the beautiful Scott fountain to marvel over, scores of flowers, an outdoor casino, and an aquarium that had the biggest catfish she'd ever seen. It was an oasis amidst the concrete and asphalt where residents threw barbecues, family reunions, church picnics, and graduation parties.

Now, she was here and older but the awe of the river and its slow-moving freighters still touched her like it had when she was young. She opened her door and stepped out. Paying Saint no mind she walked down to the water's edge. Once there she looked out over the river and fed herself on the memories of the past, the silence, and the peacefulness of the surroundings. Spying an old weather-beaten tree stump a few steps away, she thought it looked like a perfect place to sit, so she did.

Saint was still simmering over the encounter with Gus. With him in the picture, The Majesty and her supporters were facing another formidable enemy. Green had no scruples. None. A few years ago, there were rumors that he'd had been hired by various U.S. government agencies to conduct covert operations the U.S. couldn't afford to conduct overtly because of political reasons, but like most such jobs, there'd been no paper trail to confirm or deny the allegations. *Was this one of those operations?* When the President asked Saint to take on this job, he'd made it clear that no one was to know Saint was acting at his request. Nagal was a touchy subject within the administration not only because of its port but because The Majesty would not be controlled should she and her candidates carry the election.

Who is Green working for? He needed to find that answer ASAP. It was bad enough having to deal with Ridley who was probably representing his own interests in the search for the Eye, in spite of what the generals were told or led to believe. The Ridley Saint knew trafficked in drugs, illegal weapons, and young boys. In the past, political connections kept him from being thrown in jail. Saint had a sneaking suspicion those same connections floated the story of Ridley's death in a boating accident to keep him from being exposed.

Saint looked out at Narice standing beside the water. *God what a woman.* Green had probably scared her to death, but the lady refused to be a victim. Whether she was running away from Ridley or bringing Green to his knees, she was a woman a man didn't mind having his back. Being a loner, Saint had never worried much about interpersonal relationships, but having her upset with him didn't sit right, so he went to make peace.

Narice didn't say anything when he walked up and stood beside her. For a moment the chirps of the birds and the gentle lapping of the water against the shore were the only sounds.

Then he asked, "Did you ever come here for the Fishing Derby?"

In spite of her mood she smiled. "Every year until I got too old. Never caught a thing, though."

"Me either. Sarita caught a big perch one time. Named it Lucky. When Gran threw Lucky in the cornmeal and put him in the skillet, Sarita cried for days."

Narice chuckled.

In the silence that followed, Narice looked around at the fresh-cut grass and the towering healthy trees. "Did you ever rent the canoes?"

He grinned. "Yeah, we did."

"The last time I was here, the canals were so full of garbage like hamburger bags and pop cups you couldn't even see the water. Glad it's being kept up again."

"Yeah, the Isle was a mess. Trash. Crime. The aquarium closed, the casino was falling apart, but it looks like it's on its way back." Saint then said to her, "Because of Ridley I spent twenty months in a Thailand prison."

The revelation caught Narice so off guard, she was speechless for a moment.

"He was an attaché with the Canadian embassy. When I found out he was using streetkids for sex parties, I reported him, but one of his party regulars was a high-ranking Thai government official."

"What were you charged with?"

"Espionage. They planted some documents in my apartment and that was it."

Narice ached for him.

He turned his eyes to the water. "Nobody could get me out. Not our government, not my friends . . . spent the time fighting the terrible conditions, scorpions, the guards, the other prisoners . . ." His voice trailed off, then became strong again. "Hating Ridley kept me alive. I knew if I held on, one day I'd get out. Then I'd pay him back."

He looked at Narice. "But when I was released, I was told he was dead. Killed in a boating accident somewhere in the Pacific."

"But he wasn't."

"No."

He added, "You running away from that cab, and me having to chase you, probably saved Ridley's life that night. Seeing him brought back all those old feelings and I wanted to kill him the moment I snatched him out of the cab."

She didn't say it, but she was glad he hadn't. Although they hadn't been together long, she couldn't imagine being on this search with anyone else.

"Being brought up on murder charges would have made me miss all this, and you." And Saint knew that missing out on the opportunity to meet and hang out with this challenging, headstrong beauty would have been a tremendous loss.

Narice's butterflies returned under the scrutiny of his shaded eyes. He was affecting her whether she was ready to admit or not.

There was silence for a moment, and then he said, "So, now, you know."

Narice could almost feel the pain and hardship he been forced to bear. She also knew that he'd given her a look inside himself that few others had been allowed to see. "Thank you."

"If we're going to be Batman and Robin you need to know who the Jokers and Riddlers are."

She smiled softly.

"I like that."

"What?"

"Making you smile."

Narice had to take in a deep breath to make her heart slow. "Are you flirting with me?"

He gave her a grin. "Maybe. Is that allowed?"

Narice's insides were fluttering big-time. "Maybe."

"Well, while you decide, how about we do the Loop and you tell me what the book says about our quilt?"

Her eyes were shining. "Okay."

The Loop was the road that circled the entire island. On the weekends, traffic on it crawled due to the hundreds upon hundreds of cruising young people. On a workday afternoon like today, the SUV had only a few joggers and a couple of cyclists to share the road with.

Through her window, Narice enjoyed the view of the sun sparkling on the river and the white gulls gliding above, then picked up her book. "Okay, it says in here that our Monkey Wrench pattern was a call to get ready, but not just with tools to dig with. They could be any implement needed for the journey."

"Like what?"

"A compass. Weapons."

That word made her look over at him, but he kept his shaded eyes on the road.

She continued. "The journey north could be dangerous to the fugitive slaves, so they also needed mental tools like, being sly, smart, wary, and smooth."

"I got that covered."

She shook her head in amusement.

Saint said, "So by putting that Wagon Wheel symbol on the quilt, your daddy might also be warning us to be careful."

"Exactly."

"What are some of the other symbols?"

"Let's see. There's the Bear Claw, the Cross Roads. Hey, this Log Cabin looks like that box thing that's in the middle of the quilt."

"Let's see."

She held up the page so he could check it out.

He took a quick look. "It does, doesn't it? Do you think it has something to do with the *Home* he put in his note?"

Narice didn't know, but she thought she recognized another symbol from the quilt. "This Wagon Wheel looks familiar, too."

"What's it mean?"

"A couple of things. It represents a wagon, of course, but it says here it represents the runaway slaves sometimes." Narice met his eyes.

Saint said, "Maybe we're supposed to drive somewhere?"

"Who knows?"

By now their slow drive had taken them to the eastern side of the island where there were more woods. She looked into the dense trees and asked, "Do you think the deer are still here?"

"Maybe. Used to be quite a herd of them in there."

"I know." Narice kept her eyes pealed, but no deer. She straightened herself in her seat and heard her stomach rumble.

Saint heard it, too. "Was that your stomach?"

She chuckled. "Yes."

Saint glanced at the clock on the console. It was almost two o'clock. "We can stop someplace if you want?"

"Coney Island?"

He grinned. "You're a woman after my heart."

So, they left the Isle and headed downtown.

After a lunch of coneys and root beers, Saint headed up Jefferson to Sarita and Myk's place. Now that Narice had her book, they could take a good long look at the quilt and maybe get a better understanding of the markings and symbols. Then they had to hit the road. He wondered if the sleeping Green had been found by now? The next time their paths crossed, Green owed Narice a thank-you because had she not been with Saint, Saint would have put Green to sleep permanently.

Myk and Sarita weren't home yet, so Saint used his key to enter through the front door. The interior of the house was so quiet; Narice felt like they should be tiptoeing so as not to disturb the silence. "Do you have any other brothers beside Myk?"

He tossed his keys on the kitchen table. "One." He then walked across the room, opened a couple of cupboard doors until he found some boxed coffee and a grinder.

"Does he live in Detroit, too?"

"Yep. In the Manoogian Mansion."

Narice cocked her head quizzically. "That's the mayor's residence."

"Yep." He moved to the sink and filled the carafe with cold water. "Drake Randolph, Myk, and I are all half-brothers. Papa was a rolling stone."

"Where's your father now?"

He shrugged. "Dead I think. Not sure. Never met him."

Narice thought about the wonderful memories she and her daddy had made together and was saddened that Saint never had that opportunity with his own father. "Have your brothers ever met him?"

"Not that I know of."

"What about your mother?"

He shrugged. "Never met her either. She had me in prison. The state put me in foster care an hour after I was born. Records said she was declared unfit. They must have been right because she OD'd a few months after she got out."

Narice wondered about the little boy that he'd been. The terrible circumstances surrounding his parentage and birth had to have affected him deeply. Were his brothers aware of his unorthodox life? She supposed they were since she now knew that the voice of Big Brother belonged to Myk. "Does your family know what you do?"

He looked her way for a moment, then refocused his attention on filling the coffee filter with the now ground beans. "Sometimes. Most times not. Sarita has enough to worry about running her center." Saint didn't tell Narice about Myk and Nia, or that the squeegee guys had been Nia operatives.

Saint was pouring himself a cup of coffee when Myk walked in. His grim face grabbed their attention. "Did you leave a couple agents on the bathroom floor at the mall?"

Saint took a draw from his coffee cup and said coolly, "Was that who they were? Yeah, why?"

Myk sighed.

Saint had seen that look on his brother's face before and so said, "Look don't start. They came in with their guns drawn. What was I supposed to do, let them shoot me?"

Myk met his eyes and conceded. "No, you weren't, but they're both in the hospital. There's an APB out on you."

Saint shrugged. "Okay."

"And Ridley wasn't deported. Our friends at INS say it had something to do with his diplomatic status. Because of all the outstanding terrorism cases they're dealing with, it'll be at least sixty days before they can have a hearing."

Saint then told Myk about Narice's close encounter with Green at the bookstore.

Myk glanced over at Narice. "You and my wife would get along well. She doesn't let anyone manhandle her either."

He then went back to his brother. "So who is Green working with?"

Saint tossed his brother the identification he'd taken off the men in the mall bathroom.

Myk studied them a moment. "Why would the Department of Agriculture be involved?"

"Who knows? We've got more players in this game now than a bid whist tournament."

"Well, let's leave that for now. I've got something to show you. Remember the surprise I was telling you about?"

Narice and Saint followed him back out to the garage. As he led them deeper into the structure, Narice realized just how big it was. He stopped, then used the clicker to close the door. Then a light came on from overhead to reveal a large something hidden under a tarp. Myk peeled it back. Another SUV. It was black and had tinted windows, but was the biggest one she'd ever seen.

"It's made by Cadillac," Myk explained.

Saint walked around it. "This is a big sucker."

"It has to be to carry all the hardware."

Saint paused. "Hardware?" He tested the metal over the doors by knocking on it a few times. "Armor plated?" he asked with a raised eyebrow.

"Yes."

Narice didn't believe this. An armor-plated SUV?

Saint appeared excited. "What else she got?"

Myk smiled. "One-way glass. All the doors work manually or by remote. Remote start . . ."

As he continued regaling Saint with the bells and whistles, the two men reminded Narice of kids showing off their newest handheld video game.

Myk walked his brother around to the back of the vehicle. "Take a look at this."

Saint did and then crowed softly, "All right!"

Narice looked too and wondered why he was so geeked over four oversized tailpipes. And why did it have four tailpipes in the first place? The brothers seemed to be having such a good time, she decided to save her questions for later.

The still smiling Saint circled the vehicle. "Who are they building this for?"

"A couple of Saudi princes worried about terrorists.

GM asked me to field test it, so it's all yours. I thought it might come in handy the next time those helicopters show up. Try to bring it back in one piece, if you can."

Saint grinned. "We'll take real good care of her won't we, Narice?"

Amused she responded with, "I'm just along for the ride."

Saint winked her way, then asked his brother, "This baby have a name?"

"Sarita named her Lily, after my old housekeeper."

As if trying the name out on his tongue, Saint said, "Lily. I like that."

Narice did, too. Beauty and strength.

Myk added, "You have reinforced glass on the windows, headlights, and taillights. The tires are guaranteed to roll another fifty miles if they go flat."

Saint looked even more impressed. "Anything else I need to know right now?"

"Not that I can think of—other than try and keep the collateral damage to a minimum."

"As long as you e-mail that message to the other side, I'll try."

Myk didn't appear pleased by the answer, but he didn't challenge his brother. He instead directed his next question to Narice. "Any luck translating the quilt?"

"Not really. We have a few of the symbols identified, we think, but we haven't had time to look into the others."

"Well, I'm sure you'll figure it out. You two should get going. Any idea where you're going?"

"Nope, but someplace we can hole up and figure out the quilt. Once we do that, we'll let you know where we'll be heading. We'll probably do most of our driving at night. Probably be safer."

Myk nodded. "Good enough." He handed Saint the keys. "I'll take care of the other truck you were driving." Then as if he suddenly remembered something, added, "Oh, and you've got plates from six or seven different states and a few government issue. Should buy you a little time."

Saint left for a moment to go into the house. He returned with Narice's packed suitcase and the quilt. He placed them inside, then walked around to the passenger side and opened the door for her. Were it not for the strategically placed running board, she would have needed a boost to climb in.

Once in, Narice hooked up her seat belt and looked around. The inside was plush gray leather. Bucket seats. DVD player up top. Two additional rows of seats behind her and enough buttons and toggles on the dash to put a jet to shame. Green dials, reds dials. Miniature screens. What they were all for, she hoped Saint knew.

Through her window, she saw the brothers talking, then embrace in a good-bye. Then, Saint was in his seat, Lily's engine fired up, and he backed them out of the driveway. She looked back to see the garage door closing. They were now on their own.

Eight

While Saint drove, Narice continued to mull over the handwritten clue her father had hidden in the quilt. What had he meant by *Home*? Thinking out loud, she said, "Suppose we forget about my house being the place daddy talked about in his note. Where else might home be?" A blink later, she had an epiphany. "Maybe he meant his own?"

Saint shrugged. "Maybe, but where's that?"

"Grey Swan, Georgia. Little bitty town down by the Okefenokee Swamp. I went to visit right after my mother died. Haven't been back since."

"Has he been down there recently?"

"Not that I know of."

"Well, before we head off on a wild-goose chase—"

The word *goose* sent a chill across the back of

Narice's neck. "Where's the quilt?" Hastily unhooking her belt, she leaned into the back seat, giving Saint a real nice look at her behind in blue shorts as she reached for the paper-wrapped bundle. She picked it up, then with a bounce settled back into her seat.

Saint asked, "What's up?"

"When you said, goose . . ." She paused for a moment to unwrap the quilt. Sending the paper wrapper sailing into the back seat, Narice spread the quilt out and studied it. She pointed to a square. "There."

Saint glanced at where her finger rested. To him the square's symbol just looked like a bunch of stacked triangles.

Narice had her book out and was flipping through the pages. When she came across what she'd been after she said proudly, "These are the Flying Geese. I knew I'd seen them in here."

"Geese?"

"Yes. This patch tells the runaways to follow the geese north. I guess it's a clue for folks who plan to escape in the spring when the birds migrate."

Saint grinned. "You're getting damned good at this, Teach."

She inclined her head, and said in a fake British accent, "Thank you, sir."

Saint was starting to like this woman way more than he was supposed to. "What else does it say?"

She read further. "If the slaves were to travel in a particular direction, that direction was sometimes highlighted by using a different fabric within the rest of the pattern."

Narice looked at the square of geese closely. The triangles representing the birds in flight were in flocks of three. Two of the flocks were done in black corduroy. One flock flying towards the bottom of the quilt was made of black satin. "Well, we have two made of cord and one of satin."

"Which way are the satin ones flying?"

"Down."

"Meaning south?"

Narice studied it again. "I guess."

"Your theory that this quilt might be telling us to check out your daddy's birthplace could be a good one."

"Or not." Right now, she wasn't sure about anything. Narice took a moment to look out of her window. "Where are we headed?"

"Some place where we can hole up for the night and study this quilt, hopefully without being disturbed by cockroaches or helicopters."

"I'm all for that."

Were Saint traveling alone, he'd be content with the nearest fleabag hotel, but the lady with him was a *lady*; she deserved to spend the night in a decent place. With that in mind, he left the Detroit city limits and headed west. The cockroaches and their friends were probably scouring the city for them. Leaving town would make it harder for him and Narice to be found.

The motel was in Ann Arbor, about thirty-five miles away. It was nestled in a complex of six or seven other motels. If the quilt was really pointing the way south, one of the highways running through Ann Arbor was US 23 which connected with south I-75 near Toledo, less than forty minutes away.

Saint got off the highway at State Street, turned right on Victor's Way, and drove down the quiet tree-lined street to the motel. It was the same chain he and Narice stayed at in Grand Rapids. The suite's layout would allow each of them to have their own bedroom and shower, and the place was spacious enough to stretch out and relax.

Saint parked and went inside to the desk. After registering them as Mr. and Mrs. Palmer, he paid cash for the room and took the keys. Getting back in the van, he told her, "We're Mr. and Mrs. Palmer."

After settling into the room, they got the quilt out and pored over it some more.

Next to the Flying Geese was a pattern she identified as the Drunkard's Path. Its patch was made up of two intersecting lines that zigzaged across its square.

Saint read aloud, "The drunk's pattern told the runaways not to travel on a straight line so slave catchers and the dogs would have a harder time tracking them. Based on their African heritage, slaves believed evil traveled in a straight line."

He raised an impressed eyebrow. "Never knew that."

Narice noticed that the raised eyebrow seemed to be a signature move. "Neither did I."

They were seated on stools at the long white counter that divided the small kitchen from the main living area and served as a place to eat.

Saint read a little further and said, "According to this, what we have is a sampler quilt. One that has a bunch of different patterns on it. Many were used as maps."

Narice looked down at her father's midnight blue-and-black creation and marveled at the effort that must have gone into making such a beautiful work. "So, we're not crazy. This is a map."

"Yep."

"Wow. When he told us to use the quilt, he wasn't kidding."

"No."

She ran her palm slowly over the soft fabric surface. "This had to have taken some time to do—look at how intricate the patterns and stitches are. I wonder when he started it." She also wondered if he'd been scared? *Had he already been threatened or pressured?* Thinking about him made her mood gently slide to blue.

Saint saw the sadness descend upon her like clouds bringing shadows. It was time to do something else. "Hungry?"

She shook her head. "Not right now. If it's okay with you, I think I'm going to take a catnap. Give me about an hour, then I'll be ready to eat."

"Okay."

She slid from the stool and headed up the stairs to her portion of the suite.

When Saint heard her door close, he turned his mind to dinner. He didn't really want to risk eating out, so he picked up the phone and called the desk. Under normal circumstances if a guest made arrangements in advance, the housekeeping staff would stock the room's refrigerator and cabinets with groceries, but since Saint hadn't made arrangements, he figured the promise of a hundred-dollar tip would do the trick. It did. One hour later, the lady manager arrived with enough food to keep Saint and Narice fed for their stay. The bags were set on the counter and the manager took her tip. Before she left, however, Saint said, "Some friends of mine might drop by. They like surprises and gags and they especially like posing as Federal agents. If they show up, will you call me?"

The blonde said, "Sure will."

Saint gave her another twenty. "Thanks."

She smiled like Marilyn Monroe. "No, thank you," and she exited.

A pleased Saint closed then bolted the door.

Narice came downstairs at 7:30. Saint, standing at the stove, noted that she looked rested and that she'd changed into a dark blue, clingy-looking top that had long sleeves and a scoop neck that was discreet yet sexy enough to catch a brother's interest. On the bottom half she wore a pair of jeans that showed off her curves. She was dressed very casually but with the gold heart hanging from a chain around her neck, her hair fixed, makeup on, and the thin gold bracelets on her wrist, she looked like an elegant million bucks.

"What're you cooking?" she asked. "Smells good."

He found the scents of her perfume just as pleasing. "Broiled salmon, fried corn, salad, and yeast rolls. Sorry, they're frozen but no time for real ones."

Narice croaked "You make yeast rolls—from scratch?"

"Yep. Gran cooked for rich folks all of her life. No way you could be around her and not learn something. Sarita and I are great cooks."

"The secret-agent chef. What else can you make?"

He pulled open the oven door to check on the salmon. "I do a mean prime rib. My German chocolate cake ain't bad either."

"You do not make German chocolate cake."

He turned to her. "Why would I lie about something like that?"

Narice realized he was serious. Nope, she didn't know much about this man at all. "Where'd all this food come from?"

After he told her about the delivery, she said, "Well, cook on my brother. I can't wait to eat."

Unlike many men Narice knew, he appeared comfortable in the kitchen. Brandon, her ex, had been a good cook too, but Narice had rarely been home in time to sample his efforts. She turned her mind away from those bittersweet memories and refocused her attention on Saint. Lord, he was handsome; the face, the build, the way he moved. He was dressed in his usual black turtleneck and black jeans, but this set looked fresh. It was her guess, he'd showered while she was upstairs sleeping. The dark glasses were in place and the beard still made him look like an outlaw, but the magic coat was on one of the living room chairs. *Thank goodness.* She doubted the health department would clear it as a proper food preparation garment.

He looked her way and said, "There's wine over here chilling. Pour yourself some."

"Don't mind if I do."

The kitchen was small. As she reached for the bottle sitting in a saucepan filled with ice her body brushed against his and the heat of the contact was like a slow sear. "Excuse me," she whispered, hastily, trying to pretend she'd felt nothing.

"No problem."

Their eyes met and held. The last twelve hours had been hectic ones; there hadn't been time to further explore their unspoken attraction to each other; they'd been too busy with cockroaches. Now, however, they were alone and admittedly curious about each other.

He stepped back over to the stove and took the top off the corn. He stirred it with a large spoon, then scooped a small portion onto the spoon's tip. "Here, taste this."

Narice hesitated for a moment but walked the two steps to where he stood.

His voice was soft with warning. "Careful, it's a little hot."

Feeling as if she were being stroked by his eyes, she

let him feed her. The sweet, spicy taste made her moan softly with delight.

Her sounds of pleasure made him wonder if she would purr that way if he kissed her. "Like it?"

"Mmmm. More," she purred appreciatively.

He took a clean spoon from the drawer and dug her out another little portion, then slowly fed that to her as well. It was an innocent yet sensual moment that affected them both. After she swallowed she slipped her tongue around her lips in a move Saint found so provocative and blood firing, he had to turn back to the stove. "It didn't need more salt or anything?"

Narice's pulse had heightened in response to being fed and it refused to slow down. "No. Perfect. Do you want some wine?"

"Yes, please."

Narice found some glasses in the cupboard and took out two. The merlot was a well recognizable one. She poured some into each glass and handed him one, and attempted to shake off the wild sensations his nearness had a way of setting off. She raised her in toast, and said, "To the cook."

He raised his in reply, "Thanks."

More conscious of him than she thought safe, Narice matched his sip. Giving her a long look over his glass, he took another draw then went back to his cooking. Her senses flaring, she strolled over to the fireplace. A store-bought composite log, wrapped in red paper, sat on the metal grate waiting to be lit. The room's blue-patterned drapes were pulled closed and with the lamps in the sitting room lit; the interior of the suite was cozy and hushed.

Narice took another small sip of her wine and said, "I know it's July but how about a fire?"

"Sure, why not. The AC is on."

Instructions on how to operate the fireplace safely were printed on a little metal plaque on the wall, and after reading them, Narice adjusted the flue, then using the matches provided by the motel, lit the paper ends of the log's wrapper. Once the flames caught, she closed the wire grate and stepped back. "How's that?" she asked him.

He looked over. "Cool."

Narice turned back to the fire and watched the flames slowly build. The heat made her move back a short step, but the blaze was lovely to look at. Standing there with her merlot in her hand, she realized she couldn't remember the last time she'd sat with a man by a fire. With the smells of the food cooking and the crackling sounds from the fireplace, the air was romantic, even if it wasn't supposed to be.

In the kitchen, Saint knew she wasn't deliberately tempting him, but her presence, the fire, her perfume were keeping him from concentrating on what he was supposed to be doing, which was slicing tomatoes for the salad. Even as he kept glancing her way, he had to make himself pay attention to the task at hand so he wouldn't lose a finger to the knife's sharp blade.

But soon all the food was done.

He called out, "Come get it."

She walked over to the counter and eagerly took a seat.

Narice watched as he expertly removed the salmon's crisp silver back before he set the steaming browned fillet on a platter. Next came a large bowl filled with the fried corn, then the salad, and the hot-buttered rolls. Impressed, she scanned the fare. "I may have to hire you."

He sat down. "You can't afford me."

She asked teasingly, "No?"

The timbre of her voice and the look in her dark eyes made Saint's manhood quicken. "No," he told her. "When I cook for a lady, I don't cook for cash."

Narice chuckled, "Oh really?"

"Really."

"Then I need to leave that alone."

"Probably."

She met his eyes. The heat of attraction was rising in the room like heat off of the salmon. "Pass me the corn, please."

He handed her the bowl and she put some on her plate. No matter how hard she tried she couldn't stop thinking about what he'd said. Was he as good in bed as he was in the kitchen? Instinct said yes. She shook herself free of those dangerous thoughts. After adding a wedge of the salmon, putting dressing on her salad, and helping herself to two rolls, Narice was ready to eat. "Can you say the grace?"

Saint raised an eyebrow.

She eyed him back and waited, but when he didn't respond, she said to him, "Never mind." Bowing her head, she recited a soft, short prayer, then picked up her fork. "Thanks for dinner."

Saint thought she was going to light into him for not saying the grace, but he hadn't blessed his food in so long, her request caught him off guard. "I take it you're a church-going lady."

Narice was savoring the perfectly prepared salmon. "I am. This is good."

"And you had doubts."

"No, not really. You cooked breakfast for me, remember?"

"I do. Do you cook?"

"No. I don't usually get home until after eight, so I do a lot of microwaving."

"You need a housekeeper."

"I need a wife."

He smiled beneath the shades. "Did you cook for your husband?"

Narice shook her head. "No. He did most of that."

When she didn't say anything more, Saint studied her for a moment, wondering if he'd said the wrong thing. Since it appeared he had, he went back to his plate.

The meal continued and the silence lengthened. He looked her way a few times, but she wouldn't meet his eyes. "Didn't mean to bring up bad memories."

She waved her fork, "It's okay. Some marriages work—some fail. Mine, died."

He studied her.

Her tone was matter-of-fact. "It was mostly my fault—well, all my fault to be truthful."

She saw his eyebrow rise again. "Hey, this is an equal-opportunity country. Women get to wreck marriages, too."

Saint didn't know how to handle such candor.

"I was so set on climbing that corporate ladder, I had no time for him—didn't care that the brother had fixed my dinner, or had a hot bath waiting for me at the end of the day. By the time I left the office and got home, the lights were out, the food was cold, and so was the water in the tub. I was a deal-making, balls-whacking bitch. So he left me."

"When was this?"

"Ten years ago. I married him when I was twenty-two, fresh out of college with a basement-level job on Wall Street, but it was the Street and I was excited." She smiled wistfully. "Had my MBA by twenty-four, found a White mentor known for liking his women brown, and I started my climb."

"Your husband didn't support what you were doing?"

"In the beginning yes, but after my hours at the office became longer, and our time together became nonexistent, he wanted out. I didn't blame him. I wouldn't have wanted to be married to me either—not back then. I was raised by my daddy and his friends. I didn't know a lot about dating or men or how a woman was supposed to—what do they call it in the Bible, cleave to your mate. I was chasing the almighty dollar, I didn't have time to be a wife."

She looked over at him with clear dark eyes. "So, Bran made me pay him one dollar as part of the divorce settlement. He said that's all the marriage was worth to me." She took a sip of her wine, then set the glass down. "Sadly, he was right. I didn't value it or him the way I should have."

"How long were you married?"

"Almost three years."

"Where is he now?"

"Philly. Married to a real nice sister. They have two girls with one on the way. He's happy and I'm glad. Lord knows, he wasn't with me."

"So, what made you take up teaching?"

"Car accident."

He looked surprised.

"Three years after my divorce, I was driving home one night in the rain—pouring rain and suddenly there was a dog in my lights, just sitting in the middle of the highway. Daddy said, I should have hit it, but I swerved, spun out, went off the road, and hit a tree. Totaled my Z, and woke up three days later in the hospital. I was so bandaged up and hooked up to so many machines, I looked like Elsa Lanchester in the *Bride of Frankenstein.*"

Saint smiled.

"Broke a lot of bones, tore muscles. I was in the hospital for three and a half months."

"Wow."

"It was rough. Daddy came to take care of me for a

while, but I eventually hired a nurse. Once I could move around in a wheelchair, she would wheel me out onto my deck or onto the front porch so I could get some air and sun. I found out I had neighbors," she said with sparkling eyes. "And that the school bus came to pick up the kids at eight-fifteen every morning. I saw cardinals and robins and felt peace inside myself for the first time in a long time."

Narice paused as the memories of those times came back. "Anyway to make a longer story shorter, I wasn't the same person after the accident. It's that old cliché, but it's the truth. My father said it was God's doing." She shrugged. "He may have been right, but I did change. My drive was gone. I didn't have the fire in my belly anymore, I didn't care about cutting the big deal, so I quit the firm."

"That took a lot of guts."

"I never thought about it like that." And she hadn't. Maybe had she not been financially secure, walking away might have been harder, but at the time, the decision hadn't cost her any sleep at all. "After that, one of my sorors invited me to volunteer at her school a couple of days a week. I took her up on the offer, and I loved it. Loved the children, their smiles, their honesty. Loved it so much I went back to school, got an education degree, and started my own place."

"Do you regret the first life?"

"Heck, no. Well, I do regret that Brandon got hurt by it, but I'm as rich as a goddess. As the old ladies used to say, I have my own purse, and I don't have to ask anybody if I can spend it."

He grinned.

She told him frankly, "You smile, but I tell some brothers that, and they take off running."

"I'd think a brother would have to be pretty strong to take you on."

"I suppose. Haven't been many takers lately, and that's okay, too. I have a good life. A man would just be the whipped cream."

Saint realized she was not the china doll he'd thought her to be; she was a strong, determined woman who accepted responsibility for her actions and the decisions she'd made in her life. That she would share this part of her life's story with him, humbled him in a way. "I can't believe there isn't a man in your life."

"Hey, I'm thirty-seven years old. Brothers my age want skinny little video girls. Real women like me and my sorors scare them to death." She paused for a minute. "I take that back. Some of the ladies I know are married to princes. The rest of us have learned to live without whipped cream."

"I'll make you whipped cream anytime you like."

The words sent a hot streak through Narice that made her nipples tighten and reminded her just how long it had been. She tried to play it off. "Would you?"

Saint wanted to reach out and slide a finger over the curve of her lips; wanted to hear her moan like she did after tasting the fried corn. "Gran has a secret recipe that will melt in your mouth."

"Never had a man offer to make me whipped cream before."

"Never met a man like me before."

That was certainly the truth, she thought to herself. From the slim bones in his fingers to those dangerous-looking shaded eyes, he was the most tempting male she'd ever met. He seemed to have tapped into and opened up places in her feminine self she'd shut away long ago. "You don't have a hard time pulling women, do you?"

He met her bold question with a bold reply. "Be lying if I said I did, but I'm choosy. I stopped bed-hopping a long time ago, but," and his voice slowed, "I do enjoy beautiful, intriguing women, and you are both."

Narice felt his voice shimmer through her, felt his shaded eyes touch her like a hand. "I bet most women fall into your bed just like that, don't they?"

He threw back his head and laughed.

"I'm just asking, because I'm not going to do that."

He ran his eyes over the gorgeous mouth, her graceful neck, and the curve of her jaw. Imagining how his lips would feel murmuring over each, increased his desire. "No?"

"No."

"Never say never." His voice was as low as the silence in the room.

"I'm not saying never. I'm saying I'm not easy."

"No woman worth having ever is."

Narice was flowing in places that hadn't flowed so sweetly in years. "You're very good at this."

"You don't know the half of it, angel."

She drew in a calming breath. "I think I'm going to finish eating then get out the quilt and the book."

"Sounds like a plan."

The heat of his maleness wafted across the counter and Narice wondered where she might buy a fan. Being able to cool herself down was going to be a necessity. "How about I help you clean up first?"

"I'm okay. Nothing to do but put leftovers in the fridge and the dirty dishes in the dishwasher. You go and get started on the quilt."

"Are you sure?"

He nodded and said gently, "Positive."

Book and quilt in hand, Narice went to the couch and took a seat in front of the now roaring fire. She was conscious of him working in the kitchen behind her, though, and of his offer to make her whipped cream. Fanning herself with her hand, she settled in.

Aided by the clues in her book, Narice could now identify four of the seven squares on her father's sampler quilt. The Monkey Wrench, the Wagon Wheel, the Flying Geese, and the Drunkard's Path. Of the remaining three, one had a pattern that appeared to be a cross. The pattern next to it had symbols that looked a little like leaves, and the last one, the one that seemed to be a square within a square had a small yellow Star of

David in its center. She still hadn't found any references to why there was a penny attached to each of the quilt's corners, or what purpose they served, though.

Saint finished the cleanup and came and sat in an armchair close to the couch. "Find anything new?"

"Yes, this cross is, I think, the Cross Roads symbol. The cross road was a specific city."

"Which one?"

"Cleveland."

"Cleveland?" he echoed with surprise.

"Yes. It was a major fan-out point for fugitives heading to Canada. Cleveland's code name on the Underground Railroad was Cross Road. Detroit was Midnight. Sandusky, Ohio, was Sunrise. This is really interesting."

Saint thought so, too, but the woman reading to him was even more so. "So does that mean we need to go to Cleveland?"

Narice didn't know, but she read on looking for references to the Cross Roads pattern and the last two undeciphered squares. The leaf pattern turned out not to be leaves at all, but a symbol known as the Bear Paw. "The Bear Paws are supposed to represent bear tracks, and told the runaways to follow the tracks of bears through or around mountains."

"There aren't any mountains in Cleveland."

She chuckled. "No, there aren't, but you do have to go through the mountains to get to Georgia where my father was born."

"So what do we do about Cleveland?"

She shrugged. "You got me."

The last unknown symbol, the square within a square stood for a pattern called the Log Cabin, which the book explained could represent the place where the runaways could build a shelter for the winter, "Or," Narice said looking up from the page to Saint, "it also signified a safe house."

"Interesting. I'm assuming that eight-point-star in the center of the cabin means something, too."

"It says here that during the abolitionist days, the inner block would sometimes be made out of differing colors to signify different things. Isn't the eight-point-star the Star of David?"

"Yes."

"Why would daddy use it? I wonder if this was his way of putting X marks the spot like on a treasure map?"

"Maybe the star does represent the Eye. King Solomon was David's son."

"Sheba gave the Eye to Solomon. Maybe he's trying to tell us the diamond is buried in a log cabin, or in a safe house in Georgia?"

Saint had no idea.

Narice said finally, "Okay, I'm making an executive decision. I say we head to Grey Swan, Georgia, and see what we find. Daddy's sister Camille is still living there far as I know. Maybe she can help."

"Did she come to the funeral?"

"No. I didn't know how to contact her. Maybe it'll be in the phone book I found with the stuff daddy left with Uncle Willie."

"Did you bring it along?"

She nodded. "Yes."

The rest of the items like her parents' wedding picture she'd left with Willie for safekeeping. She'd taken nothing but the address book and the quilt.

"Were your father and his sister, close?"

Narice shrugged again. "There was something mentioned years ago about a falling out, but I've no idea what it was over. Like I said earlier, I've only been there once."

"Well, with all the software Lily is packing, we ought to be able to find Grey Swan with no problem. I hope."

"Me too."

He went over to his coat and pulled out his handheld. After punching in a few codes, the map feature appeared on the screen. He typed in the words *Grey Swan GA*. He got nothing. "Hmm," he muttered.

"What's wrong?"

"Grey Swan isn't in the map software."

"I know it exists, or at least, it used to. Can you pull up the Okefenokee?"

He punched in more letters. The swamp appeared on the little screen. "Yep."

"Then we're straight. Once we get there, someone should be able to tell us how to get to Grey Swan. When do we leave?"

"First thing in the morning. The better head start we get, the better off we'll be."

Narice agreed. Who knew where the cockroaches

were? The threat of an early morning departure should have been enough to send her to bed so she could be well rested at sunrise, but it was only a little past 9:30. Because of the nap she'd taken, she was wide awake. She asked herself, *Now how does one pass the time with an exciting and sexy man,* but she knew the answer, so she stopped asking herself questions.

Nine

Saint was asking himself the same question and came up with the samc answer. Problem was, she'd already stated her position on the subject, so being content to share her company was all he had. He wasn't accustomed to putting his desire for a beautiful woman on hold, especially when the attraction was mutual. He remembered the pledge he'd made about not getting involved with her, but after listening to her candid telling of her marriage, he was more intrigued than ever. "What's it like being a headmistress?"

"Hectic, fun, thankless, rewarding." She paused for a second and then said, "Now, I have a question."

"Shoot."

"Is there a lady in your life?"

He sipped fom his wine. "No."

"Why not?"

"Cheetahs don't make good pets."

That made her laugh. "I'm trying to be serious here."

"Hey, it's the truth. We don't make good pets. Ask anybody. We live in trees. Eat our meat raw. Women hate that stuff."

She shook her head at his silliness. "So you've never been married?"

He downed his wine. "Nope. Told you, I've been in love with Sarita my whole life. No other woman ever measured up."

"So now that's she's married, now what?"

He shrugged. "I'm in no position to marry anybody. My work doesn't allow it. Why'd you ask?"

"Just curious about what a cheetah looks for in a mate."

He studied her for so long she didn't think he was going to answer, but finally, he replied, "Strength, first of all. Smarts. A good heart. Passion."

He pronounced that last word while looking her square in the eye, and Narice felt her core respond to his unspoken call. "Passion?"

"In life and in bed."

The words made her flutter inside and again Narice noted that she had never met a man quite like him before. She also noted that he hadn't placed beauty or booty on his list. She liked that.

"Any more questions?"

"No. I've been nosey enough for one night."

"It's okay. Anything I don't want to answer, I won't. You seem to be the same way."

She acknowledged his assessment by saying, "A lioness doesn't make a good pet either."

That made him laugh.

The phone rang, jolting them both. It rang again. Saint picked it up. "Hello."

He listened to the person on the other end for a few moments, then placed his hand over the mouthpiece, and said quietly to Narice, "Get your suitcase," adding, "quick now, angel. Cockroaches are here."

Narice hustled up the stairs. Grabbing her suitcase, she flung it open, then hurried into the bathroom to grab her toiletries from the counter. She tossed them into their plastic travel case, then threw the case and her dirty clothes into the suitcase. Luckily she hadn't unpacked much. A quick zip and the luggage was closed. She took hold of the handle and rolled it to the stairs.

She saw Saint loading foodstuffs into grocery bags and shaking ice from the fridge's ice maker into trash bags. While she moved over to the couch to retrieve the quilt and the book, he explained, "That was the manager on the phone. From the description she gave me, it sounds like Gus Green. I asked her to keep a lookout for him." Now that he had the food bagged and the perishables iced, he met her eyes. "You ready?"

A serious Narice shook her head.

"Okay, let's head out."

It was dark outside now. Small, ground-level solar lights illuminated the way to the parking lot. Cradling the quilt and pulling her suitcase, Narice hurried with him to where Lily sat parked in the shadows. A quick scan of the lot showed no one. He used the clicker to open Lily's tailgate, then put the food and Narice's suitcase inside. Taking long precise strides, he turned the remote on her door. She climbed in and hit the lock. He ran around to the driver's side and was behind the wheel and belted in, in no time flat.

He keyed the ignition and fired up the engine. Cool air poured out of the AC vents, and the green lights and dials on Lily's dashboard glowed at the ready. Grasping the stick shift, he slid it into reverse, and backed out of the spot. They had no way of knowing where the cockroaches were, but neither wanted to wait around and find out.

Saint drove with the lights out hoping he'd be able to spot the cockroaches before they spotted him. He glanced over at Narice. She looked scared but in control. When this was over, he planned on making love to her in a thousand different ways, but right now, he had to get them out of here and onto the highway—preferably in one piece.

Getting out proved to be a problem. There was a big black sedan barricading the motel's main exit to the street. Saint stopped the SUV just out of sight and sat a moment weighing the advantages and disadvantages of just ramming the sucker out of the way. Deciding he didn't really want to wreck Lily so soon into their relationship, he backed up, hoping to find a less hazardous egress.

Narice saw the car too, and was glad he wasn't planning on confronting them. His last game of chicken hadn't been fun; she wasn't ready for another heart attack so soon.

Saint grumbled, "There has to be another way out of here."

They drove past parked cars and saw an occasional guest going to or from their room, but no other exit.

Saint backed up into a space, then whipped Lily around. Time was running out. They couldn't keep circling forever. If they didn't find an escape route soon, Gus Green was bound to find them.

Narice said excitedly, "Fence!"

He stopped then took the risk of turning on the headlights so he could see the barrier better. The wire fence didn't appear to be very tall, nor did it look to be made of heavyweight metal. He threw the stick into neutral, set the handbrake, and got out. Out of his pocket came another prototype; one that looked like an everyday aerosol can.

Narice watched him through the windshield. Illuminated by Lily's headlights, he raised the can in his hand and quickly began to spray the fence. Confusion wrinkled her brow. Because she had no idea what he was doing, she kept one eye on him and the other pealed for cockroaches. A split second later, he used a booted foot to kick the fence. To her amazement, the section fell to the ground, leaving behind a gaping hole.

He ran back to the SUV, jumped in, and closed the

door. Seconds later he drove through the hole, over the curb, and down to the street.

A surprised Narice asked, "What was that stuff?"

"A spray that breaks down the chemical bonds in metal. Got it for testing from the good scientists up in Minnesota. It's strictly experimental. They also have one that rebinds metals."

"So, you could have put the fence back together?"

"Yep, but didn't have time. Right now, I wish had, though. We have company."

Narice checked her side mirror and sure enough there were lights on their tail. "Are you going to try and loose them?"

"Yep."

"Where should we go?"

"Grey Swan, Georgia, sounds good to me. You game?"

She grinned. "Yes. Let's see how much gas they've got."

He laughed at her enthusiasm. "Woman, I can't wait to make love to you."

Narice sparkled in response, then laughed, "Well it won't be now, so step on it, Cyclops."

"Yes, ma'am."

Saint roared Lily up to eighty. The two cars behind them sped up in hot pursuit.

He tore through the red light and made a squealing left to head west onto Eisenhower, leaving behind a trail of cursing angry drivers in the intersection. Saint paid them no mind.

Ahead was State Street a main artery in Ann Arbor that intersected with Eisenhower under four large hanging traffic lights. All of the lights were red, but he barreled through the intersection at full speed, then had to swerve to miss hitting a pizza delivery car and a hoopty with one headlight. A crash sounded. Narice swung her head around. The pizza car and the hoopty had crashed into each other. Three seconds later the two black sedans blazed through the red lights, too. Like Saint the sedan's drivers ignored the blaring horns and thrown fingers coming from the angry drivers of other cars on the street.

Saint had been to Ann Arbor a few times to see the University of Michigan football teams play, so he had a pretty good idea where he was. Briarwood Mall was on his left now, and if his memory served correctly, he could take a left at the next set of lights and hit the highway. He hoped Cadillac had built Lily as solidly as she looked because she was in for the run of her young life. First order of business was to ditch the jokers on his tail before he got on the highway so with that in mind, he glanced to his left. There was a smaller strip mall and a couple restaurants, maybe he could shake them there.

When he spun the wheel and made a sharp tire-screaming turn into a one-way street, Narice grabbed the armrests and closed her eyes—if she was going to die she didn't want to see it, but the adrenaline made her open them again. She watched him side-swipe cars, run over trash cans, and generally scare the hell out of pedestrians and drivers alike, but he kept Lily rolling, while the sedans did the same.

Since the cockroaches seemed intent upon staying hot on his trail, Saint gave up trying to shake them and led them out onto Ann Arbor–Saline Road. Sideswiping an Escort, he shot down the ramp to 94 East. The tires screeched in protest, taking the sharp downwardly spiraling curve, but when the pavement leveled again, they grabbed the road and powered the Caddy forward.

Saint's eyes snapped up to his rearview mirror and then to the mirror on his door. He didn't see them. Had he lost them? No. There they were, closing fast. "Hang on!"

He eased the big engine up to 110 mph. Cars ahead of them scrambled to get out of the big truck's way, but one car, bearing an Ohio license plate seemed oblivious to the Cadillac walking it down. Faced with no options, Saint passed the car on the left shoulder, sending gravel and dirt flying. Only his driving skill kept them from tipping over, or side swiping Mr. No Driving Ohio, and careening off into the ditch that doubled as the median on most Michigan highways.

By now, Narice could hear sirens behind them and she was breathing so fast and holding on to the front of her armrests so tightly she was surprised her knuckles hadn't popped through the skin. The SUV was traveling at such a high rate of speed, the cars it passed seemed to be standing still. It was a car chase worthy of Hollywood and she was scared to death.

A large green road sign indicated that US 23 South

was a half mile ahead, so Saint swung Lily into the right-hand lane. He hadn't let up on the speed, but he hadn't lost the cockroaches on his tail, either. Lily hit the ramp and again took the steep incline on screaming wheels. Saint braked just enough to keep the Cadillac on the road, then merged them into the sparse traffic doing 105.

Narice turned back and looked up the ramp just in time to see the first sedan begin to spin out. Whether it was lack of driving skills, the excessive speed, or an unfamiliarity with the road, she didn't know, but the driver lost it—big-time. Every thing around her seemed to slow as she watched the car became airborne and fly trunk-end first over the side of the ramp and disappear. Moments later a flash of light filled the night sky and her hands went to her mouth in dismay. "Saint—"

"I know, baby, but we can't stop."

She was horrified by the carnage they'd left behind, but in her heart she knew he was right. She forced herself to face forward. With her eyes now glued on the dark ribbon of the road ahead, she tried not to think about what she'd just seen.

Twenty minutes later, they rolled through Toledo and headed south towards Bowling Green. Once they made it there, they drove on to Dayton.

The highway troopers in Ohio were notorious for ticketing out-of-state drivers, so as he headed towards Dayton, Saint slowed his roll as much as he could while still maintaining a good speed. He had no way of knowing if another black sedan was back there lurking in the dark, so he kept alert. He glanced over at Narice. She'd been pretty quiet since the accident. He supposed she was thinking about the men in the car. In his business, deaths or injuries were known as collateral damage, and sometimes it couldn't be avoided. Saint had taken lives in defense of his own, but never just for the hell of it. Truthfully, there was no place in his line of work for sentiment—not when it came to the other side. Although he'd been trained not to internalize collateral damage, Narice hadn't and he needed to remember that. "I have a friend we can stay with in Dayton. We'll lay low for the day and head out again after it gets dark. Traveling at night is probably going to be safer from here on out."

"Okay." Narice added the remembrances of the tumbling car and the resulting fire to the memories of the dead man on Uncle Willie's floor. She wondered how many others would be hurt or killed before this was over.

It was now three A.M., and raining. Lily's wipers kept the glass clear in rhythmic time. They were riding around Dayton's inner city. Faded billboards touting cigarettes and cognac stood on tall poles above storefronts and empty lots. There were very few people out. The ones she did see were hurrying to cars to get out of the rain. Two female streetwalkers were the exception. Wearing Daisy Dukes, spike heels and filmy transparent blouses, the sisters looked wet and miserable. "Where's your friend live?"

"About fifteen miles south of here."

"In the city of Dayton?"

"No, suburbs."

"Then why are we cruising the neighborhood?"

"Just making sure we aren't being tailed again. My friend won't appreciate us showing up with cockroaches on our shoes."

"In other words, we're taking the Drunkard's Path."

Saint grinned and wondered if she knew being witty was also high on a cheetah's list of preferred attributes in a mate. "Exactly." He also wondered if now might be the time to discuss the car crash. "There was nothing we could do about that car back there."

Her voice was resigned. "I know, and I keep telling myself those people will hurt me if they get the chance, but, seeing a crash like that isn't something you can just up and forget."

"I understand, but the folks after us *will* hurt you, Narice. Don't ever lose sight of that, okay?"

She met his eyes.

"It's real important."

"I haven't forgotten what they did to my father." And she wouldn't.

He drove them around for another thirty minutes. When he was finally convinced there was no one behind them, he left the inner city and headed west.

They rode through suburbia with its condos and wide four-lane streets lined with car dealerships, restaurants, and strip malls. They drove past drugstores, electronic stores, and mile-wide discount outlets. Narice waited for him to turn in somewhere, but he kept driving. In fact, he drove until the streetlights vanished and the road they were traveling became dirt and rutted with holes large enough to make Lily rock back and forth like a toddler taking its first steps. Out of her window Narice could see nothing but black. "Where are we?"

"Farm land."

"Your friend lives on a farm?"

"Owns the farm to be exact."

Because Saint impressed Narice as being overwhelmingly urban, it never occurred to her that he might have friends who farmed; she certainly didn't.

She sat silent when he turned onto a narrow dirt road and drove on another few miles. He lowered his speed to a crawl, then made another turn onto another dark, narrow road. Eventually the headlights illuminated a house that appeared to be a good-sized two-floor place. The structure was a weathered gray and had a wide old-fashioned sitting porch on the front.

Saint blew the horn. Twice. A light mounted on the roof of a big barn right in front of them came on and the beam lit the surroundings like day for night. A few moments passed, then the barn's corrugated metal door began to rise, and as it did, he drove in.

Once they were inside, Narice could see that the barn was filled with tools of all kinds: shovels, hoes, rakes, wheelbarrows. There were handtools like saws, hammers, and screwdrivers hanging from a board on the wall nearest her side of the Caddy. Narice tried to pick out more of the interior's details, but her attention was grabbed first by the barn door slowly closing behind them, and then by the wall they were sitting in front of. It began to rise, not horizontally as the barn door had done, but separating vertically into two. She stared curiously at the halves now sliding farther and farther apart, and at the lighted corridor she could see ahead. "Where the heck are we?" Being around him was like traveling with a human amusement park.

"Underground."

She stared at the shiny metallic walls lining the passageway; walls that certainly weren't put in by any farmers. The place resembled more the entrance to a secret installation or bunker. *Lord, where is this man taking me now?*

A woman with Hispanic features, maybe in her fifties, waist-length black hair with silver streaks stood at the end of the passage. She had on a long multicolored robe and was leaning on a cane, but what really drew Narice's attention were the two huge black-and-brown Rottweilers seated statue-like on either side of her legs. Their heads were big as ponies, and they looked powerful enough to take down a grown man. Oddly enough, both canines were wearing heavy vests around their massive bodies. The garments reminded Narice of bulletproof vests, but who would put that on dogs? . . . *Curiouser and curiouser,* Alice said to herself.

Saint smiled at the welcoming committee and was

glad to see Portia up and around. She still had her cane, but she'd assured him when he talked to her last week that she was healthy and on the mend. Jesse and James looked healthy, too.

He sensed Narice's curiosity, but right now he cut the engine, then leaned his weary head back on his seat and let the adrenaline slide from his soul. *It's good to be home,* he noted genuinely. For a few long moments he savored the relief of arriving here in one piece, then turned his head Narice's way. "Stay here for a moment. Have to prepare the dogs."

Narice didn't know what he was talking about, but complied and remained in the van when he stepped out. She watched the woman on the cane give him a strong hug that, yes, made Narice wonder about the woman's identity and her role in his life. Not that it was any of her business; but still . . . Reminding herself that she had no ties to Saint, she waited to see what would happen next. He clapped his hands and the dogs charged. Startled for a moment by the sight of the dogs eating up the short distance, then knocking him down, Narice relaxed when she realized he and the dogs were playing. He wrestled them and rolled on the ground while they played, barked happily, and repeatedly licked him in the face. It was obvious the man and dogs were friends. He finally stood, gave them both a scratch behind the collars, then signaled them to follow him over to Narice's side of the car. He opened the door and said to Narice. "I want you to step out kinda slowly, then ball up your fingers and let the dogs smell the back of your hand. Okay?"

Narice eyed the dogs. "Okay."

"Are you scared of dogs?"

"Not usually. No."

"Good. Come on out, slow though."

Narice did as she was told. She exited, then held out her hand for the dogs to sniff. They approached her individually. Saint introduced her to the first one. "This is Jesse."

Narice extended her curled up hand. Jesse sniffed the skin, looked up into her face as if memorizing it, then sat beside Saint.

"And this is James."

Narice stood silent for the second encounter. James checked her out much the same way Jesse had, then went to sit down on the other side of Saint.

"And I am Portia. Welcome to our home," the woman said with a Spanish-inflected voice.

Narice looked to the beautiful woman whose long thick hair almost hid her face. "Thank you. I'm Narice."

Portia gestured towards a metal staircase. "Come. Would you like something to drink or eat?"

Narice asked for the facilities instead and Portia said, "Of course. Right this way."

When Portia turned her head, hair fell back to reveal the left side of her face and an ugly red scar that ran from just below her eye to her chin. The wide scar marred the otherwise unblemished beauty of a woman in middle age. Narice dropped her eyes so she wouldn't embarrass herself or Portia by staring. When Narice looked up again, she found Saint watching her from behind his shades.

Metal stairs framed by wooden walls led up from the underground room, so after Saint retrieved the quilt and Narice's suitcase, humans and dogs began the climb. Narice looked back to see the lights going out behind them. It soon became so pitch black, the Cadillac appeared to have disappeared.

At the top of the steps was a wall of wood. Portia pushed on a panel and the wood slowly swung inward. She led Narice and the rest of the small party through the opening and into a dimly lit pantry. A surprised Narice watched the wood swing close again and realized it was the pantry's back wall. A few steps later, past shelves of canned goods and other food stuffs, they stepped out into a large shadowy kitchen lit only by the light on the stove.

Portia said kindly, "This way, Narice."

Narice was shown to a restroom near the kitchen. When she returned, the kitchen was lit up and an apron-wearing Saint was at the stove cracking eggs into a bowl. Portia was seated in a chair at the table. The dogs were lying on the floor at her feet.

Saint said to Narice, "I'm making omelets. Want one?"

"No. Thank you, though."

Narice took a seat at the table and wondered if he had

lied to her about having a wife. Rather than make herself crazy, she let the subject go and concentrated on what he was doing. He was going in and out of the fridge and pantry gathering items for cooking as if he lived here. The proverbial lightbulb went on above her head. She asked without ceremony. "Is this *your* home?"

She thought she saw a smile flash across his outlaw's face for just a second, but she decided it had to have been her imagination.

He glanced over at Portia, who appeared impressed that it hadn't taken Narice long to figure out the situation. "How'd you guess?"

"You look like you're real comfortable cooking over there. You know where all the pots and pans are, and where the food is stored. Then, there's the dogs."

"What about the dogs?"

"They were so happy to see you."

He looked over at the dogs. "You guys hear that? You blew my cover."

Jesse barked. James didn't move.

Portia reached down and patted Jesse's head. "This lady's real smart, isn't she Jess?"

Jesse barked again.

Portia laughed. "You're right, much smarter than that model he had with him last summer."

Saint cracked, "Both of you need to see a pet shrink."

Portia met Narice's eyes and winked.

A short while later, Saint sat down at the table to eat his omelet and toast. While eating, he checked out

Narice and wondered what it might be like to have her at his table all the time. Granted it was fantasy; Narice was far too fancy for a man raised in foster care, but fantasy was all he had. He wanted her and he wanted her bad. He glanced over at Portia. "So what's been going on?"

"I should be asking you. All the chatter says you've upset quite a few people over the last few days."

He shrugged. "So what else is new?"

Narice studied them. Was Portia privy to his secrets, and what had she meant by chatter?

Saint bit into toast. "I ran into our old friend, Gus Green."

Portia's eyes flashed distaste. "That bastard. Did you slit his throat?"

"No, we were in a bookstore. Narice didn't want blood all over—" He looked at Narice, "Who were those people again?"

Narice chuckled softly, "Clifford the Big Red Dog and Dora the Explorer."

Saint waved his fork. "Yeah, them."

Portia dropped her head in what appeared to be amusement at Saint's ignorance of children's books and programs. "You were right, Narice. My granddaughters love them." She then cocked her head and asked, "Do you have children?"

"Yes, about two-fifty."

Portia's eyes widened.

Narice laughed. "I run a school."

"A teacher?" she said with surprise. She then bent

and said to Jesse, "Did you hear that, Jess? She's a teacher."

Jesse barked, twice.

Portia replied to the dog. "You are so right. It is about time he brought home someone with an IQ higher than James over there."

Narice laughed.

Saint rolled his eyes and went back to his food.

Ten

Once Saint was done eating, he turned to Portia. "Now, tell me about this chatter."

In response she gave him a questioning look, but Saint nodded for her to continue. He knew Portia was concerned about Narice being privy to their conversation, but he wanted her included. Narice was smart and a member of the team. Keeping her in the dark would be disrespectful to her and to her intelligence.

Portia silently deferred to his judgment, then spoke: "I heard your old friend Gus Green cursing over the wire earlier, so I sat down and listened."

"What was he cussing about?"

"You," she said with a smile. "Come. I recorded it. You can hear it for yourself."

They rose and Portia and the dogs led them down a

hall that led to a large metal door. Portia then reached into the pocket of her flowing robe and pulled out a small gray device. Holding it like a remote, she pointed it at the door. In response the door slowly swung wide, showing that it was as thick as the door on a bank vault.

The first thing Narice noticed when she stepped inside the room was the coolness of the air. The second was the jaw-dropping display of electronic equipment. It was as if she'd stumbled into a wizard's workshop. There were computers and scanners, printers and monitors. There were large audio speakers against one wall and components with dials and screens that glowed with green light. The equipment filled tables, sat on shelves and on boxes. All of it seemed to be pulsing with life, but Narice had no idea what most of it was used for.

Saint gestured her to a seat.

Narice sat down and stared around like a tourist in the command center at Kennedy Space Center. "This is very impressive, Cyclops. Very impressive."

His response was pitched low. "Glad you like it."

His voice was as vivid as his shaded eyes, and Narice's heart tripped over itself. Needing some calm, she turned her attention to Portia only to see a very knowing smile on the woman's scarred face. Portia didn't say anything, however, instead she took a seat at one of the tables and hit a button on one of the units. Electronic static came over the speakers and filled the room, followed by what sounded like people arguing. A second later, a man could be heard clearly shouting,

"How the hell am I supposed to know how he did it? Just find his ass! No! Leave the damn fence there! The techies will pick it up later. There they are! Get the car!"

The sounds of footsteps and car doors slamming followed that.

Portia pushed another button. "Now listen to this. It's a phone call Gus placed about an hour ago."

Green was saying, "No, sir. He managed to elude us."

An electronically altered male voice spoke next and said, "Explain to me how he got away again." In spite of the distortion, the speaker's impatient tone was very clear.

"The tech people say it's some kind of spray. It melts fences."

"Melts fences?" the other man demanded skeptically, disbelievingly.

"Yes, sir." Gus's voice was small. His guilty voice reminded Narice of the children sent to her office for discipline.

The echoing voice then asked Gus, "Do you know where they are now?"

"No."

"Then dammit, find them! Kill St. Martin if you have to, but bring me that woman."

"Easier said than done, sir. St. Martin's no chump."

"I don't care if he's Batman. Get him out of the picture and bring me the Jordan woman, or I'll get somebody to do it for you."

Narice felt fear run down her spine. Who did the

voice belong to? Was there yet another player at the table of this deadly game?

Portia turned it off and looked up at Saint. "So, now you know what the chatter was about."

Narice was almost afraid to ask. "Who was the man speaking with Green?"

Portia shrugged and admitted. "I don't know. I should have his identity in another few hours."

Narice wanted to ask how, but decided she didn't want to know.

Saint asked Portia, "Have you heard anything from The Majesty?"

"Yes, she called in by pic phone this morning. Look over at that monitor there."

Portia rolled her chair over to a keyboard and began to type. A few moments of silence followed, then The Majesty appeared on the screen. She was veiled and robed in her signature purple and black. "St. Martin," she said from the monitor. "I hope you and the Keeper's daughter are well. The cockroaches have been so bold as to try and poison me, but did not succeed."

Narice was shocked by the news, but glad to hear The Majesty had survived the attempt on her life.

"Keep me abreast of your progress. May the Eye keep you safe."

Then she was gone.

Saint said, "That's it?"

Portia nodded. "Yep."

He then said, "Do we know who Gus is working for?"

"So far, no. And no one wants to claim him. My preliminary contacts think this is a rogue operation."

Narice looked to Saint for an explanation.

He said, "It means, Gus and his buddies were sicced on us by someone without proper authorization."

Portia added, "Somebody that probably doesn't want to be found, but we'll find him. I'm really hoping it's someone tied to Ridley." Then she added venomously, "I knew he wasn't dead. I would have felt it if such evilness had left the earth."

Saint said, "I don't care who he's tied to as long as he's found and stopped."

"I'm on it."

Narice knew that there were a lot of twenty- and thirty-something women who were tech masters, but someone Portia's age was a rarity and Narice was impressed. How had Saint and Portia met? Why did Portia have such animosity towards Ridley? Was it because Ridley was responsible for Saint's imprisonment? Narice's questions were stacking up like rush-hour traffic on the freeway.

Portia asked Saint, "So where do we stand on the Eye?"

Narice thought, *We?*

As a result of the conversation that followed, Narice learned that Portia knew all about the Eye, but Saint spent the next thirty minutes bringing her up to speed on the most recent developments: like the bomb in the Grand Rapids garage, their visit with Uncle Willie, and the high-speed chase in Ann Arbor. Portia didn't know about the quilt, though. Narice showed it to her and Portia seemed moved by the beauty. "This is phenomenal. And your father did this before he was killed?"

"Yes." Narice then told her about the symbols and what they meant.

"So, it's like a treasure map?"

"Yes, in a way."

Portia ran her palm over the fabric. "Your father was very talented. A man with such creativity didn't deserve such a terrible fate."

"I agree."

Portia looked up at Narice. "He'll be avenged. You'll see."

"I hope you're right."

Portia stated firmly, "No, he *will* be."

Narice didn't argue. An unexpected yawn escaped Narice then. It had been a long day.

Saint could see her tiredness. He wanted to take her upstairs, put her in a warm tub, and hold her while she slept. The fantasy took him by such surprise, he had to mentally shake himself to remember what he'd been about to say. "Ready to crash?"

Narice nodded. "Yeah. I'm dead." And she was. Now that she'd had an opportunity to relax, she could feel fatigue slowly creeping up and taking over.

"Portia will show you where you can sleep."

"Thanks." In reality, she wouldn't have minded cuddling in bed with him, but she buried that thought.

Saint didn't want her to leave. "I'll see you in the morning."

"See you in the morning." Narice gave him one last backwards glance, then followed Portia and the dogs back into the hallway.

The room Portia took Narice to was upstairs on the second floor. It was large and old-fashioned. Starched white curtains covered the windows that ran the length of the back wall. There was a big four-poster bed made of brightly polished cherrywood. A matching nightstand stood beside it. A sit-down vanity with a big wooden mirror stood against another wall. The hardwood floors and a ceiling fan also caught Narice's eye. "This is nice."

"I like it in here, too. There's a bathroom through that door. Has a shower. Towels are in the cupboard. Is there anything you need?"

"No. You've been very kind." Narice put her suitcase on top of the bed spread then undid the zipper. "How long have you lived here?"

"Almost seven years. We bought this place together."

"Really," Narice replied looking over at Portia.

Portia's dark eyes danced with amusement. "It's not what you think. He and I are the best of comrades, and that's all. I needed a place to live and so did he. It turned out to be an ideal investment."

Narice didn't want to admit how relieved she felt

hearing Portia define her relationship with Saint. "I just can't see him as a farmer."

Portia laughed. "He couldn't either, at first. Now I think he enjoys being out here in the quiet. Helps him heal."

Narice wondered what kind of healing Portia was referring to, and realized she now had more questions than ever about the mysterious Saint. She yawned behind her hand. The questions would have to wait for another time, though. Right now, all she wanted was a shower and some sleep. "What time is rise-and-shine around here?"

"Usually seven A.M.," Portia replied, "but we'll let you sleep in."

Narice replied gratefully, "Thanks."

"You get some rest. And Narice, thanks for bringing him home."

In light of what she'd seen and heard over the last few days, all Narice could say was, "You're welcome."

After Portia's departure, Narice took her shower. Done, she dressed herself in a pair of blue silk man-style pajamas she'd picked out at Myk Chandler's in-house department store. Her crawl into bed was interrupted by a knock on the door. She answered, "Yes?"

"It's me."

Narice couldn't help it. His voice made her smile. She climbed off the bed and went to the door feeling like a sixteen-year-old.

She opened the door and found him standing on the

other side. The magic coat was gone. He was dressed in all black and the shades hid his eyes.

Saint knew he didn't really have a reason to be standing at her door, but he'd convinced himself it was because he wanted to make sure she was okay. In reality he just wanted to see her. "The room okay?"

"Yes. Portia told me I could sleep in in the morning."

Saint could smell the freshness of her skin and the scents she'd used in her shower. "Portia lies, a lot. I clang the breakfast bell at six."

Narice shook her head. "It's four now. I am not getting up at six."

"Not even if I make you whipped cream?"

The words touched her like she imagined his kiss would; deep, dizzying. She remembered him declaring he'd wanted to make love to her; not that she'd taken him seriously, but she did remember. "That's a very tempting offer," she admitted softly, "but, no, not even for whipped cream."

His smile stroked her. "You make it hard for a brother to please you."

The phrase, *"please you"* made her heat rise, but she set it aside and told him truthfully, "You've been keeping me out of harm's way. That pleases me more than all the whipped cream in the world."

Saint smiled down. "Then I'll go with that." He wanted to raise his hand and slowly trace the shape of her jaw. Forcing down the urge, he said instead, "Sleep tight."

Narice could feel her body responding to his unspoken call. Her nipples had tightened and a warmth was spreading out from her thighs, reminding her again how long it had been since she'd been with a man. "You, too." Reluctantly, she backed up and then shut the door softly.

Saint was left standing there looking at her now closed door. Portia passed him in the hall on her way to bed and cracked, "Not accustomed to being on this side of the door are you?"

He smiled.

"I like her. She's classy and she's smart. Try not to mess it up."

"Go to bed," he told her with a grin. "I'll see you in the morning."

She lifted herself on her toes and gave him a kiss on the cheek. "Glad to have you home. Don't stay up too late."

He gave her a squeeze then went to his room.

After taking his shower, Saint picked up the phone by the bed. The line was a secure one so calling and checking in with Myk and Sarita wouldn't compromise them or him. He talked to Sarita first, and then to his brother.

Saint asked, "Any repercussions from harboring a known fugitive?"

Myk laughed. "No. I got a few calls asking if I'd seen you. I just told them no. Simple lies are always the best. Everything okay?"

"Yeah." Saint caught him up on the events since leaving Detroit.

Myk said, “Well watch your back. I forgot to tell you the full manual on Lily is in the glove box along with the registration and authorization from GM giving you permission to drive their test vehicle. Is it still in one piece?”

“Barely.”

Myk’s resulting silence made Saint chuckle. “You’re so easy to get. The Caddy’s fine. You go on back to bed. I’ll check in when I can.”

“I’m holding you to that.”

“Good night, big brother.”

“Bye, Saint.”

Saint set the phone back into its cradle, then while the women slept, he and the dogs went back downstairs to check out the Caddy. He found the manual just where Myk said it would be. He read a bit then said to the dogs, “Hey listen to this. The windows are one and half inches thick and bulletproof.”

Jess watched him intently. James was asleep.

“It says the body panels are kicked up with bullet-resistant steel panels.” Saint looked down at Jess and asked, “I wonder what the difference is between bullet-proof and bullet-resistant?”

Jess didn’t seem to know either, so Saint read on. “Let’s see. She can face down a .44 Magnum, a 9mm submachine gun or an Uzi, but we’re on our own against rockets or grenade launchers. Hmm. Guess we’ll stay away from those. The undercarriage and gas tank are armored, too.”

Jess yawned and stretched out beside James. "You sleepy, too?" Saint asked her. "We'll head up in a minute. I need to see what else the Caddy is packing."

Saint read about the communications systems, and how to deploy the four on board missiles. By the time he came up for air an hour had passed. He yawned and stretched. Tired, he stuck the manual back in the glove box, woke the dogs, and the three of them climbed the stairs for bed.

The next morning, Narice awakened to a room filled with sunlight. She felt refreshed and rejuvenated from the deep uninterrupted sleep. As she left the big bed and headed to the bathroom, the hardwood floors felt cool under her bare feet.

She took care of her morning needs and dressed. Today's outfit was a sleeveless white linen shell worn over beige lightweight drawstring pants. On her feet were a pair of brown leather short-heeled mules that showed off the red paint on her toenails. Hair and light makeup came next, followed by hoops for her ears and a thin gold chain for her neck. She looked at herself in the mirror and liked what she saw. In her head she could hear her daddy saying, *"Narice, when you look good, you'll feel good."* She sent a prayer of thanks up to his spirit. A knock on her door made her look over. "Come in."

It was Saint carrying a tray loaded down with what appeared to be breakfast. "I was hoping to catch you in bed."

It took her a moment to get her bearings because he wasn't wearing the shades. Nothing stood between her and those devastating green eyes, and she couldn't decide which man was more overwhelming, the one with the shades or the one without. She finally responded to that loaded statement. She flirted back, "I'll bet you were. Maybe next time."

"Guess, I'll take this back then."

"Hey! Get back here. If that's my breakfast. I want it."

He faced her and for a moment said nothing, just drank her in. Only then, did he say, "Good morning, Narice."

She held his eyes. "Good morning. Did you get some rest?"

"Yes."

Narice wasn't sure she believed him. Up close she could see the weariness in his golden face. "Did you bring enough for two?"

"Yep. Let's eat on the porch."

He set the tray on the edge of the vanity table, then crossed the room to the windows. He pulled back the curtains to reveal the French doors that centered the glass wall.

Once the doors were thrown wide, sunlight entered unencumbered along with a cool breeze. Narice walked over and was surprised to see a porch attached to the room. It looked out over a small tree-lined stream that ran the length of this side of the house. She leaned over the edge and looked out. To her left and right were acres and acres of open land. Below her, a path had been cut between the house and the stream but the rest had been left wild and natural. Birdsong filled her ears as did the quiet hiss of insects. "This is fabulous," she whispered in awe.

She turned back to see if he was affected too, but he was transferring the items from the tray to a small glass-topped wrought-iron table. Next to the table were two iron chairs. The slope of the roof shaded that portion of the porch, offering a perfect place to sit and enjoy what looked to be the beginning of a glorious but hot Midwestern summer day. Narice supposed he'd grown accustomed to the glorious vista and therefore took it for granted, but she doubted she ever would.

He was seated and pouring orange juice into her glass. "Come and get it."

She went to join him. He began taking tops off of dishes and showed her hash browns, bacon, eggs, and grits. Narice preferred a bowl of cereal and a toasted bagel or English muffin for her morning meal, but when a brother brings breakfast on a tray, a sister eats it; especially if he prepared the food himself.

Saint looked at the small portions Narice was placing on her plate and a bulb went on in his head. "You probably don't eat like this in the mornings, do you?"

She didn't lie, "No. Cereal, toast, juice and I'm good to go."

"I'll remember that."

"That's not necessary. I'll eat whatever you cook."

He held her eyes. "A lady should have what she prefers."

"Yes, sir." Narice could feel the essence of him playing over and around her like a sensual fog. "Thanks for breakfast."

"You're welcome.

"Tell me about this house."

He put salt and pepper on his grits. "Not much to tell. Portia had a friend of a friend who knew the owner. Government foreclosed on the place. Portia made the owner a very generous offer and he took it."

"It's very peaceful."

He looked around, then nodded his agreement. "I didn't think I'd like being out here in the sticks, but coming back always feels good."

"How long have you been away?"

"Almost six months. I was in Belize before hooking up with you."

"Belize?"

"Yes. Grave robbers looted an archaeological dig. The government wanted the stuff back, so I helped out."

"What is it that you do, exactly?"

"Exactly? This and that. I find things, lose things. I listen here, talk there."

"You're being deliberately vague, aren't you?"

Saint told the truth. "For now, I have to."

"Does that mean that sometime in the future you won't?"

He shrugged but said nothing more. Narice accepted the answer without taking offense. The stuff he seemed to be into would probably scare her to death. "Can I ask how Portia got that scar?"

"From her ex-husband. He thought she was having an affair."

Narice was appalled. "Even if she was—"

"She wasn't though. She needed almost thirty-five stitches to close the gash. He told her he wanted to make sure no other man looked at her."

"She's still a striking woman."

He smiled. "Yes, she is."

"Where'd you meet her?"

"In Rio many years ago."

"Her husband sounds like a real peach. Is he still alive?"

"No. A Great White had him for dinner a few years back. Accident. Portia called it divine retribution."

Narice thought she agreed with Portia.

Saint studied Narice across the table. The sleeveless top showed off her arms. They were firm and brown and had just enough definition to make him wonder if she lifted weights. He liked that she was fit. He liked the light makeup, the hoops in her ears; seemingly everything about her earned his approval. Now, if he could just get his attraction under control he might be able to be around her and not want to seduce her every time their paths crossed. Like now.

Narice had been around him enough to sense when his interest in her was rising and she sensed it now. Today he was dressed like a construction worker; ragged sleeveless sweatshirt, shorts, socks, and a pair of brown hikers. Had he been working at a building site in

Baltimore, sisters on their lunch hour would have been lined up at the fence trying to get a good look at him. The green eyes were heart-stopping enough—throw in his smile and that very sexy voice . . . Yet, he was here with her; having breakfast, and in his own understated way, exuding such a strong male vibe that keeping herself from succumbing was becoming a full-time job.

"So, should I court you?"

The bluntly asked question caught her by surprise. Narice placed her elbows on the table and rested her chin on her clasped hands. "What do you know about courting?" she asked, her eyes skeptical, playful.

He leaned back in his chair and checked her out. "Probably more than you think."

"You're not going to want to marry me when we're through, are you?"

Saint's turn to be surprised. He had never met a woman like this before in his life; she could ride shotgun for him anytime. He chuckled. "I promise, there'll be no rings at the end."

"Good. Because I don't want to get married again, and I know you aren't interested in settling down."

Saint was truly blown away. "Are you this confident in bed?"

Her eyes sparkling, she shrugged. "One man's frigid woman is another man's freak. I don't have a whole lot of experience but I do enjoy myself when it's done right. . . ."

Saint was so turned on by her candor, he wanted to

drag her into his lap and kiss her until Halloween. "Are you always this frank?"

"Only with men threatening to court me."

Saint's smile was all male. "I'm going to eat you up."

"And I can't wait," she tossed back in her softest lioness voice.

"Well, before we start acting like teenagers in the back seat, we should get some work done."

"Whatever you like."

Saint's manhood rose in response and in anticipation; only discipline kept him focused on what he should be doing as opposed to what he wanted to do. So, from the back pocket of his shorts, he pulled out a folded map and a yellow marker.

He removed some of the dirty dishes from the tabletop then spread the map over the cleaned space. The map was of the United States. Using the marker as a pointer, he showed her I-75 near Dayton. "This is where we are, and this is where we are going to wind up." The end point was the Okefenokee Swamp in southern Georgia.

He began to draw a line down 75. "If we take this route and keep the stops to a minimum, we can probably do it in under fourteen, fifteen hours."

Narice stood up and leaned over the map so she could get a better look. The route he'd highlighted took them through cities like Lexington, Chattanooga, Atlanta, and Macon. Her calculation said the drive would be 700 miles from Dayton to the swamp on the Georgia Florida border. "That's a long way."

"Yeah, but as long as we don't have to dodge cockroaches all the way down, it should be okay."

"Do you think they'll find us?"

Saint refused to lie to her. "Probably, but we'll be ready."

"What about flying?"

"I considered that too, but if I need my weapons, I don't want to have to wait for them to come off the carousel."

To Narice that made sense. They were standing fairly close to each other. Her bare arm was only inches from his. Unable to stop himself, Saint reached out and gently lifted her chin, then kissed her lips softly. He'd planned to kiss her just once then let her go, but as she responded and began to return the kiss, passion flared.

One minute Narice had been studying the map, and the next, he was kissing her and she was melting. When he pulled her closer, the heat of their bodies coming together made her slowly wrap her arms around him and hold him as close as he held her. The taste of his lips left her breathless; shimmering. In reality they'd both been waiting for this, pining for this, and they didn't waste the moment.

Saint transferred his kisses to her ear and then down the soft edge of her jaw. The heightened rush of her breathing matched the rush in his blood. He wanted to kiss her until sundown and then, until sunrise. Her lips were as intoxicating as the perfume teasing him from the silky brown column of her neck. He placed a kiss against the golden heart hanging from the chain around her neck, then brushed his warm lips against the skin.

Narice drew in a shuddering breath. He was *good*—real good. Her arms had fallen to her sides and she was supporting her weight by holding the edge of the table. Every cell in her body was singing, pulsing as he traveled bold yet lazy kisses over her throat, her jaw, the gold heart around her neck. His hand moved to her breast and mapped it slowly. Each touch singed her skin and she sensually arched for more. In response she slid her tongue erotically against the edges of his mouth. He groaned and tasted the pink tip, while his hands tugged at her shirt to pull it free. Their tongues danced and mated; their breathing filled the morning silence, a silence that was suddenly spoiled by the insistent barking of a dog.

Saint turned and said, "You got lousy timing, Jesse. What do you want?"

While Narice tried to catch her breath, the dog barked twice.

"Tell her I'll be there in a minute."

Jesse trotted back into Narice's room.

"Portia wants us for something."

Narice held his green eyes. She would have questioned him about his talking dogs, but she was too busy trying to come down off the sensual rocket ride he'd taken her on. Yes, he was very good but then she'd sensed that about him the night they met. "What do you think she wants?"

"We'll deal with that in a minute. . . ." he whispered, kissing her again. A few hot moments later, he reluctantly drew away. Tracing her kiss-swollen mouth with a gentle finger, he then asked huskily, "So, will you go with me, as we used to say in middle school."

She smiled. "No commitments, no ties?"

"None."

"Then I guess I can let you walk me home every now and then."

He leaned in and kissed her deeply, so deeply, her eyes closed and her body soared again. He broke the kiss and escorted the dazzled Narice back inside.

Eleven

Portia was seated in front of a monitor, fingers flowing over the keyboard. On screen were four wavy lines moving back and forth like something out of an old sci-fi flick.

Without looking up, Portia said, "Sorry to interrupt your breakfast, but there's something you need to hear."

Saint walked over. "What's up?"

"I've managed to isolate the true voice of Gus's boss from the scrambled one." Her lyrical voice was harsh. "Take a listen." She hit a key and a very familiar voice came over the speakers.

It was Ridley's and Narice fought off a shiver.

Portia spat, "May The Majesty cut off his tiny little balls."

Saint nodded his agreement, then said, "Knowing Gus and Ridley are working together makes me feel better, though."

Narice asked, "Why?"

"Because I thought we were facing three groups: Gus, Ridley, and the general's thugs, but with Gus and Ridley teamed up, that means only two packs of dogs are after this meat."

Portia cautioned, "He could still be working for the generals. No way to verify it one way or the other right now."

Saint understood, but in his mind, it did pare down the opposition. "Anything else? How about word on the election in The Majesty's country?"

"Nothing new. United Nations has reps on site attempting to set up polling places. Word is, the generals are being very cooperative."

"All the while making attempts on The Majesty's life."

"Exactly."

"Well, Narice and I are going to hit the road around eight tonight, so anything else you can find will help."

Portia nodded, then said, "In the meantime, it's such a glorious morning. How about taking the dogs out and letting them run for a while. Jesse's been pestering me since she got up."

"No problem." He turned to the dogs lying near Portia's chair. "You two ready?"

Both canines hopped up excitedly and trotted to his side. He grinned and rubbed their strong black-and-brown necks affectionately. "Then let's go."

Outside, the dogs took off like prisoners on the lam. Narice had traded her mules for tennis shoes and the open field seemed to stretch forever. The silence of the country wasn't something a city girl like Narice was accustomed to, but she found herself enjoying being able to hear the birds singing and the rustle of the breeze through the tall grass instead of traffic, planes overhead, and the rest of the noise associated with civilization. Even at her South Carolina time-share, the quiet often competed with the drone of power tools, jet skis, and drunks partying at night on their boats. Here, though, silence ruled. "I could learn to like this."

Saint ran an admiring eye over her womanly curves. "Could you?"

"Yes, I could."

"How about the owner?"

Narice looked up at him for a moment, remembering his kisses on the balcony. "I like Portia a lot."

He growled and cut her a warning look.

Narice laughed, "Oh, you mean, you?"

Amusement made him shake his head. "You're hard on a brother's ego."

"Me?" she asked innocently.

"Yes, you, Headmistress Jordan."

"No, I'm not. I love brothers."

"Uh-huh."

"I do. Otherwise I would have accepted Lars's marriage proposal last year."

Saint stopped. "Lars?"

"Yep. Lars Hansen. Norwegian. Investment banker. Bucks on both sides of his family."

"You were dating a Norwegian?"

"Hey. No brothers were asking me out."

"So, what happened?"

"The cultural divide was too big. He didn't know Frankie Beverly and Maze from Morris Day and the Tyme."

"I wouldn't have married him either," Saint laughed.

"He took it well. In fact, somewhere in the Mediterranean he's sailing his yacht, the *Narice.*"

Saint stared. "He named his boat after you?"

"Yes. I was pretty flattered, but not enough to marry him."

Saint was suddenly jealous of a man he'd never met. "How'd you meet him?"

"He's the uncle of one of my students. We met a couple of years ago at her birthday party."

"I see."

Conversation died after that.

Saint didn't like hearing about her and another man, especially one who'd probably held her in his arms and tasted her kisses. As dynamic and fiery as she was, it was stupid of Saint to assume she'd been a hermit since her divorce. Now, illogically, he wanted to know about every man who'd ever so much as spoken her name.

Narice sensed the story had disturbed their interlude and his male ego. *Men,* she thought. Keeping her voice nonchalant, she told him, "You know, some men would have sulked or pouted knowing some other man named his yacht after me. Glad you're not like that."

Busted, Saint looked her way and smiled, "Me too."

Narice chuckled to herself and kept walking.

Their meandering steps took them farther out into the fields and past a large stand of sunflowers. The plants were well over six feet tall and were crowned with multiple stems filled with flowers. Some were the traditional yellow petals with brown centers but others were exotic varieties she'd never seen before. "Red sunflowers?"

"Yep."

The petals were a dark red bordering on black and the centers were even darker. Narice found them quite beautiful. She saw others that had pale pink leaves and a few that had snow-white petals. "These are amazing."

The variety of sunflowers was exceeded only by the variety of bees and other insects buzzing around the sturdy blooms.

Saint watched her walking amongst the tall flowers, and thought she was pretty amazing, too. His mind flowed back to last night when she'd come to the door in those blue pajamas; she'd looked good. The kiss they shared this morning on the balcony was good too, so good it was still pulsing in his blood. "These sunflowers are Portia's babies," he said to her, knowing he wasn't going to be able to keep his hands off of her for much longer. "She sells the seeds to a local birdseed packager—when the local finches don't eat them all."

Narice continued to pick her way through the flowers. "Where'd Portia get her technical training? She seems real comfortable with all that technology."

"Here and there, but she picked up most of it while working for the Brazilian government."

Narice thought about Portia's skills, the contacts Portia talked about having, and her ability to ferret out secret info. "Did her job entail, *this and that,* too?"

Saint hesitated for a split second, then told her the truth. "Yes."

Narice was pretty sure he wouldn't answer any more questions along that line, so she didn't ask another. Instead she let rise the heated memories of the kisses they'd shared at breakfast. Being out here with him brought it all back, along with her bold admission that the dog-interrupted interlude hadn't come close to satisfying her.

Saint said, "You know, in a way, sunflowers are like mistletoe."

"How so?" Her face was a study of amusement and skepticism.

Green eyes sparkling with mischief, he slid an arm around her waist and eased her close enough for her to feel his body heat. "If you're near sunflowers and a pretty lady comes by, you can kiss her."

Narice learned that drowning in a man's eyes was not just a figure of speech. "Oh, really?"

"Naw. I made it up."

She dropped her head, laughed softly, then met his smoldering gaze again. "Well, let's pretend that you didn't. . . ."

Convinced that she was the most fearless and fascinating woman alive, Saint used his right hand to raise her chin and brushed his mouth across hers, murmuring, "I'm game . . ."

The sweet power he slowly poured into the kiss melted Narice's knees. Heat bloomed, and this morning's passion on the balcony picked up where it left off. Her lips parted in shuddering response and he nibbled seductively on her bottom lip. His tongue slid over the parted corners of her mouth, then delved inside to coax hers to come out and play. In the meantime his hands were slowly exploring the curves and planes of her body, setting off tiny flames of desire that made her want more. He left her lips and grazed his bearded cheek ever so lightly over cheek, her jaw, her chin; inhaling her scent, savoring the softness of her skin, tempting her with fleeting touches of his body's heat. A brazen fire began to build in the core of all that made her woman and she whispered, "Touch me . . ."

The force of those two words hardened his manhood and sent heat spiraling through his veins. He undid the buttons on her blouse, then ran a hot palm over her lace-encased breast. "Here . . . ?" He boldy slid a hand down her body and gently cupped the warmth between her thighs in the thin, lightweight pants "Or here . . . ?"

He gave a meaningful stroke to that damp, blossoming spot and Narice responded with a low, sensuous groan.

He slid her bra free and tongued a nipple. He bit the tight bud gently, expertly, causing Narice to suck in a shaky breath. Only when each nipple was hard and throbbing did he raise his head and kiss her mouth. His hand between her thighs was doing marvelously wicked things.

In a voice that was as hot as she was, he asked, "What's a headmistress doing wearing such sexy underwear . . . ?"

Narice couldn't have answered if she'd tried. Speech was gone; mind was gone; only the sensations rising from his naughty explorations below and his expert fingers on her half-bared nipples above, remained. With a touch he coaxed her to widen her stance and she complied shamelessly just so she could continue to be fed. The flimsy cotton of her pants and the thin material of her panties made it easy for him to find the bud whose only purpose was pleasure. His fingers were erotic, knowing, and fed her so full and so well the orgasm that tore through her long starved body made her grasp his wrist and fall against his chest so she could ride the waves of pleasure.

Saint took her weight and felt his own desire roaring. She'd come so quickly, he had to ask softly against her ear, "Has it been that long?"

She whispered back. "Yes." But she glorified in all he'd made her feel.

Saint knew that were she his, she'd never go a day without him leisurely pleasuring her the way her sweet woman's body deserved. He slid a fingertip over the shuddering vent between her thighs wanting more than anything to sheathe himself in her tight heat. He wanted to explore, kiss, and coax her until she forgot about men named Lars, and remembered only him.

But he couldn't take her here amongst the sunflowers because—he slapped at a horsefly as it bit his neck—there were too many bugs.

Narice finally came back to herself. The pure want in his eyes made her shiver sensually.

He pressed his lips to hers. "You shouldn't look at me that way."

Narice kissed him back. "Why not?" She wanted to be naked for him right here and now.

He circled his hand over her ripe behind and murmured, "Because I'm about two seconds away from stripping you naked, woman, and our first time shouldn't be in the middle of a sunflower field."

She gave his lips a series of tiny seductive little kisses and asked again, "Why not?"

He dropped his head and traveled kisses up the column of her warm throat until her head slid back. "Because the only thing I want biting you, is me . . ." He gave her a gentle nip on the soft skin below her jaw and she groaned her pleasure.

He said against her ear, "Remember the mosquitoes at Uncle Willie's . . . ?"

She did only too well.

He gave her a long parting kiss then stepped away.

Very conscious of the steam rising between them, they viewed each other through eyes hazy with desire. Narice wanted to find the closest bed and pay him back in kind for the glorious pleasure he'd given her. Her breasts were still throbbing and the echoes of her orgasm continued to pound in her blood. He was right, of course, making love out here wouldn't be wise. She slapped at a horsefly the size of a quarter and he raised an eyebrow knowingly.

He asked, "You ready to continue our walk?"

"No," she said with a blaze in her eyes, "But lead on, McDuff."

He face looked at her quizzically.

"Line from Shakespeare."

"Ah." He ran his eyes over her kiss-swollen lips and felt himself grow hard all over again. "A lioness who quotes Shakespeare. You, are one of a kind."

"You're not so bad yourself."

He took her by the hand and they set off again, passing plots of tomatoes and trellised green beans. They played tag in a field of corn and kissed themselves senseless in the middle of a melon patch. Her blouse was again opened and he helped himself to the twin prizes inside.

Saint spotted a fallen tree trunk. They sat and rested. The openness and quietness of the surroundings were a marked contrast to the heat pulsing through her body. Saint looked her way and grinned.

"What's so funny?"

"You. Me." He leaned over and kissed her slowly and thoroughly again.

Eyes closed, she asked, "What do you mean?"

"You're the classiest woman I've ever had the pleasure to chase down a dark street."

Narice's eyes were smoldering. "And you're the hottest man to ever catch me."

"Never thought we'd end up like this."

"Me either."

When it was time to move on, Narice wasn't sure her legs would hold her. She was so dizzied and dazzled by desire, putting one foot in front of another took a lot of effort. She realized they were now quite a ways from the house. They were standing on a rise and the house below looked very small. "I didn't realize we'd walked so far."

He eyed this woman who had the sweetest nipples on the planet, and damn if he didn't want to taste them again. "Time passes when you're having fun."

She grinned. She had had fun. "Be nice to spend a few more days here."

He took in the expansive land spread out before them like God's tablecloth and couldn't agree more. "I know."

But they knew they could not.

Narice glanced over at him from beneath her lashes

and again couldn't decide which of his personas moved her more—the man who wore the dark glasses or this one with the contacts over his green eyes. "Do green eyes run in your family?"

"Supposedly. According to my father's mother, I'm the spitting image of one of my great-, I don't know how many greats, grandfather. Man named Galen Vachon."

"Sounds French."

"French, Spanish, Black, he was all of the above. Light-skinned Black Frenchman from Louisiana. Married an escaped slave woman named Hester he met in Michigan back before the Civil War. He supposedly loved her very much."

Narice wondered if he would ever slow down enough to love a woman very much. "So, what's your full name?"

"Legally, it's Galen Anthony St. Martin."

"Galen," she rolled that around on her tongue. "What name do you prefer?"

"Saint, is fine."

"So you met your father's mother?"

He didn't speak for a moment, then nodded. "Yeah. After Myk tracked me down and told me we were brothers, he took me to Louisiana to meet her. She's in her eighties but she is a pistol. I stop in and see her every now and then. She lives in Louisiana."

"She didn't know about your birth?"

"No. She didn't even know I existed until Myk

found my birth records." He then turned to her and said, "Enough about me. Tell me about your school."

Narice knew that he'd shared as much of himself as he would for now, but she was hungry for every detail about him and his life. Only then would she know the man inside. "Sorry, if I'm prying."

"No problem."

His face was unreadable. It was almost as if he still had on the shades.

Since he'd asked for a change in the conversation, she was just about to tell him about her school when the dogs bounded into view. They were barking, but it sounded more like a whine; like a kid in need of mama. As they came closer, a foul putrid odor filled the air.

Narice wrinkled her nose. "What is that terrible smell?"

Saint's face reacted to the odor too, and in an exasperated voice he said, "Skunk."

Narice had never smelled a skunk before in her life. It was now unforgettable.

The dogs were almost on them when Saint, his face still soured from the smell, yelled at them, "Stop!"

The well-trained Rottweilers immediately halted. They were a few yards away but close enough for Narice to see their faces. Both dogs looked absolutely miserable.

Saint walked up close, then bent down to their level and asked, "How many times are you two going to have to get sprayed before you leave those stupid skunks alone? We talk about this every summer. You know that stuff can blind you if it gets in your eyes. You think I'm going to go out and buy you seeing-eye dogs?"

They dropped their heads like guilty children. Narice tried not to chuckle. She felt sorry for them.

Saint's voice softened with affection. "Dummies. Go on to the house and wait by the barn. I'll be there in a minute."

The dogs walked slowly towards the house. The stench was so strong, Narice could feel her eyes starting to water. She had no idea skunk spray was so acrid and potent.

Saint used a hand to fan the foul air. "Good grief."

"Do you just give them a bath when that happens?"

"Yes, but with tomato juice, and Portia's not going to be happy having to deskunk them with the tomatoes she planned to can and turn into salsa. Those two are in *big* trouble."

Narice considered herself to be quite intelligent, but *tomato juice*? She'd never heard of such a remedy. Being with this man was giving her a whole new education.

Saint was right, though, when they got back to the house, Portia was so upset over having to use her precious tomatoes, she fussed at the dogs in her native Portuguese the entire time she and Saint were washing them down. Narice was in charge of the blender. Her role was to puree the tomatoes, add a little water, and bring the juice out to the yard.

Portia took another full pitcher of puree from Narice and switched languages from Portuguese to English just long enough to thank Narice, and say to Saint, "These are *your* dogs."

Rubbing juice into Jesse's coat, he chuckled and asked, "Why is it when stuff like this happens, they're *my* dogs but when they save the world, they're *yours*?"

"Because," she told him, but she was smiling.

Narice blinked. *Save the world?* Surely he was kidding, but with Saint and Portia it was hard to tell.

By early afternoon, the humans were so covered with splatters of tomato juice that showers were necessary. Portia was sure the dogs would need to be treated again before all the stink was gone but decided to give them another bath later in the day. Saint prepared a lunch of BLTs and freshly made coleslaw, and they all sat outside under a big umbrella and ate. Narice appreciated having a man around who could cook, and cook well. As for his other talents . . . She glanced his way, and he gave her a quick lust-filled wink. They were well appreciated, too.

After lunch, Saint and Narice were in the kitchen cleaning up when Portia walked in with a letter. She set it down on the kitchen table. "Mail, Saint." Then she left them alone.

Saint hung up his dishrag and picked up the envelope. He opened it, scanned it a moment, then handed it to Narice. It was a bank statement from a financial institution in Zurich.

She glanced up at him, confusion on her face. "Why

are you getting bank statements from Switzerland?"

"It's where I keep most of my money."

The bottom line showed he had a little over 1.6 million stashed away, give or take a few thousand Euros. "Why did you want me to see this?"

"So you'll know I'm not just a scrub who can't afford a new coat."

She chuckled. "If I'm attracted to a man, his bank book doesn't matter."

"It does to the man."

"Why are men so insecure?" she asked getting up and walking to him. She wrapped her arms around him and placed her head on his chest.

He held her close. "Because we are," he confessed and kissed her lightly on top of her head.

"Why Switzerland, though?"

"Because they're discreet."

"And you need discretion?"

"Yes. Because of what I do."

"Is that for your safety?"

"Mostly. Only certain people know where to look to find me."

"And you prefer that kind of life?"

"I do." *Or at least I used to.* Having her around was making him question things about his lifestyle he'd thought were engraved in stone.

"So, if at some time in the future I need your unique talents, what do I do, just send up the bat signal?"

"If you need me. I'll know."

She studied his eyes; she believed him.

* * *

Since Saint had already stated his plans to leave the farm around eight P.M., Narice went up to her room around ten to seven to gather her suitcase and belongings. She'd enjoyed the short respite here at his home and didn't want to leave, but they had an Eye to find and her daddy's death to avenge. She wasn't looking forward to the intrigue surrounding the search. The idea that Ridley and Gus Green were in cahoots didn't sit well, but if Saint wasn't bothered by the revelation, she supposed she could take it in stride, too. Gripping the handle of her pull-along suitcase, Narice, wearing a blue sleeveless blouse, blue shorts, and white running shoes took one last look around her borrowed bedroom and wondered if she'd ever see it again.

Narice was a little melancholy when she joined Saint in the underground tunnel where he'd parked Lily, but she kept it to herself. The dogs, still looking sheepish, seemed to sense the imminent departure and followed Saint's every move with sad eyes. While he loaded up the Caddy with provisions like coolers, bedding, and digging tools, Portia stood beside the dogs, looking grim, as if she knew the degree of danger ahead. Saint just looked like Saint. He had on the glasses again and his coat. The temperature outside was in the mid eighties yet he didn't look a bit uncomfortable wearing the boot-length trench and the long-sleeved black Henley and black jeans he had on underneath.

When Narice walked up, he held his hand out for her case. "Ready?"

"Yes."

Portia said, "It's been nice meeting you, Narice. I'm sure we'll meet again."

"Thanks, Portia. I hope I'll be seeing you again, too."

Portia then walked over to Saint and gave him a strong, long hug. Her voice was thick with emotion. "Stay safe. Okay?"

He hugged her back. "I will. You keep the home fires burning."

"I will. I'll get in touch with our satellite friends and cut a patch into their system, that way if you need help you can just yell."

"Will do."

Saint hunkered down next to the dogs and ruffled their necks affectionately. "You two still stink, but take care of the house and Portia. Okay?"

Jesse barked. Twice.

James barked. Once.

He gave each a final hug. When he walked over to the Cadillac, Jesse raised her head and began to whimper. Saint didn't look back; he hated leaving the dogs as much as they hated seeing him go.

Narice said, "Poor Jesse."

Saint shook his head and said quietly, "She does this every time I leave."

Placing his emotions under control, he stuck the key into the ignition. The head lamps came on, casting light on the shiny metal wall of the underground chamber. A few moments later the wall in front of them rose. As the car moved forward and the wall lowered soundlessly behind them, Jesse howled as if her heart were breaking.

Once they were underway and could no longer hear Jesse's mournful good-bye, Narice stared around at the metal tunnel they were driving through. Small lights were set in a horizontal line about midway up the walls. "Where'd this tunnel come from?"

"Originally, it was an underground railroad route that connected four Quaker families that shared this land. I guess they moved a lot of escaped slaves through here. When Portia was thinking of buying the farm, the owner took her down to see the original tunnel, but most of it had collapsed."

"How long is it?"

"About a mile. We had a company reopen it and shore it up, then had it excavated so it would accommodate cars, then put in these metal walls. It's an alternative route out, just in case."

Narice wondered if he spent his whole life looking for alternate routes out. She supposed she was glad he had such experience, otherwise she might be somewhere with a gun-wielding Ridley in her face. Turning her mind from that she looked around at the darkness and the lights and wondered what those escaped slaves would think if they could see the tunnel now. "Where's the exit?"

"Inside of an old barn at the end of the tunnel."

"It isn't noticeable?"

"No more than the entrance was."

Narice remembered how the entrance had been camouflaged as an ordinary, every-day barn wall and was impressed by the cleverness of the builders.

He drove on slowly. Moments later they emerged inside a dark, dilapidated barn. Through the barn's missing slats, she saw a narrow dirt road outside. Before turning out, he waited for a moment; she supposed to make sure no one coming up or down the road would see them, but once the coast seemed clear, he glanced her way. "We'll get some gas and head south."

She nodded and the search for the Eye of Sheba was on again.

To Narice the drive back to civilization seemed to take less time than it had to leave it. After the dirt road turned back into a paved one, they were once again cruising through suburbia.

The gas station they stopped in belonged to a well-known chain. Time wise, it was almost half past eight. The sun was low in the sky but light would be with them for a while longer.

There were only a few customers at the pumps so Saint swung Lily to an empty spot then cut the engine. He undid his seat belt and reached deep into one of his pockets and pulled out a thick square of stuck-together bills.

As he unwadded the paper, Narice looked on amused. "You have something against wallets?"

He continued to unfold the bills. "No."

"Looks like it was put in a trash compactor."

He look up at her from behind the shades. "It was."

Her laugh shook her shoulders.

He leaned over, gave her a quick but serious kiss, then got out.

A happy Narice watched him stride confidently towards the door and thought back on the walk through the sunflowers this morning. His hands were as magical as that coat. Thinking about the pleasure he'd given her made her long for a nice hotel room, complete with a big bed and clean crisp sheets. Chastising herself for being so scandalous, she settled back into her plush leather seat and smiled contentedly.

After paying the clerk inside, Saint walked back out to the pump. Lily was equipped with a double gas tank designed for long-distance driving, so filling her up was going to cost a fortune, but with half a fortune in his coat pocket, Saint didn't care. He stuck the nozzle into the hole and watched the numbers on the pump dial begin to rise. It was going to take a few minutes for the tank to fill, so his eyes strayed to Narice. *Lord what a woman.* Just thinking about her made him hard all over again, a state he seemed to be in constantly lately. Her fault, of course, for being so bewitching and sexy and all those other adjectives. The memory of her soft plea of *touch me* was going to keep his blood hot for days.

The Caddy's tank was now filled to capacity, and the thump of the pump shutting off brought Saint back to the present. Shaking himself free of vivid thoughts involving Narice, a bed and himself, he pulled the hose free and closed the gas cap. A few seconds later he was back in the driver's seat heading Lily towards I-75.

Twelve

Lily had a V-8 engine and 345 horses under her hood. With Saint behind the wheel and the cruise control set on eighty, it didn't take long to cover the fifty-seven miles from Dayton to Cincinnati. The sunlight was fading, dusk was now descending, and Narice looked out of her window at the lights of Cincinnati. She'd never visited the city before, but knew it was on Ohio's border with Kentucky.

A bridge over the Ohio River took them into Kentucky. According to the map software Saint punched up on the dashboard's small monitor, Interstate 75 ran 193 miles from the Ohio Kentucky border, then south to the Kentucky Tennessee line.

Narice wondered where the cockroaches were, but told herself not to worry about them; they'd show up soon enough, she was sure. She looked over at the shadow-shrouded Saint. Since leaving Detroit they'd traveled over 250 miles; dodged helicopters, led a high-speed chase, and managed to not get blown up in Myk Chandler's sports car. She'd stayed at his home, met Portia and his dogs, and now Narice felt as if she knew much more about Galen Anthony St. Martin, the person. She was glad to be with him; he was keeping her safe. That he kissed like he invented the concept was just the whipped cream.

Saint's voice interrupted her thoughts. "Can you drive a stick?" Lily's transmission was standard.

"Yep. Since I was sixteen."

"Good. In the glove box is an extra set of keys. Hold on to them just in case."

Narice pulled opened the compartment's door. The little light inside revealed a small stack of manuals, maps, and two keys on a ring. She took them out and put them in her purse.

"Can you shoot a gun?"

Narice's answer was blunt. "No, and no desire to learn."

"You need to be able to protect yourself."

"I understand that, but I've never liked them. When the son of one of my sorors was shot and killed in a drive-by three years ago, that was it. No guns."

"Being able to handle a weapon could save your life."

"It didn't save his."

"Narice—"

She held up her hands: "No. No guns. I'll hit the cockroaches over the head with a lamp or something, but I'm not learning how to pull a trigger."

"All right. I'll leave it alone, for now."

"For-ever," she responded.

Saint could hear the finality in her tone. He shrugged tightly. "Okay. For-ever."

"Thank you," she said curtly.

"You're welcome."

They both felt the tension in the air. It wasn't thick, but it was there.

He asked, "Are we having our first fight?"

The question was so out of the blue she chuckled softly. "Feels like it."

"How about we kiss and make up?"

His outrageousness filled her with humor. "You are such a man."

To her surprise he pulled off the road, set the stick and brake, then turned her way. He beckoned her with a finger, and she leaned over the console separating their seats. In her sultriest voice, she asked, "Yes?"

Saint met her lips with his. After what seemed like a sweet eternity, he murmured, "When a man wants you to learn to shoot, you're supposed to listen."

He was slowly undoing the buttons on her blouse. Kissing him back with all the power of Eve, Narice countered, "When a woman says, to hell with a gun, you're supposed to listen. . . ."

He put an arm around her waist and eased her to her knees on the seat so he could bring her closer, then temptingly brushed his mouth against the bared skin above her exposed bra. "What am I going to do with you?"

As he began to explore her with his hands, she arched and stretched, "Whatever you like, as long as it doesn't involve me and a gun."

Saint was unable to resist the lure of her mouth. He kissed her again, deeply, then pointed out, "You didn't mind Uncle Willie having *Arnold*." Saint was enjoying the way her nipples were rising under his passing hand. He slid the demi cup aside and bit her gently.

Narice dissolved. She was finding it hard to keep up her end of the conversation, especially with him wickedly tonguing her nipples that way; she was pulsing everywhere. "And I don't mind the one you have in your pocket either."

He backed up and looked at her speculatively, then said slyly while continuing to pleasure her breasts. "The one that goes bang-bang or the one that goes bang."

"Both."

He threw back his head and laughed. "Oh, my my my. You are going to be in so much trouble when we finally find a bed."

Narice purred softly. "So are you."

Saint truly enjoyed Narice Jordan's company and wondered if she was his reward for having sacrificed so much for God and country. Lord knows, if he had a normal life she would make the perfect mate. Problem was, his life wasn't normal. At a moment's notice he could be in Zimbabwe, Turkey, or jailed in Thailand. Doing *this and that* wasn't a nine-to-five gig; he couldn't come every night and say, "Honey, I'm home." Looking at her, he felt a pang go off inside himself that made him think about what might have been had he chosen a different path. The moment was not only memorable but scary in a way, because until now, Saint had never questioned his plan to journey through life alone. "I'd better get back on the road. We need to cover a lot more miles before we find a place to sleep."

Narice plainly felt the change in him. "Something wrong?"

"Nope."

That said, he let down the brake and steered the car back onto the dark road. Fixing her clothes, Narice didn't believe him for a minute.

For a while, the interior was quiet. Narice didn't mind the silence, it let her release her frustration with him and to turn her mind to other things: like this search they were on, her parents, particularly her father, and how he may have spent his last days. Was the Eye really buried somewhere in his hometown? The silence also gave her an opportunity to think about the man behind the wheel. He didn't impress her as being traditional when it came to gender issues, but maybe she was wrong. "If I'm being more aggressive than you like you need to say so."

Saint looked away from the road. "Who said anything about that?"

Narice shrugged. "One minute you're getting me all hot and breathless, and the next you shut down and go far away."

"Personal issues. Nothing to do with you."

That only added to her skepticism, but rather than call him on it, she put him out of her mind and fished around in the console between them. "Mind if I put in some CDs?"

"Help yourself," he said emotionlessly.

So she did, then settled back.

Because of the APB Saint had been warned about by Myk, he didn't want to be stopped by any member of the Kentucky law-enforcement establishment. With that in mind, he kept Lily's speed under seventy during the hour or so drive to Lexington. He noticed that Narice hadn't said a word since asking about the CDs. He supposed that had a lot to do with him, he hadn't exactly been chatty and he'd broken off their last encounter pretty abruptly. He was still thinking about that, his life, and the choices he'd made. An old mentor once told a much younger Saint that when you start questioning the value of what you do, it's time to get out of the business. Saint didn't question the value of his work; he knew very few brothers who'd been privileged enough to carry messages from the Dalai Lama, climb Mt. Kilimanjaro, watch snow leopards at play in the wild, or go diving off the Great Coral Reef. He'd also helped topple foreign governments, infiltrated drug cartels, and posed as a Saudi prince. Doing *this and that* defined him, but who would he be when it became time to hang up his coat? It was a question Saint couldn't answer.

It was almost ten P.M. when they entered the Lexington city limits, and the streets were fairly deserted.

"I need to make a pit stop," he told her. "And I'm sorry, Narice. See why cheetahs don't make good pets?"

He turned to her.

She studied him for a long moment. "Takes a big man to apologize."

He didn't reply.

"Thanks," she finally told him. "And, yes, a pit stop sounds good."

"No more being quiet, okay?"

She could see him studying her in the dark, so she said, "You're driving. I didn't want to be distracting."

"You can forget about that."

"Why?"

"Angel, everything about you distracts me—from your perfume to my thinking about your hot underwear."

His candor widened her eyes and she stared in amused amazement.

He defended himself. "Hey, I'm a man. What can I say? It's what men think about."

She couldn't suppress her chuckle. "What else do men think about?"

"Whether she liked your kisses? Whether she'll really let you make love to her when the time comes?"

The embers of Narice's passion slowly stirred. "And the answer to both is, yes."

He laughed. "See what I mean about distracting?"

Narice smiled and sat back.

On a spur off the main highway they found a combination gas station convenience store, and got out. Narice noticed a black sedan parked on the side of the brightly lit building. She beat down the urge to stare over at the car's shadowy occupants and felt a shiver of something cross her soul. As she and Saint reached the door, he opened it for her and she asked, "Did you see that car?"

"Yep."

"Our friends?"

"Maybe."

They went inside. The restrooms were in the back. Saint kept an eye on the door and said to Narice, "You go on. I'll be right here. Careful coming out, though, just in case I'm entertaining guests."

Narice knew what he meant by guests, so she nodded and headed for the door marked *Ladies*.

Although there were lots of munchies stashed in the SUV, Saint bought himself a hot cup of coffee, a couple of chocolate candy bars, and a bag of chips. Carefully positioning himself so he'd be able to see the door and Lily, he asked the young brother behind the counter, "Cops got you under surveillance?"

The kid shrugged, "You mean that car outside?"

"Yeah."

"Guess so. Last few nights, we had some people drive off without paying for their gas. The manager tried to fire me but I told her it wasn't my fault. She said I should've stopped them." He looked at Saint and said plainly, "She can kiss my ass. They not paying me for that."

Saint chuckled. "You're right man."

The kid took Saint's money and bagged his items. "Nice-looking lady you came in with. She your wife?"

"Yes," Saint lied, pulling his bag from the counter.

The kid then looked nervous. "I wasn't beaming on her or nothing, man."

"It's okay. Do me a favor. I'm going in the john. If anybody gets out of that car, holla." Saint gave the clerk a hundred-dollar bill. "Think you can do that?"

The kid held the bill up to the light. Seeing that is was true and not counterfeit, he told Saint, "Hell, yeah."

Saint grinned then headed off.

Saint was inside the restroom washing his hands when he heard. "Yo! YO!"

He moved quickly to the door. Easing it open just a crack he saw Ridley, Gus, and a man with carrot-red hair Saint had never met entering the store. He quickly closed the door, then tried to plan what he wanted to do. First, he needed to hope Narice would see them before they saw her and he needed to get out of this bathroom. The dimensions were too small. There were three of them and only one of him. If a fight broke out in here he'd get his butt kicked big-time. To negate that scenario, he stuck his hand in his pocket, positioned his fingers on his gun, then walked out of the bathroom as if he didn't have a care in the world, saying, "Well, look what that cat drug in."

But his swaggering stopped when he saw the gun pointed at the temple of the scared clerk.

Ridley said, "St. Martin, if you would be so kind as to hand over the weapon I know you have in that coat of yours, this young man will live to see tomorrow."

Saint slowly brought out the gun. The redhead took the weapon.

Ridley pulled his gun down and told the kid, "Shift's over. Go home."

The wary kid looked from Ridley to Saint.

Saint held the clerk's eyes and said quietly, "Go on home."

The clerk didn't have to be told twice. Grabbing his cell phone and CD player, he made a quick exit.

Narice opened the door, but remembering Saint's warning, she cracked it just a little and looked around the store to make sure the coast was clear. It wasn't. She closed the door and scanned the bathroom for another way out. The small window by the sink was all she had.

"Now," Ridley said to Saint. He walked over and placed the nose of his gun against Saint's temple. "I'm assuming Ms. Jordan is in the restroom. Gus, go get her. Jacobs, get the lights. If the citizens think this place is closed, we won't be disturbed."

The redheaded Jacobs hit the switch and plunged the store's interior into a state of semi-darkness cut through with beams of light from the street lamps outside.

The patch-wearing Green hustled back from the ladies room. "She's not there. Window's open, though. She must've lit out. I'll go look outside."

Even with Ridley's gun ready to blow his brains out, Saint cheered Narice's spine and spunk.

Narice had already slipped into the driver's seat. When she saw Green come out and begin walking to where Lily was parked, she almost panicked then remembered the glass was one-way; he couldn't see her. The fact that the lights were now out in the store gave her a queasy feeling. Where was Saint? Had they already killed him? She fed Lily the key and revved the engine. She had no choice but to take matters into her own hands.

Green jumped back like a ghost had appeared. It took him a moment to figure out what was happening, but by then Narice had thrown the stick into reverse and Lily was moving fast. Gus had the good sense to leap out of the way. Bracing herself for the impact, she and Lily came through the glass in an explosion of power and sound, knocking over shelves, displays and everything else in their way.

Saint wanted to cheer. He elbowed Ridley hard in the nose, then followed that with a quick uppercut that staggered his nemesis to his knees and sent a stab of pain through Saint's hand. Ignoring if for now, he looked around for Jacobs and saw him running from the big Caddy barreling down on him like a runaway locomotive. Saint couldn't decide which was louder, the store's alarm, the big Cadillac-rumbling engine, or Jacobs's screams of terror. A grinning Saint scrambled past the wide-eyed Ridley and tried to wave his lady down.

By now Green had run back into the semi-dark store, but Narice was doing her best to keep him and Jacobs occupied until she and Saint could hook up. She chased them like dogs after a rat. Turning the wheel and crushing everything in her path that wasn't moving, she turned the inside of the store into shambles, but kept them in her lights and on the run. In their mad rush to stay out of her way, they tripped over canned goods, stepped on loaves of bread, and slipped and slid through the liquids on the floor left by broken bottles of everything from beer to tomato sauce. She didn't see Ridley anywhere, but she could see Saint waving her down. She spun the wheel and charged forward. A blink later, Narice had the door open, Saint was in, and she barreled Lily out through the hole she'd made. As the tires peeled off the narrow sidewalk the Caddy bounced high, but Narice held the wheel firmly and headed out of the lot. In her mirror she could see Green limp out of the store, his gun raised. A few pings hit the SUV. Bullets she assumed, but she was too busy driving.

Saint swiveled around in his seat and stared back at the carnage. The store looked like it had been hit by a tornado. Eyes wide, he turned to her and said, "Damn girl!"

Narice could feel the adrenaline pumping and the rush of excitement singing in her blood. "Hey, couldn't leave you behind."

"I'm glad you didn't, but the only thing still standing back there is the sign."

"I'll get it next time."

He shook his head and settled in.

When the sign for 75 finally came into a view, Narice said, "I think we should take the real Drunkard's Path now."

Saint agreed. Every policeman in the state was going to be on their tail. Since the police would probably concentrate their search on 75, heading for another road seemed like a good idea. He reached down and punched up the map software. A new route using secondary roads showed on the screen. The drive across Kentucky would now take longer, but Narice and Saint didn't care.

As they distanced themselves from the scene of the crime, Saint had no words to describe Narice. When he first met her she'd been just a name in a file; Narice Jordan—schoolteacher and daughter of the man The Majesty called the Keeper. He knew where she lived, how much taxes she'd paid last year, and that she'd never gotten so much as a parking ticket from the law. All the facts and figures had been in the file, but nothing that spoke to her strength or courage. "Want me to drive?"

"Nope. I'm fine."

"Okay, well, I'm going to ice this hand before it swells up like a pineapple."

"How'd you hurt it?"

"Busting Ridley in the jaw."

"Good for you," she said with gusto.

Saint undid his belt and leaned around the seat to flip up the lid on the large blue cooler sitting amongst the tools, boxes, and other stuff he'd brought along.

Narice asked, "Do you want me to pull over so you can get what you need?"

"No. You keep driving. The more miles we put between us and the scene of Hurricane Narice, the better."

She agreed.

Saint put the ice in a small plastic bag, then slid his aching hand into the cold cubes. After a few more moments the hand was so cold and numb the ache toned down.

Narice looked over at him in the dark. "Do you think it's broken?"

"Hope not."

The next big city on the original route was Knoxville, Tennessee, 181 miles south of Lexington. After that they'd twist and turn their way through the mountains to Chattanooga and then on to Atlanta. Right now, Atlanta was a good 300 miles away. They had a long way to go.

A few minutes later, the sign appeared for Reed's Crossing, where according to their map, they could pick up Highway 421 that ran a drunken path parallel to the interstate. They'd still be traveling south, but the highway made enough of a swing east before reconnecting with 75 that Saint hoped it would throw the dogs off the scent.

Being a city girl, Narice didn't like driving the backwoods, but tonight because 421 was shut down for some type of repairs they were following the detour. "Do you think we should turn around and go back to 75?"

Saint shook his head. "No. This may be a blessing in disguise."

"The road is certainly disguised. Where the heck are we?"

Saint used his free hand to bring up the map. A cursor blinked their position. "There."

"Doesn't matter. I still don't know. Country people need to get some streetlights."

It was as dark as Narice had ever seen. Third-world countries probably had better lighting. To make matters worse the road was narrow and unpaved. Good thing Lily did all-terrain well, otherwise they might be sitting on the side of the road with flat tires. "I can't believe I tore up that store that way."

"I felt like I was in Bonnie and Clyde."

"I know. Can I go to jail?"

He smiled at her question. "We'll tell them you did it for God and country. Don't worry about it. The government has a budget line for stuff like that."

"Really?"

"Yeah."

"So I won't get a visit from someone's lawyer down the road?"

He chuckled. "No, Narice. I'll take care of it, soon as we find the Eye."

"I'm holding you to that."

"I know you will."

She turned her attention back to the road. "How do you think they found us, again?"

"Don't know. Last time they saw us we were heading south. Ridley and Gus are smart but it doesn't take a whole lot of brains to station a few teams along the road south and wait. We were at the farm overnight. That would have given them plenty of time to set something up."

"So we stumbled on them—they didn't find us?"

"Exactly."

"Lucky us," Narice cracked. "Now they know what we're driving."

"Plate too, probably, but Myk gave me plenty of fake plates. We can be from any state or country in the world."

Narice didn't know why she was surprised. "You two thought of everything."

He looked around at their dark surroundings. "Everything but this detour. Where the hell are we!"

Neither of them knew, but Narice kept driving and prayed she didn't miss a detour sign in the dark.

Thirteen

After another thirty miles of twists and turns on the narrow road, Saint made an executive decision. "Angel, we passed a campground sign a little ways back, I say we hole up there until morning. Even with the GPS it's too damn dark out here."

Being an urban African-American Narice wasn't sure how she felt about camping out in nowhere Kentucky in the middle of the night, but decided she'd come too far to wimp out now. "I'm game." In the meantime, all the ruts and holes were rattling her spine and teeth. Lily might be an SUV but this road with its posted speed limit of 45 mph was more suited for an F-150 than a souped-up, tricked-out Caddy. Narice felt like she was driving a stagecoach.

A sign appeared in the headlights: CAMPGROUND CLOSED.

She turned to her ever-resourceful companion. "Now what?"

"Guess we keep driving."

So, that's what they did.

Narice gave up the wheel an hour later and Saint took over. His hand still ached but he'd sustained worse injuries, so he just dealt with it. "You can stretch out in the back if you like."

The two rows of seats behind them were folded down. Piled on top of them were various long-handled tools, coolers, boxes, Narice's suitcase, and myriad supplies he'd brought along. *Lie down where*? "I'm tired, but not tired enough to sleep on a cooler."

They shared a grin in the dark.

She added, "Besides," and she cuddled up next to him as much as the bucket seats and the console between them would allow, "you stayed awake while I drove. I should at least do the same."

Saint enjoyed her closeness. The fading notes of her distinctive perfume played over his senses like the soft teasing notes of a jazz tune. "I think you just want to share my scintillating company."

"I think you're right."

Her eyes and sexy voice made him hard as a beam. He needed to find them a bed as soon as possible. Yes, he was on a job, and yes, he was supposed to be on business, but the woman cuddled next to him was making it difficult to concentrate on anything but her. With that in mind, and the realization that taking this off-road had not been a good idea, Saint made another executive decision. "Okay, enough of this drunkard's path. Let's find the highway, the GPS says it shouldn't be far."

"Hallelujah."

Saint loved her exuberance. "If the police show up, we'll deal with it, somehow, and if more cockroaches show up we'll just step on them."

"Did you know a cockroach can live a week without its head?"

He laughed. "And you heard that, where?"

"One of my science teachers. She swore it was true."

Shaking his head, Saint turned his attention to the GPS to plot their course. I need to give you a quick tour of this dashboard just in case something happens to me." So while he drove he acquainted her with all the bells and whistles. He finished up by showing her how to deploy Lily's missiles and the red button that set the firing cycle in motion. When he was satisfied that she knew as much about Lily as he did, they drove on.

They reconnected with Interstate 75 just outside of London, Kentucky, which according to all the roadside signs was the gateway to the Daniel Boone National Forest. Because of the late hour, traffic on the highway was light. Narice looked out of the window beside her. The area around the highway was pitch black, but off in the distance were the twinkling lights of towns and cities. She wondered about the people using those lights: who they were, what they did and believed. She doubted any of them would believe the ride she'd been on since burying her daddy; she was finding it hard to believe herself.

Saint looked her way. "Penny for your thoughts."

"Just thinking about all that's happened since my father died. You. The Majesty. Cockroaches."

"It's been interesting. You've been interesting, too. You're one of a kind, Madam Jordan."

"That's probably a good thing. The world doesn't need more thirty-seven-year-old women driving Cadillacs through store windows."

"You came through like the cavalry, though."

The praise in his voice warmed her. "Glad I could help a brother out."

They rode in silence for the next few miles, but Saint was very aware of her presence. He knew that adrenaline sometimes stoked the libido and he'd be the first to admit that, yes, he'd sampled a few honeys while caught up in dangerous situations more than few times, but being around this Brainiac woman with her curvy body, gorgeous mouth, and fearless ways had his heat turned up like a furnace. "How about some music?"

Narice thought that an excellent idea. Now that they'd left Ridley and that sorry excuse for a road behind, music would be nice. She clicked on the light on her side of the console and looked through the cache of CDs in the console. Seeing a Grover Washington made her smile. The legendary sax player was one of her favorite jazz musicians and always good on a nighttime drive.

Narice leaned forward to put in the CD when out of nowhere came the angry roar of helicopter rotors. Her panicked eyes flew to the windows.

"Can you see it?" Saint yelled while quickly checking his mirrors.

"On my side! Tree high."

He growled a curse and floored the accelerator. "I should have killed Ridley when I had the chance." He cursed again.

Narice could see the black chopper flying above the shoulder of the road and parallel to their position. It kept pace; a lurking, ominous presence.

An angry Saint had had enough cockroaches for one day. At this rate, he and Narice were never going to find that bed.

When the helicopter made no move to approach, Narice asked, "Why's it just laying back like that?"

The reason appeared a heartbeat later. Another helicopter swooped in and showed itself on Saint's side. "Reinforcements."

"Then that means they're scared of us."

Saint grinned. "I like the way you think, angel mine."

For a moment, the endearment made Narice forget all about helicopters and cockroaches. Although she knew better than to read anything deep into the words, she was touched just the same. However all that was set aside as the helicopters swung out of position and headed towards the Caddy. "Here they come!"

"I see 'em. Tighten your belt. This baby doesn't have airbags."

Her eyes widened. "Why not?!"

"You can't drive away from the bad guys with an airbag in your face."

She stared, then because she couldn't help it, she laughed at his logic. "Remind me to never elope with you again."

"Hey, you love this."

What sounded like metal rain began hitting the car. Narice ducked instinctively. "No, I don't. I don't like being shot at." She knew the vehicle was bulletproof, but it didn't matter to her innate sense of self-preservation.

Saint didn't like being shot at either. Never had. More bullets strafed Lily's armored body; others struck vehicles nearby. The chopper pilots didn't seem to care where their bullets went. In the rearview mirror Saint saw a mustang rolling behind them in the middle lane. The sleek Ford was moving fast, trying to get the hell away from the choppers when suddenly there was an explosion that sent chunks of pavement and the underlying steel rods flying into the air. The road turned into a fireball. The mustang veered crazily and spun out into the median. "That was a missile!"

Narice's eyes widened. "A missile?"

"Yeah, those bastards are shooting missiles!" Saint

knew that Lily was equipped with a variety of built-in weapons; James Bond's rides had nothing on her, but her guns weren't meant to bring down a helicopter, let alone two. Lily did have something on board that might even the odds, though. "We've got to get off this road!"

Narice agreed. She looked back helplessly at the now burning mustang and then angrily out at the choppers on their tail. *What kind of people use missiles on a public interstate? The kind that burned your father in his bed,* a voice in her head reminded her.

Saint kept the pedal on the floor while swerving all over the road. Lily was now rolling at plus 100 mph.

Narice watched the choppers flying in and out of their path like deadly dragonflies. They let fly another missile. It missed—barely, but did hit a semi rolling in the right-hand lane. While the trucker fought to keep the rig on the road, the trailer burst into flame.

The choppers' ammo was now coming at them like something out of a war zone. Narice was tight-lipped as she held on to her seat. Saint was driving like a bat out of hell and Lily didn't miss a beat. Narice thanked the lord for General Motors and building Lily like a brick house.

Saint knew that with any luck one of the other drivers had already called 911. Ridley's diplomatic status wasn't going to matter in this situation; this part of the country was small-town America. The local police were not going to be happy with a helicopter shooting missiles at its citizens, no matter the cause.

For now, though, he and Narice were on their own and the choppers were flying close enough for them to see the pilot's grin in the dim light of his cockpit. Saint shouted over the din of the rotors. "I'm going to head into those trees. Then I want you to take the wheel."

"Okay." At the speed they were traveling she had no idea how such an exchange would be accomplished, but she was sure he had a plan.

Apparently the choppers didn't want the Caddy to head into the trees and used the machine-gun fire to try and stop it. Saint kept driving. While one copter continued to fire, its companion swooped down and attempted to ram them. Saint turned the wheel sharply and sped through a fence and towards the safety of the trees. The copter had no option but to increase altitude or collide with the dark branches.

Under the protective canopy of night-shrouded green, Saint stopped the Caddy and threw open his door. "Change places with me. Quick now, angel."

Narice didn't have to be told twice. Outside, she ran around, jumped in, and slammed the door. Belt on, she waited and watched him climb into the back. She listened for the choppers while watching Saint lift the lid on a large black footlocker.

"Should I start driving?" Seeing him pull out what looked like military hardware made her ask, "What's that?"

"Grenade launcher. Let's see how *they* like being shot at."

Narice went still. "Grenade launcher?"

"Yeah. No more questions. Have to work now."

The *work* involved putting the weapon together. He did it so quickly and efficiently; it was real obvious he'd done it before. She wondered what other weapons of mass destruction he had on board.

The choppers sounded above. Narice craned her head to try and spot them through the windshield, but saw nothing.

By now Saint was done. He and his piece were ready. The concern on Narice's face made him pause but he was too well disciplined to be distracted by it. "I want you to take off towards that open field just as fast as you can drive. Stay close to the trees. If anything happens to me, get the hell out of here, okay?"

"Not okay. We're a team, remember?"

"Not if I'm blown away."

"Didn't we already do this rescue thing once tonight?"

He shook his head. "Why are Black women so hard-headed?"

"No idea."

Amusement and affection shone from behind the dark glasses. "See you in a minute."

"Be careful."

He shot her a smile then disappeared into the night.

Narice took off towards the field, bumping over the uneven terrain. There was no way she was going to leave him behind—under any circumstances. She supposed her confidence stemmed from being a novice at this intrigue stuff. If she had more experience maybe she'd be more inclined to follow his orders, but right now, she didn't know enough to save her own neck.

The sounds of the helicopter swooping down instantly scared Narice back to reality. Driving fast, she careened across the open terrain in front of a low-flying chopper. Its predator lights gave the inside of the Caddy an eerie glow. She was the bait. Prayers went up that a missile wouldn't blow her to bits, and that Saint wouldn't miss.

The ground to her left suddenly exploded and she screamed. The aftershock shook the Caddy, but Narice somehow kept herself together enough not to crash into the trees, some of which were now ablaze.

Another explosion shook the world, then another and another, sending fire and chunks of grass and debris into her path. By now, she was a cussing, screaming crying mess, but she swung the wheel hard, doing donuts, one-eighties, and three-sixties in her mad dash to stay out of the way.

Suddenly the biggest explosion yet assaulted her ears, and in her mirror she saw fire in the sky. Her shouts of joy filled the cabin. Pieces of burning and twisted metal began to fall, hitting the roof, the ground. She powered Lily back the way they'd come. Some poor farmer was going to be real mad when he came out in the morning and found tire tracks and dead chopper parts all over his field, but right now he wasn't on Narice's list of concerns. All she wanted to do was find Saint and get the hell away from this place.

Saint grimly waited for the second chopper to appear but it instead rose up into the night sky and headed south. Apparently the pilot didn't want to share the fate of its friend. Saint was glad. There'd been enough mayhem for one night.

When he looked up, Narice had the Caddy's door open and she was running to him. He swooped her up with one arm and held her close. He could feel her tears wetting his face. He dropped the launcher and hugged her even closer. "You okay?"

She nodded.

He kissed the tears in her eyes. He was so proud of how she'd handled herself. Seeing that she was indeed in one piece was worth every dollar he'd ever made in this business "You sure?"

She ran her hand down his bearded cheek. "Yes. Are you?"

"Now I am."

He pulled her in against him again and the kiss that followed was inevitable and wonderful and oh-so-welcome. Off in the distance sirens could be heard. Saint eased his lips from hers and murmured against her ear. "Time to go, angel."

She responded by kissing him again with such sweetness, he groaned and whispered, "Stop it woman. We need to split."

But he couldn't fit actions to words. The taste of her lips, the feel of her soft body pressed against him made him want to stand there until sunrise. That was out of the question, though, so he placed his hands on her waist, lifted her bodily and gently set her down a few inches away. "Let's go."

She grinned. He grabbed up the launcher and they raced back to the Caddy.

Saint shot the stick into first. Leaving behind the burning carcass of the crashed helicopter, they headed out of the field. Once Lily had pavement under the wheels again, he took the speed up.

In Narice's door mirror she could see dozens of flashing red and blue lights pulsating in the darkness behind them. "Here come the cavalry."

Saint took the speedometer up to eighty-five. "And we're getting out of Dodge."

Saint looked over at Narice. No words could describe how impressed he was by her. With her elegant and unorthodox ways, she'd already stolen a big chunk of his heart. When the time came for them to go their separate ways he would miss her a lot. The thought of never seeing her again didn't sit well, he realized. Usually he had no problem cutting ties to people he met on the job. "You did real good back there."

"I was scared stupid. I never want to do that again. Ever." Memories of the earth exploding around her made her fight off a shiver of delayed reaction. "I'm going to have nightmares for the rest of my life."

He chuckled in the darkness. "Lean over here a minute."

When she did, he kissed her softly, fully. "Damn good."

He went back to driving. She settled in and enjoyed the way his praise warmed her insides, but the darkness of the last hour hovered on the edges of her consciousness like the copters hovering over the highway. She hoped the driver of the Mustang had gotten out before the fire, but she was less charitable about the chopper pilot.

A while later, they drove past a large highway sign that welcomed them to the State of Tennessee. "Are we going to stop?" She was hoping for a nice soft bed.

"Just for gas. I want to be in Atlanta by morning."

"Then what?"

"Get a room, lose ourselves for a day or so, get our bearings, grab some sleep. . . ."

The tone of his voice on the word *sleep* piqued Narice's interest. "Sleep, huh?"

"Yeah, you know—like in a bed."

"I thought cheetahs slept in trees?"

He gave her a slow grin. "Not when there's a lioness around."

Even in the dark that smile of his stroked her. "Do you know where this bed in Atlanta is going to be?"

"How about something five-star for the lady?"

Narice liked that idea. She was so tired and sleepy she'd almost trade the grenade launcher for a good meal and a long hot soak in a tub filled with scented bubbles. "Shouldn't we be in some hole in-the-wall hotel keeping it on the down low?"

"Yes, and it'll be the first place Ridley will look. By the time he and his people figure it out and run us down, we should be checked out and on our way to the Okefenokee."

Narice didn't know if she agreed with that logic, but since he was the secret agent, she deferred to his expertise. "Well, we should share the drive. Atlanta's almost three hundred miles from here."

Saint looked at the numbers on the map she'd brought up on the green scope of the GPS. "I can handle it," he said easily. "I'll set the cruise and we'll be there in no time.

Narice was again skeptical, after all they were both too tired for words, but she didn't argue.

Saint wasn't worried at all. He had driven longer distances on less sleep hundreds of times. He appreciated Narice's offer to help with the drive, but with flying cockroaches on their trail he needed to be behind the wheel. Narice was a damned good driver, but he was trained. That the choppers were carrying missiles still blew him away. Ridley and his crew were playing hardball, which meant this chess game was only going to get uglier. The rocket launcher caught them with their pants down, though, just like he'd hoped. The knowledge that the chopper had flown off in a southerly direction did not bode well.

As the night hours passed, Saint drove from Jellico to Knoxville and then through the mountains to Chattanooga. One hundred and eight miles after leaving Chattanooga, they rolled into Atlanta.

The fact that she and Saint were still in one piece

was cause for champagne, Narice decided, and planned to order some just as soon as they got to where they were going. It was early morning in Atlanta and the city was just waking up. She on the other hand wanted to sleep so badly she didn't care if it was on a street corner, but as he'd promised, Saint drove the scarred and battered Lily up to the gold and glass doors of one of the city's most prestigious hotels. She looked the place over and smiled. "I've stayed here before. Very classy choice, Cyclops."

"How about the best suite in the house?"

"Fine with me. Can we afford it?"

"Yep."

"Will they give us a room, though? We're not exactly freshly dressed." With her travel-wrinkled shorts and blouse, and him in that coat, they'd be lucky to get a room at the Y.

He cut the engine and turned her way. "Quit worrying."

"Okay," she said skeptically.

While a blue-uniformed doorman waited patiently by the Caddy's closed doors, Saint ran his eyes over her lips and thought about the kisses he planned on enjoying later on.

Narice had become so attuned to him, she didn't need to see his eyes to know what he was thinking, and right now, his thoughts were in a place easily read. He reached out with a finger and gently traced her mouth. His touch made her eyelids lower and heat race through her veins.

Her response thrilled Saint to his core. Unable to resist, he leaned in and kissed her; the more he kissed her the sweeter she tasted.

By now the scarred, mud-covered Cadillac was drawing very skeptical looks from the brother doorman.

Saint in his flowing coat and dark glasses hit the button to lower the window and said to the brother, "I'll park her myself."

After parking Lily in the back of the large lot, Saint escorted Narice inside.

The hotel was done in royal purples and gold. It's signature chandelier, supposedly one of the largest in the world, sparkled overhead like diamonds. The establishment was well known for its superior service, luxurious rooms, and catering to people who didn't mind paying up to six figures per night.

The perfectly coiffed, redheaded sister behind the desk took one look at Saint in his coat and Narice in her travel-wrinkled clothing and said, "I'm sorry. We don't have any rooms available."

Narice knew the woman was lying. She was just about to challenge the woman when Saint put up his hand. "I got this." He then said to the woman dressed in her red hotel suit. "Can I see your manager please?"

"She's unavailable."

Narice wanted to snatch her.

Saint reached into his pocket and pulled out a small blue business cardholder. He opened it, flipped through, and handed her one. "Read that out loud for me, please."

She sighed impatiently. "Jeffrey Galen. Vice President for Quality Assurance"—her eyes widened and her voice dropped to a whisper—"you work for our hotels?"

"Yes, I do. My assistant and I travel the country looking this way to make sure all of our guests are treated fairly. Now, your name? Ms. Cooper remember this name."

Narice assumed she was Ms. Cooper, so she piped in seriously, "Yes, sir, Mr. Galen," and she stared smugly at the now terrified clerk.

"My name is Sheila Stump. I'm so very sorry. I'll get you our best room."

Galen said, "And Ms. Stump, you are not to tell anyone on the staff that I am here. Do you understand?"

She nodded.

"As far you are concerned I am just another guest. Do that and I may let you keep your job."

She looked ready to burst into tears. "Yes, sir."

Saint reached into his pocket and pulled a wad of hundred-dollar bills. "Will fifteen hundred cover my bill for one night?"

The woman nodded so quickly Narice thought her head might bounce off her neck. Narice had no idea what other business cards Saint carried, but she loved the way this one put Ms. Sheila Stump in her place.

The clerk was now hustling to handle the paperwork. "Do you need help with your luggage?"

"Nope. Just a key and a room."

And what a room it turned out to be. Narice was accustomed to traveling first-class, but even she was impressed by the chandelier hanging above the entranceway and the large bank of windows overlooking the city. The twin bathrooms had large walk-in showers and sensual Jacuzzis. The two bedrooms had big beds sumptuously covered in ivory and gold. There was a bar, a sitting room, which sported black leather furniture, three TVs, and a killer sound system. The refrigerator was fully stocked. From the drapes to the carpeting on the floor, it was a room fit for a queen.

Standing before the windows enjoying the view, Narice said, "I like the way you roll, St. Martin."

He grinned.

"Jeff Galen. Quality Assurance."

He came up behind her and wrapped his arms around her waist. "Right now, though, I'm with the Narice Quality Assurance," and he brushed his lips across the edge of her jaw. Narice rippled in response to the unexpected caress. She turned up her lips for a kiss and he complied deliciously.

Soon one kiss turned into another, and before they knew it, the fire between them was fully involved. His hands began moving slowly over her breasts, rolling the nipples between his fingers and sliding his palms over the tightened points. She could barely breathe. "I should take a shower . . ." she managed to say.

The buttons on her blouse were conquered, the halves opened, and his lips were saluting each newly bared inch of skin from the hollow of her throat to the soft flesh rising and falling above her lacy black bra. "If you leave, you'll miss this . . ."

He unhooked her bra and filled his palms with the trembling weight of her soft breasts. He tongued each nipple in turn, letting the scents of her skin turn up his heat even more, then sucked until she gasped from the heat filling her.

He captured her mouth again while his expert hands and fingers continued to play her breasts like a gifted musician on a prized instrument. When he dropped his head to once again taste the buds he'd prepared so lavishly, she crooned like a lust-filled Stradivarius.

The pleasure pulsing through Narice was wonderful. To be in the hands of a man who knew his way around a woman's body was priceless. His lips on her throat, his mouth on her breasts, the heat of his hard thighs against her own all set her on fire.

Saint was on fire, too; a slow burning, white hot variety that made him want to lay her across the bed and fill her until she moaned his name. He didn't care about showers; he wanted her now. He whispered boldly, "How 'bout we move to the bed?"

Narice nibbled his bottom lip, then licked at the parted corners of his mouth, before saying in a passion husked voice, "Thought you'd never ask. . . ."

They kissed their way through the suite to one of the bedrooms; opening the fronts of pants, discarding clothing, and lingering over the caressing of heightened flesh. He picked her up, then gently laid her on top of the elegant spread. Next she knew, her shorts were taken from her and the founder of the Jordan Academy was lying below him wearing her opened blouse, undone bra, and matching black lace panties.

Saint had been wanting this woman for over a week now. He traced the waistband of her panties and then the whorl of her navel. "Love your underwear," he murmured.

His hand cupped that hot warm place between her thighs. When she spread her legs in wanton invitation, his hands sent back an erotic rsvp. "We can shower later, angel. I can't wait."

Neither could she. His touches were magic; scandalous. She wanted to touch him like he was touching her, but every time she tried to reach for him her efforts died because he was stroking her through the fabric of her panties in bold and magical ways that made her so hot and filled her with such hazy desire, she couldn't complete her goal.

Saint had wanted this first time to be slow and unrushed but touching her, kissing her, and hearing her moan in response made him feel like a teenager in his girl's bedroom and her mama was due home in twenty minutes. He had to have her now or explode.

Narice was breathless and wet from the passion flowing between her thighs. As he slid her panties off her hips and stroked the dampness of her core, she thought she'd explode into orgasm then and there. She held his eyes while he eased the condom on. When he entered her, then filled her, her eyes closed and she growled like the contented lioness that she was.

Saint made a mental note to make love to this woman early and often; she was passionate, uninhibited, and oh-so-sexy, but now he concentrated on stroking her, teasing her, making her beautiful body rise and fall to his rhythm. He filled his hands with her soft hips and lifted her so she could feel every possessive inch of his thrusts. Wanting to brand himself into her memory, his rhythm increased. Her soft cries of response floated in the silent room. It didn't take them long to find paradise. She finished first and he exploded right behind her. The cheetah growled, the lioness purred, then they slept.

Fourteen

Hours later, Narice awakened in the bed. The slow realization that Saint wasn't beside her made her sit up. Her eyes swept the room. The clock beside the bed showed five after seven, which meant she'd slept a good ten hours. The opened drapes showed dusk falling, but where was he? Still wearing only her blouse, she got up, intending to search the rest of the large suite, but a note on the table beside the bed made her stop. Picking it up, she read: *"Gone for whipped cream."* Laughing, she set thc note down and padded into the shower.

Twenty minutes later, a revived Narice wrapped herself in one of the hotel's thick black terry robes and stepped out of the bathroom feeling all the world like a woman who'd been thoroughly loved. Her nipples tightened at the memories of his hands plying her nipples and the hard promise of his body sliding into hers. Just thinking about him made a soft pulse begin its familiar beat between her thighs. The smell of food cut into her reminisces. Tantalizing aromas filled her nose and captured her attention. *Surely he wasn't cooking?* Throwing on some clothes, she went to find out.

He wasn't cooking. Dressed in a black tank top that showed off his lean muscles, and wearing a pair of well-fitting black jeans, he was standing beside a beautifully set table for two. The cloth on it was the color of indigo and the china and silver reflected the twin flames of the ivory candlesticks in the center. Ornate silver dishes covered the food and a bottle of champagne chilled in a silver bucket packed with ice. The table was positioned right beside the windows and offered a dazzling view of Atlanta, twinkling like a constellation against the shadows of evening. The subtle glow of the dimmed lamps in tandem with the sounds of the soft jazz floating from the speakers made the atmosphere sensual and romantic. "This is very nice."

"I thought we could do with a little room service."

He didn't have his dark glasses on and once again Narice had trouble deciding which of his personas intrigued her the most. She concluded that it didn't really matter; the man moved her in every form and the scandalous woman growing herself inside couldn't wait to be *moved* again. "Did you get your whipped cream?"

"Yeah, I did," he told her with a gleam in his green eyes, then gestured her to the table. "Shall we?"

Narice inclined her head royally, then walked to one of the two chairs. Always the gentleman he came to assist her, lingering just long enough for the heat of his nearness and the fresh scent of his clean body to tease her senses, then took his own seat.

Saint thought she looked even more beautiful by candlelight. She was casually dressed in a sleeveless green top and a matching pair of lightweight blousy pants. Her bare feet sported red toenail polish. The row of dark buttons fronting the shirt brought his attention to her curves. The fabric was thin, showing the points of her nipples and making him remember the passionate gasp she'd made when he took them in his mouth.

Narice forced herself to look away from the brilliant hunger in his eyes so she could clear her mind and say a silent prayer before starting in on the meal. Once that was done, she looked up and found him still watching her. His intensity seemed to raise the temp in the room a good fifteen degrees. "We really should eat."

"Do we have to?"

Both knew what the other wanted.

"Yes."

"Why?" He began taking tops off of the food.

"Because we'll need our strength."

He answered with a smile. "You're right."

Anticipation stroked Narice with a sensual shiver, and because she'd never meet another man quite like Anthony St. Martin, she vowed to enjoy this interlude.

The dinner included roast chicken seasoned with rosemary, a salad with Caesar dressing, side dishes featuring everything from green beans to spiced apples, hot yeast rolls, and a chocolate hazelnut gateau for dessert.

Saint popped the cork on the champagne. After pouring some of the fine beverage into two crystal flutes, he set the bottle back into the ice then raised his glass for a toast. "To a beautiful sexy lady named Narice."

"To a handsome sexy brother named Saint."

Eyes mingling they sipped in unison, then set the glasses down.

Fixing their plates came next, but as Saint picked up his silverware, he paused to watch Narice's fingers slowly and deliberately undo the top three buttons of her shirt. "And what are you doing?"

"Playing."

He surveyed her hot eyes. "Playing what?"

"A new game I just invented called, *Seduction.*"

Saint's blood began to roar. "Are there any rules?"

"I don't think so."

"Can I play?"

Narice's nipples tightened deliciously. "Yes."

He slowly set down his silverware, then walked over to where she was sitting. The desire blazing in his gaze made Narice tremble a bit. When he leaned down and brushed his lips ever so softly over hers, her trembling increased.

He coaxed her to come and play with kisses that were featherlight yet potent enough to make her reach up and slip her hand behind his head to bring him closer. Their earlier coupling had been as frenetic as two teenagers in the back seat of a car, but Narice wanted to go slow this time so she could thoroughly explore every golden inch of him. The kiss deepened and their tongues mated provocatively, reigniting their inner fires and their need for each other.

Moments later, he slowly backed away then straightened, only to slide a possessive palm down over her breast. As he caressed her, teased her and made her lips part, he husked out. "I think we should call this game, *Make the Principal Hot*."

Narice thought he had hands of magic. The sensations caused by him expertly rolling her pleading nipples between his thumb and forefinger made her arch and preen with uninhibited delight. "I think she already is."

"Good." He dallied with her breasts and lips for a few more steamy moments. Only when she groaned out her pleasure did he seem satisfied. He silently slipped away and retook his seat.

Narice was breathless, weak, and rocked. Her vision was hazed over, and if he touched her intimately he'd find her already flowing. *Make the Principal Hot* was a good game.

Saint liked the way his game was progressing. Everything about her made him want to lay her down on the nearest flat surface and see how many times he could make her explode beneath him, on top of him, in front of him; he wanted to make love to her in so many different ways it would take two lifetimes to experience them all. He was falling for her and falling hard, a voice in the back of his head pointed out, but Saint didn't want to deal with that now. Right now, all he cared about was pleasuring her until sunrise.

So, they ate. It was a slow process because what they really wanted was each other. As a result they spent as much time making love with their eyes as they did sampling their meal.

Narice had never considered herself a very sexual woman, but being with Saint seemed to have opened a new channel within herself. All she could think about was being naked for him, having him run his hands slowly up and down her thighs, and having him fill her to the hilt. Her ex had been just as inexperienced as she the first few times they'd gone to bed, and Lars had been more focused on his own pleasure. Her best time in bed had been three years ago. A Canadian financial guru. The brother's talent as a financier was surpassed only by his talent in bed. After a torrid six-month affair, they'd gone their separate ways. Last she heard he was serving time in a Canadian jail for embezzling 14 million from a mutual fund.

But here in the present the *new* Narice boldy undid the last three buttons. The now gaping top made the sides of her breasts very visible.

Saint eyed the tempting brown beauties waiting for him to claim, and his manhood rose to the occasion. "Come here for a moment, Narice."

She set her napkin on the table and walked over.

When she reached him, he took her by the hand and guided her to sit on his lap. Without further ado, he kissed her slowly and fully, sending desire surging through her veins. In response she met him willingly, boldy, running her hands up and down his strong arms. He pulled her closer, teasing her tongue with his, then brushed his mouth over the soft skin covering her jaw. "Are you hot, Ms. Principal?"

Narice's eyes were closed. She wanted to answer but gave a croon instead as his hands filled themselves with the trembling weight of her breasts. Dinner was momentarily forgotten because the diners were hungrier for passion.

Saint didn't think he could get any harder, but the scent of her perfume, and the silken feel of her breasts increased his need a thousand times over. How was he going to let her go when this adventure came to an end? No brother in his right mind would relinquish skin this soft or a mouth this divine. She wanted no ties yet he wanted to tie her to him for life. Instead he had to take what she offered, which was her spirited mind and body.

It was thc body he was concentrating on now, and so leaned her back and took a sweet dark nipple into his mouth. She growled low in her throat and he turned his attention to the neglected twin, tonguing it, sucking it while his hand beneath her shirt explored her back and the planes of her waist. He tugged at the waistband of her pants and she lifted her hips to accommodate their removal. They fluttered to the floor leaving Narice on his lap wearing her opened green top and a black lace thong.

"God, you look hot . . ."

He began trailing kisses down her arched throat and over the soft tops of her breasts. The scents on her skin were driving him wild as was the heat of her hips atop his hardness. Capturing her mouth again, he kissed her as if he needed her essence to live while touring a slow hand over the yielding brown flesh of her thighs. He explored her languidly, learning the shape of her while his palm burned over her skin as he moved it up and down her limbs.

Narice took it all back; the Canadian brother was an amateur compared to this master. The hand now working slow magic between her thighs made her part her legs so he could do whatever he wished. Her wish had already come true. The knowledge that he was wickedly caressing her through the thong sent her senses racing.

"Is the principal hot . . . ?"

His steamy voice and the feel of the lace being circled so wantonly over her honey-filled core made speech impossible for Narice.

"Are you hot enough to come for me?"

He raised his finger to her breasts and circled a wet finger around the aureole. Leaning down, he bit the nipple gently before sliding two long fingers into her core. It was so good Narice buckled, twisted, and came with a hoarse scream that ruffled the silence.

Saint's manhood was so thick and full he felt like he was going to burst. Watching her come with such awesome abandon pushed him right to the edge, but he held on. He had more in store for the Lady Narice. Then it could be his turn.

It took Narice a few long seconds to come back. Lying over his arm, like a rag doll, she tried to find her brain. She'd never had such a powerful orgasm. Never. But then she'd never been with a man like Saint before.

Something cold awakened her nipple, making her instinctively draw away and open her eyes. The sight of the whipped cream he was dabbing on her made her chuckle and then groan with renewed excitement as he sucked and licked her clean.

"Dessert . . ." he murmured, and after setting the silver bowl of cream closer at hand, dipped in a finger and boldly and slowly coated the other bud. He flicked a hot tongue over it until it too was hard and clean. "Nubbins and cream. My favorite."

He sucked her in fully and Narice drew in a loud shaky breath. She could feel his sensual tugs on her nipples down to her toes. When he raised his head, she was spiraling. In the past it took her body a while to bounce back for more loving, but with him things were different. Her body was more than eager for another round.

Dipping his finger in the cream again, Saint drew a white fluffy line down the valley of her breasts, then slowly kissed her clean. He repeated the action across each soft top and then moved to the succulent under curves. He wanted to eat her up, but forced himself to wait. There was no guarantee they'd make love again, so he wanted this night to be memorable.

Next Narice knew he was carrying her back to the bedroom. He eased her down onto the gold and ivory spread, then reached down to play between her parted thighs. She held his sparkling eyes for as long she could, but when the heat from his ministrations took her higher and higher, maintaining contact became impossible. Her hips rose, her eyes closed, and her head fell back. She felt the bed give as he joined her on top of it, but his wicked, wicked hands never stopped.

He took her thong, and once she was bare, he spent a few long moments making certain she was still flowing. Narice arched sensually, purring for him, blooming for him. Her navel was adorned with a small dollop of the cream from the dish he'd brought along, but it soon disappeared beneath his sorcerer's tongue.

Saint dipped his finger back into the dish of sweetened cream. Certain images really turned him on: a scantily clad school principal dabbled with whipped cream stood at the top of list. "How do you like my whipped cream?"

"I think it and you are scandalous," she breathed.

"I'll take that as a compliment." He placed a bit on the other inner thigh and lingered over the taste of it against her brown skin. She was, as the old song said, *the sweetest thing this side of heaven.* Circling her damp heat with his fingers, he couldn't resist and so flicked his tongue against the lodestone that made her woman. Her gasping reaction made him want more so he opened her gently and feasted lustily.

Narice didn't think more pleasure was possible, but this blazing hot encounter proved her wrong. Spreading her legs wantonly, she let him nibble taste and delight her until her hips rose to offer him more. He took the offering gladly, increasing his ardor and making her mewl in response. "I'm going to come . . ." she pleaded, whispered.

"Anytime you want, angel."

Narice's senses were towering higher and higher. His fingers slid into her gates and impaled her deliciously, he then took her bursting bud fully into his mouth, and she came screaming like a crazy woman.

Only then did he step back and sheathe himself with a condom. While she was still pulsing and echoing, he eased himself inside and she groaned with the glory of it all. "Oh, that's good," she breathed.

Saint grinned and began his rhythm. "You're a hot little teacher. Do you know that?"

She growled in response because there were no words to describe the carnal rush in her blood. "Are all cheetahs this good?"

He stroked her with movements that teased and coaxed. "Why? You in the market for another one?"

"Oh no. You are more than enough."

Stroking her lustfully, he let her feel just how much he liked hearing her words. Saint didn't want anyone touching her ripe brown body but him. In his world, only his hands would tease the dark buds of her breasts until they sang; only he would kiss her lips until they were swollen and tender; only he would slide in and out of her like this until she begged him to return. Just the thought made him increase the pace.

Soon he was caught up in the whirlwind of desire and all thought was left behind. His rapid thrusts met her answering rhythms. Passion grabbed him, sending him higher and higher. Unable to hold back any longer Saint's orgasm exploded and he roared loud enough to be heard in the lobby. Narice came next and for the third time cried out her joy.

In the aftermath they lay tangled together, their breathing the only sound in the quiet room. Narice was sticky from the whipped cream, but didn't care. His loving had left her boneless, breathless, and oh-so satisfied. She could lie here with him like this until winter.

Saint looked into her eyes and kissed her mouth softly. "Did you enjoy yourself?"

Her answer was a contented smile. "Oh yes. How about you?"

He kissed her again and grinned, "I want to do it again."

She shook her head. "You are a mess."

"And you are the hottest thing this side of the Mississippi."

She slid over so that they were belly to belly and thigh to thigh, then lightly wrapped her arms around his neck. "You're not so bad yourself."

He eased her down into the yielding bed and kissed her deeply. "How fast can you take a shower?"

"Depends on whether you're with me or not."

Saint raised his head. "Could take a long time with me in there."

"Then let's synchronize our watches."

Filled with all the happiness and joy she made him feel with her sassy brown self, he gathered her in his arms and began rolling them around on the huge bed until she was screaming with laughter. "Let me go you, Mutant!"

"Never, little girl. Never," he countered in a mock evil voice. He continued to roll them around for a few more silly minutes, then stopped and looked down into her face. For a moment he studied the flare of her lips, the brilliant intelligence in her dark eyes, the silken cut of her jaw, and the hoops in her perfectly formed ears. It was official, Anthony St. Martin was in love, really in love, but with a woman who'd made it clear she didn't want or need a man in her life.

The sudden solemness on his face made Narice go still and she felt something pass between them that lodged itself inside. She could already feel the hole he'd leave in her life when the time came for them to part and she realized it wasn't something she wanted. How could she go back to being a proper headmistress after being on the lam with him? Raising her hand, she very gently cupped his bearded face then leaned up so she could reach his lips. Her kiss said all the things her words could not, and as it deepened, he lowered himself and gathered her close.

Saint had never kissed a woman with all of his heart

and soul before, but he seemed unable to do anything else. Having Narice in his arms and in his life felt natural, good. As he kissed her cheek, her ear, her eyes, he reminded himself that in few days he'd have to let her go.

Narice broke the kiss slowly, and in an effort to bury the feelings for him that had bubbled to the surface, she purposefully changed the subject, by asking with a purr, "Still want that shower?"

Saint slid a hand down over her ripe behind, liking the way the flesh yielded to his touch. "Want the shower, want you, want to finish eating, too. Sometime tonight."

"Then I'll race you!" And Narice took off for the shower.

Saint was stunned. "Hey!" he yelled laughing. "Cheating woman!" He rolled off the bed and took off after her.

The shower was equipped with six shower heads evenly spaced up and down the green marble wall. Narice had them all on and was basking in the powerful spray when he slipped in behind her. Honestly, Narice had never taken a shower with a man before, but when he began to slide the bar of scented soap over her wet skin and followed it with the loofah he retrieved from the basket of toiletries provided by the hotel, she knew it didn't matter; he knew what to do. He washed her with hands that were seductive and oh-so scandalous, hands that had her arching and shimmering by the time she was clean.

Narice turned to him and redid the favor. She slid the loofah over him slowly, purposefully, and by the time he was clean, they were both on fire again.

They stepped out and he wrapped her in a large purple bath sheet, then made her stand in front of him while he dried her off. Narice thought she'd died and gone to heaven. The feel of the fluffy towel slowly drying the parts of herself he'd made love to so fiercely had the principal hot all over again. He took full advantage too, and with his lips and hands turned up the heat.

She countered by taking him in her hand and savored the feel of him rising warm and hard. Her eyes blazing into his, she squeezed him meaningfully. He growled and pulled her into his arms. The kiss was hard, possessive, but her hand continued its wanton teasing.

"You keep that up and you'll be riding me schoolmarm."

"Is that a threat or a promise?" she husked back, her hand still moving.

He grinned through the fog of desire and steam. "I may have to ask for your hand in marriage after all."

"And I might have to say yes, but right now, I'm interested in that ride."

"Greedy woman."

"It's your own fault. I was an innocent schoolteacher until I met you."

"And now look at you."

"Yes. Look at me."

He eyed her curves and valleys, then bent down and pressed his lips to hers. "Shameful."

"Shameful," she echoed.

He picked her up and walked her back into the bedroom.

Later as they both lay across the bed too sated to move, Narice looked up at the shadows cast on the ceiling by the dimmed chandelier, and smiled.

Saint raised himself on one elbow and began to trace a meandering finger over her belly, "What's so funny?"

"Nothing. I was just wondering if this is how the James Bond women feel?"

Her silliness made him shake his head. "Oh really?"

She chuckled a moment, but as she ran her hand over his golden chest, she became more serious. "You have a lot of scars, Cyclops."

"Yeah, I do."

Narice saw remnants of wounds on his arms, his chest, and thighs. Some looked like large healed-over cuts, while others appeared to be what she imagined bullets would look like.

"Goes with the territory." He eased away and sat on the edge of the bed, his back to her.

Narice sensed she'd stepped into uneasy territory and wished she'd kept her mouth shut. Then the faded stripes across the skin of his back caught her attention. *Had he been whipped?* She wanted to ask about them, but didn't. Instead she confessed, "Didn't mean to send you away."

He looked back over his shoulder and said into her eyes, "I'd never go far."

The sincerity in his voice made her heart pound. At that moment, Narice knew she'd never forget this conversation no matter how long she lived. She knew because she was in love with him. Recognizing that fact made her happy, but it also scared her to death. "I'm going to take a quick shower."

Saint watched her go and in spite of the slight tension between them, smiled at the way her bare behind moved provocatively as she walked. Truthfully, he wanted her to come back so he could make love to her again. Amazed by that fact, he put his head in his hands; he couldn't remember ever wanting one woman so much and so often. He already knew that Narice Jordan was one of a kind, but he hadn't expected her to weave herself into the fabric of his soul so completely. He thought about her silent exit. Had he hurt her feelings? Legally, the stories behind most of his old wounds were classified and he couldn't tell her about them even if he wanted to, but that was just a cop-out. The truth was he was so accustomed to being a loner and an outcast, he found it difficult to share the details of the darker parts of his life with someone else.

He got up and went out to the table and cut himself a piece of the chicken. What he really wanted to talk about was the dilemma he found himself in. Delivering the Eye to The Majesty was what he'd been hired to do, and until that was accomplished everything else was supposed to be secondary. Him being distracted by Narice could get them both killed. However, asking himself not to focus on her was like asking his heart not to beat, so he was really in uncharted territory.

In the end, Saint knew that the best way to deal with this unexpected complication was to let things flow and to go with the bit. He and the curvy Ms. Jordan had no future; all they had was the here and now, so he planned to enjoy it. When it was over he'd have content himself with the memories. With that settled, he washed down the chicken with a small slug of champagne, then headed off to the shower connected to the suite's second bedroom.

Drying off behind the closed doors of the luxurious bath Narice contemplated her relationship with Saint. She told herself that first of all, she didn't need a man in her life; life as she knew it was pretty okay. Truthfully, she did get lonely for companionship sometimes, but hey, that's why God made girlfriends. Saint on the other hand was a woman's fantasy, he was dangerous, intelligent, and made love like nobody's business, but he'd said cheetahs make lousy pets and she didn't doubt him for a minute. Although she had developed feelings for him, they had no future as a couple, so there was no sense in her contemplating anything else. They were having a great time. Real life would return soon enough.

Fifteen

After slipping on the hotel's robe, Narice padded back into the suite's living area and found Saint seated on the fancy celadon-colored loveseat, studying the screen on his handheld computer. When their eyes met, his smile made her heart pound. Coming closer, she asked, "What's up?"

"Just checking out the Okefenokee." Saint wanted to take her back into the bedroom and pleasure her all over again. The curvy Ms. Jordan was good for the soul but bad for business. "Says here, the swamp covers about a half-million acres." He was glad the tension between them seemed to be a thing of the past.

"People don't actually live there, do they?"

"Not in the protected areas. It's a wildlife reserve."

"Is Grey Swans on the map?"

"No."

Narice was disappointed. "Wonderful. How are we going to find Aunt Camille?"

"Good question, but we'll come up with something."

Narice didn't doubt that for a minute; after being with him these past few days, she knew he was a man who could literally pull a rabbit out of a hat.

Saint could smell the fresh scents of her body and it was playing havoc with his decision to concentrate on the job first and her second. "I need to make a call. You read up on the Okefenokee." He tossed her the computer.

Narice caught it deftly. "Aye, aye, mon capitaine."

He grinned and walked over to his coat lying across one of the upholstered chairs. While Narice read why the waters in the Okefenokee had a reddish color, and folklore tales about swamp yetis and UFO abductions, he began a search through his pockets. Watching him out of the corner of her eye, she wondered what kind of magic lamp he was after now. It turned out to be a small plastic square that he plugged into the back of the phone. "Another prototype?" she asked.

"Nah, just something to keep the line secure. If anybody's trying to listen in, all they hear is a dial tone."

"I see."

"Have to check in with Portia."

"I can go back into the bedroom if you want some privacy."

"Thanks, but not necessary."

Soon he was talking with Portia, and Narice went

back to scrolling through the info on the swamp. Located in southern Georgia and northern Florida, the land was originally inhabited by Native American tribes. The Cherokee named the area *Okefenokee,* which roughly translates to *The Land of the Trembling Earth.* Interestingly enough, the Seminoles, one of Narice's favorite historical groups, also inhabited the swamps before being forced west, and the great Seminole chief Osceola lived in the Okefenokee as a child. She linked into a few more websites and read on.

As she did, she kept one ear on Saint's talk with Portia. He gave her their location, spent a few more moments discussing their run-ins with Ridley and the helicopters then, after asking after Jesse and James, he clicked off.

"Portia says hello."

"Next time you talk to her, tell her I say hello back. How are the dogs?"

"Jesse is still moping, but otherwise they're fine. I told her I'd check in every two hours, and if four hours pass with no word, she should come looking."

They'd left the farm less than twenty-four hours ago yet to Narice it seemed like days. "Are we hitting the road, or spending the night here?"

"No, I want to get on the road, but let's take a look at that quilt one more time."

She went into the bedroom and pulled the quilt and the book from her suitcase. Returning to the other room, she spread it out on the coffee table and silently studied the patterns and symbols. The Monkey Wrench and the Flying Geese were now as familiar as the Bear Tracks and the Wagon Wheel. The only symbol that hadn't come into play was the box within a box, the Log Cabin, and she still wasn't sure if it stood for her father's birthplace or not. She really hoped they hadn't come all this way for nothing.

She looked up to find Saint studying her instead of the quilt. "I thought you wanted to look at the quilt?"

"I did, and my mind is supposed to be on the job, but having you around makes that hard."

"Good," she said with soft triumph. "Every woman wants to be memorable."

"Well, you're that and more, believe me. But."

"But."

"Me being distracted by your curvy little body could get us killed."

"Which means?"

The coolness of her tone made him search her eyes. "It means, I need to keep my stuff in my pants until we find the Eye."

She smiled. "You do have a way with words."

He grinned.

"Coming from any other brother, I'd say you were just making excuses to quit it now that you've hit it."

He raised an eyebrow.

"But I don't think that's what you're about. At least not with me."

Pleased by her accurate assessment, Saint inclined his head.

"What you said makes sense, though, so I suppose I should keep my stuff in *my* pants, too." Then she added, eyes shining temptingly, "If I can."

Saint felt his manhood rise. "All right, now. What did I just say?"

She sidled close enough to smell the soap on his skin. "Something about keeping this . . ." and she slid her hand provocatively over the front of his jeans, "in your pants."

Saint's eyes drifted closed.

Narice purred, "I'm just trying to make a point. With all that superhero discipline, you probably don't even notice my hand." She squeezed the hard promise of him gently, "Am I right?"

He captured her wrist and guided her hand over him with more purpose, "Yeah, you're right."

Narice's arousal flared between hot and scalding. "If I slipped off this robe, you probably wouldn't even notice."

Fitting actions to words, she undid the belt at her waist, then let the robe crumple noiselessly to the floor. She was naked as a jaybird underneath.

At the sight of all that chocolate loveliness, Saint drew in a shuddering breath. Mission be damned, all he could think about was the taste of her nipples and bringing her to orgasm. With that in mind he pulled her close, kissed her possessively, then eased her down onto the expensive cushions of the loveseat. Soon they were playing one last round of *Make the Principal Hot*.

An hour and a half later they were ready to leave the suite. He had on his coat and shades. She had on a white sleeveless blouse and a snug-fitting pair of capris. With her purse over her shoulder and her suitcase in hand, she waited for him to finish one last walk through the suite to make sure they hadn't left anything behind.

A knock sounded on the door. "Room service," a male voice called out. "I've come for the dishes."

Narice started to the door, but Saint walked out, saying, "I'll get it."

Ever cautious, he looked through the peephole first. To his surprise he saw The Majesty's prime minister, Farouk, standing on the other side of the door. He was wearing a hotel-staff uniform and pushing a cart filled with dirty dishes and table linens. The cart's bottom shelf and legs were hidden by the thick white cloth draped over it. Saint wondered what he was doing here, and more importantly how he knew he and Narice were in the hotel. He'd given his location to Portia, but that was only a little while ago. Farouk was looking up and down the hall nervously, as if afraid of something or someone. Had The Majesty sent him here with a message? Had something happened that he needed to know about?

Farouk solved the mystery by saying, "Please, Mr. St. Martin, I bring an urgent message from The Majesty."

Saint hesitated before undoing the locks; something about this didn't smell right. "Hold on a minute," he called, then told Narice, "Go back in the bedroom and take this." He tossed her a gun. She caught it as if it were a dead rat.

"Don't come out unless I call, and if anybody comes in that room beside me, shoot them. Period. Okay?"

She nodded reluctantly, then hurried back into the bedroom.

Only after he was sure she was safe did Saint draw his gun and open the door.

Farouk entered pushing the covered cart. When he saw the gun he smiled. "That isn't necessary, Mr. St. Martin. I'm a friend."

"Then you won't mind me hanging on to it. How'd you find us?"

"The Majesty has her ways." Farouk then looked around the suite. "Where's Ms. Jordan?"

"Out shopping."

"At a time like this?"

Saint shrugged. "Who understands women?"

Farouk smiled. "I certainly don't, but I have a message for her from my queen."

"Give it to me and I'll make sure she gets it when she gets back." Saint didn't believe him for a minute.

The man appeared frustrated then.

Saint asked, "What's the matter? This not playing out like you thought it would?"

Farouk's eyes hardened. "No. I didn't expect you to have your gun drawn."

"Oh, you just expected to waltz in here and do whatever it was you came to do?"

"Yes."

"You must be new at this."

Saint raised the gun higher. "If you have a weapon, I want you to place it on the table beside you, real slow now, this gun will splatter you all over that wall."

Moving slowly and precisely, Farouk raised the top of one of the dishes and revealed the Luger hiding beneath.

Saint said, "Just leave it there. Back away."

Farouk did so, then Saint called out, "Narice. Need your help out here, angel."

Saint was so busy concentrating on Farouk he saw the movement of the cloth draping the cart a split second too late. Fulani was hiding beneath it, and the dart from the blowgun in her mouth was already on its way. The tiny arrow pierced his hand. He growled and tried to get off a shot but the world was already spinning.

Narice came out of the back pulling her suitcase just as Saint hit the floor. With wide eyes she saw Fulani and the now armed Farouk standing over him. They both looked over at her pleased.

Farouk said, "Drop the gun, Ms. Jordan."

She didn't protest. Saint was the only thing on her mind.

Fulani came over, picked it up.

Farouk said, "Now, have a seat."

Narice hurried to Saint's side instead. She placed her hand on his chest. Mercifully, his heart was beating. "What happened to him?"

Fulani showed her the small blowgun. "He'll be asleep for an hour or so, no longer."

"But long enough for us to do what we came to do, which was to fetch you."

"I'm not going anywhere."

He raised the gun. "Oh, but you are."

Narice was worried about Saint. She hoped Fulani had been telling the truth about the drug. "I thought you loved your queen."

Fulani scoffed. "No servant ever loves her master, no matter how privileged the service may be. Besides our country doesn't need an old woman running the government. When the rebels come home with the Eye, we will decide Nagal's future."

Narice shook her head. She didn't care about the politics, just Saint's welfare and her own.

Farouk took out a phone and dialed. When he got his connection he said, "We have them."

Narice wondered who he was talking to. A few minutes later a knock sounded on the door. While Farouk held the gun on her and the sleeping Saint, Fulani moved quickly to answer the summons. In walked Gus Green, his partner Jacobs, and Ridley. All three had bruises and welts on their faces. The silent Narice was pleased to see she'd done some damage, but the big gun in Ridley's hand brought her back to earth.

Ridley said to Farouk and Fulani, "Good work. Let's get them out of here."

Narice was dragged to her feet by Ridley. "Jacobs,

Green, bring Mr. St. Martin along. Farouk get out of that uniform."

He stripped it away and revealed the casual shirt and khaki pants beneath.

"Ms. Jordan, I assume you still have the keys to that SUV of yours."

She did.

"I want them please. That vehicle will be far more comfortable than all of us piled together in Green's car."

Narice didn't move.

Ridley saw the defiance in her face and said brittlely, "The keys, Ms. Jordan, or Mr. St. Martin's dead body will be found in an alley in the morning. You may not be expendable, but he certainly is."

An angry Narice glanced over at Saint hanging between Green and Jacobs like a passed-out drunk and steeled her feelings of concern. She had to stay strong if she wanted to help him, so she dug into her purse for the keys and tossed them to Ridley. He caught them and winced. Narice wondered if he had a busted rib, too. She hoped so.

Farouk grabbed up her suitcase and Saint's gun, then they led her to the door. She shot the smiling Fulani a sinister glare, then walked with them down to the elevator.

The ride down was a silent one. Narice kept glancing Saint's way to make sure he was still breathing. He hung between Gus and Jacobs with his toes dragging the ground.

Ridley said to Narice, "When we get off this elevator, I wouldn't try and enlist anyone's help if I were you. Remember what I said about that alley where St. Martin will be found."

Narice remembered, so when the doors opened, she kept her mouth shut.

Because it was two in the morning, the fancy lobby only had a skeleton crew of clerks behind the desk, and a couple of bell man outside the big gold framed, glass doors.

A brother in a red-and-gold uniform stepped up and opened the door for Narice's party. He shot a questioning look at the unconscious Saint, and Green offered an explanation, "Never could hold his liquor."

The brother smiled knowingly. "Got a brother-in-law the same way. You folks have a good night."

When the men replied in kind, Narice's jaw tightened angrily but she didn't say a word.

Under the lights of the parking lot, Ridley used the remote to spring the locks on Lily's doors. Narice saw him smile triumphantly in response, then look inside. He eyed the jumble of items cluttering the second row of seats and said to Green and his partner, "Clear this mess."

The two eased Saint to the pavement, then spent the next few minutes tossing tools, coolers, blankets, and the rest into the back. With the job done, they stepped away. Ridley motioned impatiently for Narice to enter. Before climbing in, she shot a quick look back at Saint lying so still. Green and Jacobs hustled Saint to the vehicle and propped him up on the seat next to her. He immediately listed over, so she eased his weight down and gently cradled his head on her lap. She carefully removed his glasses and placed them in her purse. Stroking his brow with a slow hand, she prayed he'd come to soon.

Ridley climbed in next and sat beside Narice. Farouk took the wheel and Fulani rode shotgun. Green and Jacobs got into a nearby black sedan and started the engine. Their car swung in behind the Caddy.

As the SUV rolled out of the parking lot, Narice's concern for Saint equaled her concern for herself. Without a doubt, once Ridley and his crew got the Eye her value dropped to zero. She'd always been a take-charge kind of girl and being around Saint for the past few days only added to that attitude, so as she looked down at her unconscious Cyclops she vowed she'd get them out of this mess as soon as the Lord made a way.

Ridley had been observing Narice stroking Saint's face and said, "He'll be all right, you know. A few years ago, I gave him fifty strokes with a cat-o'-nine tails, and he survived. A simple sleeping drug won't kill him."

"Why'd you lash him?"

"He stuck his nose in something where it didn't belong."

Narice remembered the story about Ridley and his sex parties, but when had Saint been beaten? "So you beat him."

"Like a runaway slave."

His smugness made Narice's mouth curl with disgust. She turned away and looked out of the window at the darkness and the city's lights.

From the front seat, Farouk asked her, "Where in this swamp are we going, Ms. Jordan, and how do we get there?"

Narice tossed back grudgingly. "Your guess is as good as mine. The town isn't on the maps."

Ridley asked, "What's the name?"

"Grey Swans."

He replied with a knowing tone, "Ah, that's right. I remember now."

Narice turned to him with a puzzled look. "You remember what?"

"Your father talking about Grey Swans when I met him in North Africa."

Narice remembered him mentioning knowing her father that night in the cab. "Why were you there?"

"I was a journalist covering the war for Canada. I flew in to do a story on America's Negro troops, and he and I struck it up. We became friends or as much friends as men of different races could be back then. I'd heard rumors that he'd taken the Eye, but it never occurred to me that he would hide it and refuse to reveal the location."

It was obvious to Narice that her father didn't consider Ridley as much of a friend as Ridley believed. Narice didn't pull her punch. "Did you kill him?"

"No, his stubbornness did."

That answer just pissed her off. "Did you set the fire?"

He didn't respond.

"Did you?"

"Let's just say I gave him every chance to live a long life but he chose otherwise."

Narice could feel ugly emotions rising up in her body; emotions that wanted to strike out and hurt Ridley in ways that would leave him maimed and barely alive, but she couldn't act upon them. She wanted him convicted then incarcerated; going off on him wouldn't make either of those things happen. Besides, he had the guns. For now, she'd just have to live with her hate.

In the front seat, Fulani was leaning forward and checking out the buttons and dials on the dash. "Ms. Jordan, what do all of these knobs do?"

Narice gave her a disinterested, "This and that."

Ridley snapped. "Leave them alone. Who knows what kind of booby traps this car has."

Fulani stared him down. "The only reason you are here, Mr. Ridley, is because of your ties to the generals. You are not in charge."

She then pushed the button that brought up the GPS. When the glowing green screen appeared she giggled like an excited child.

Ridley snarled, "Didn't you hear me?"

When Fulani continued to ignore him, he said to Farouk harshly, "Do something with her."

Farouk was not impressed by Ridley's blustering. "She is just curious. I doubt she can hurt anything."

Fulani managed to get the two-way radio to work, but because she didn't know the password, she couldn't access anyone.

Narice said, "Fulani. Open that little silver panel."

Ridley snapped, "Shut up."

But Fulani was already in motion. She opened the panel then asked Narice, "What does it do?"

"Push that button to the left."

In response a red screen with a circular map complete with black grids and cursors appeared. In the center a small white light began to pulse like a heartbeat. Next came the sound of Lily's computer-generated female voice over the interior speakers. "Target locked. Five seconds to impact."

Ridley's eyes widened as did the eyes of Fulani and Farouk. Before they could react further, the metal beneath the seats began to vibrate. There was the high-pitched sound of jets (?) and then the sound of an explosion behind them. Through the window, Narice saw the fireball that had once been Gus, Jacobs, and their black sedan. Narice didn't like being the cause of anybody's death but these people had already killed her father and were probably going to kill her once they found the Eye. She was just evening up the odds.

The occupants stared at her in shocked silence, then Ridley backhanded her so hard, she reeled and saw stars. Suddenly Saint was up and his knife was at Ridley's throat. Farouk and Fulani's eyes went wide as plates. The car was silent again, but this time for another reason. His voice was deadly: "Farouk and Fulani, I can kill him before you can blink, stop the car."

Farouk pulled over to the side of the road.

"Hand Narice your weapons, and do it real slow. My head's on fire, and I'm not seeing real clear."

They did as they were told.

Narice's face was throbbing. She turned the guns on them and was so angry she planned on squeezing the trigger on the first one who moved.

Saint pushed the tip of the blade far enough into the soft skin beneath Ridley's jaw, tiny drops of blood slid down the gleaming metal. "Narice, say the word and I'll slit his throat."

Furious over the slap, she snapped, "Just get him away from me."

Saint told him, "She's saved your rotten life twice now. You won't get a third one. Remember that."

Ridley didn't move. Saint stuck his free hand into Ridley's coat and relieved him of his weapon. "Reach back and open the door." Saint wanted to carve him up and toss out the pieces.

Ridley did as he was told.

"Back out."

He stepped out and Saint went with him, never removing the thirsty point of the knife. The quietness of the night surrounded them. A few cars blew by but Saint didn't pay them any mind. "I'm going to kill you the next time we meet, so be ready."

Ridley's blue eyes glittered dangerously.

"If you don't believe me show up again and they'll be measuring you for a casket. Now start walking."

Nagal's prime minister glared but headed off. Saint waited until Ridley was a ways down the dark highway before going around to the driver door of the SUV and snatching it open. Farouk drew back fearfully.

"Out! Both of you."

Farouk began to protest, "We know nothing about this part of your country. Suppose we offer to cut you in—"

The speech was cut short by the sharp jab of Saint's knife in his ribs.

Farouk promised, "You'll pay for this."

"Yeah maybe, but The Majesty is going to have your balls in cream sauce when she finds out you're working for the other side. Now get going. Narice and I want to be alone."

Narice's eyes flashed in her stinging face.

Less than a second later, Farouk and Fulani were out and Narice and Saint were driving away. "I'm damn sick of them," Saint groused.

Behind the wheel, Narice noted how good it felt to have him back. "So am I. How's your head?"

"Terrible. But after a couple Advil, I'll be good to go—in a few hours. How's your face?"

"Terrible, but after some ice, I'll be good to go, too."

She glanced his way. He looked like Grumpy of the Seven Dwarfs. "Welcome back."

"Thanks. Pull over for a minute and let me look at your face."

She coasted to a stop and he reached up and turned on the light. The redness beneath her skin was evident. He climbed into the back and got her some ice. He handed her the small plastic bag. She placed it against her face.

Saint said, "I'm sorry."

Narice shook her head. "You didn't hit me. He did."

"I'm sorry I couldn't prevent it."

She understood.

"The next time he shows up I'm going to kill him."

"I know."

He reached out and gently removed the ice pack. He looked at her cheek again and hoped the ice would help stall the swelling. "I'll drive."

She put the pack back and said softly, "I'll drive. You can drive later."

He leaned over and kissed her, whispering, "I'm sorry."

"Let's get out of here."

He didn't argue.

Sixteen

Saint reached into his pocket for the small bottle of over-the-counter pain meds he always carried. After removing one of the tabs and swallowing it dry, he sat back and waited for relief to kick in. To take his mind off the wait, he thought back on this latest cockroach encounter. Under normal circumstances, he would have turned out the lights on Ridley and been done with him once and for all, but these weren't normal circumstances; Narice was with him and not wanting to show her his assassin side was making this job a whole lot harder than it needed to be. Saint was sure Ridley wasn't conflicted about any of this. Given the opportunity, Ridley wouldn't hesitate to do whatever it took to come out on top, but Saint had let him off the hook again and he wasn't happy with this sudden emergence of a conscience. He knew where it was rooted, though. He glanced over at Narice behind the wheel. She was the reason. The beautiful Ms. Jordan with her schoolmarm vocabulary and sex-kitten ways had cast a spell over him that he couldn't shake. Even with his head still hurting like hell the pain was dull compared to the intensity of his feelings for her. He turned his attention to the darkness outside his window. Now he understood why folks in his line of work weren't supposed to fall in love; it made them soft.

Saint brought up the GPS in order to determine where they might start the search. Waycross Georgia was one of the main gateways to the Okefenokee, and he guessed that's where Ridley and the rest would probably begin their search, so he opted to travel farther south and go in via Fargo, which was near the Georgia–Florida border. Waycross was a good 250 miles south of Atlanta. Bypassing it for Fargo would make the drive longer, but he wanted to make it hard for the cockroaches to find them.

Narice looked over at the green screen and asked, "And if Aunt Camille lives up there by Waycross?"

Saint shrugged. "We'll just have to take our chances."

Narice had her misgivings, but he was the expert and he had gotten her this far, so she deferred to him and drove on.

She and Saint didn't talk much. She drove and he sat silent in his seat. Because of the shadows she couldn't tell if he was sleeping or not. She worked about the aftereffects of whatever Fulani shot him with. Are you awake?"

"If I wasn't, I am now."

"My, aren't we Oscar the Grouch?"

Saint couldn't help but smile. "Anybody ever tell you women are supposed to be docile?"

"A few times. Mostly when I was being promoted over some man back on Wall Street."

Saint shook his head. "Pull over a minute, would you?"

Narice looked into her rearview mirror to check for traffic, then pulled over to the side of the road. She left the motor running. "What?"

He sat up. "Lean over here so I can give that mouth of yours something better to do."

Narice's desire flared. She leaned over and he fit actions to words. The kiss deepened and they both caught slow fire. Tongues mated, lips were nibbled, and his hand explored the curves of her breasts. Soon Lily's interior was filled with the soft sounds of their heightened breathing.

Saint whispered, "We should get going."

She knew he was right. "Yeah, we should."

After a few kisses more, Narice headed them back to the road. Like him, she wanted to further explore the passion neither seemed able to get enough of, but they needed to get to the Eye as soon as possible.

They were thirty miles from Waycross when the sun began to peek through the horizon, dazzling the eye with colors of reds, oranges and pinks. The beautiful sky reminded Narice how much she'd always enjoyed the beginning of the day. She said to Saint, "My daddy used to call this time of day the edge of dawn. He said every new sunrise gives you another chance to do right."

Thinking about her father brought her back to the mission ahead. "After this last cockroach visit, I really want us to find the Eye so I can go home."

Saint's headache was still pounding, though not as much. "Tired of my company?"

"Nope, just tired of the company you keep."

He smiled. "Me too."

"How do you think they found us back at the hotel?"

He shrugged. "Satellite, maybe. Who knows?"

Truthfully, Narice didn't really care. What she did care about was getting this adventure over. She turned his way and asked, "How long were you really knocked out?"

"I think the rumble of the missiles brought me around."

"You should have seen the look on their faces when that car blew up." Her face was still smarting from Ridley's backhand.

"Who was in the car?"

"Gus and the man with him at the store."

"So much for them."

"Yeah. No one should be blown up like that, but the less cockroaches we have to deal with, the better."

She looked out of her window and sighed. "I can't

wait to go back to my slow, sedate little life in Maryland. All these guns and mayhem is not good for a sister."

He grinned. "Only a schoolmarm like you would use the word *mayhem.*"

In mock offense she planted her fist on her waist. "You weren't dissin' my vocabulary back in Atlanta."

"That's because you were panting *'Daddy give me more. Give me more.'* "

She burst out laughing and tried to smack him in the arm. "You liar! I did not."

He laughed loud, "Oh Narice, I may never let you go back to your dull little life. Who's going to be my side-kick when you're gone?"

Narice felt a sharp sadness grip her heart at the thought of maybe never seeing him again. "I'm sure you'll find somebody."

"Not like you."

They shared a strong unspoken look for a silent few seconds, then she went back to driving. He said, as he turned his eyes to the view out of his window, "Tell you what, when I get lonesome, I'll just come get you. Okay?"

"I'm not touching that with a ten-foot pole. Knowing you, you'll show up in the middle of the night talking about let's fly to Tahiti."

"And you'd say?"

She studied him for a long moment. "Probably, yes."

He grinned and said, "Once a Bond girl, always a Bond girl."

Narice said to herself, *No, once in love, always in love.*

By the time they began seeing road signs for the Okefenokee, Saint's head was still a bit cloudy but the pain had subsided a lot. The ache in his hand was also almost gone. "If Grey Swans isn't on the map, we need to find a local who knows where it is."

"How about we look for a gas station or something."

"Sounds good. Just so we don't drive Lily through the front door."

She laughed. "Probably be the most action this little burg has had in a while."

"Yeah, and our court trials would be second on that list."

They passed a hospital where out front an old brother was slowly sweeping the parking lot. Since the man looked like a likely candidate, Saint did a sharp U- turn that made Narice grab for her armrest. Heading Lily back, he stopped and she lowered her window and called out, "Good morning, sir."

He looked up. "Morning. Can I help you?"

He was of average height and looked to be in his late sixties, early seventies. He had an age-lined black face and wore a short gray 'fro.

"Do you know where Grey Swans is?"

"Sure do." Then he went back to sweeping.

Narice's outdone face made Saint chuckle, "Hey, you asked him a question. He answered it."

Narice rolled her eyes and got out of the truck. "Sir, can you tell me how to get there?"

He stopped sweeping again and studied Narice for a moment before saying, "You can't. It's part of the wildlife refuge now. Restricted area."

"But my aunt still lives there as far as I know."

"What's her name?"

"Camille. Camille Jordan."

That seemed to surprise him. "Really?"

"Yes, sir. Do you know her?"

"Yeah, I know her. Everybody over sixty-five and Black knows Camille Jordan—know she's crazy."

"Crazy?"

"As a bedbug. Last time the reverend went out to check on her, she ran him off with her rifle. She don't like visitors. At tall."

"Well, I need to get in touch with her and let her know my father, her brother, Simon, died last week."

"Then he's the last. James Ohio died a few years back. My condolences."

"Thank you. Who's James Ohio?"

"Your daddy's third brother."

"Daddy had brothers?"

"Three. Curtis California, Spencer Kentucky, and James Ohio. You look surprised."

Narice didn't lie. "I am. I didn't know he had any kin besides Camille."

"Well, them Jordans always was a secretive bunch. After their parents died back in the forties, the boys all went their separate ways. Family split apart like the seat of an old pair of pants. Camille stayed, though."

"How do you know all this?"

"Well, if you're Simon's girl, I'm an ex in-law. Curtis California was married to my sister, Jerdine. Name's Mitchell Bewick."

Narice smiled and stuck out her hand. "Pleased to meet you, Mr. Bewick. I'm Narice Jordan."

He shook her hand. "Pleased to meet you, too." He then asked, "You having Simon buried here?"

"No, he died in a fire."

"I see."

There was an awkward silence, then Narice sought to change the subject. "Were your sister and Curtis California married a long time?"

"Nah. Lasted maybe all of six months, but he always sent her money back from where he was staying in Chicago."

Narice didn't know about any of this, and admittedly could spend the next three days quizzing him, but she had to find Aunt Camille. "Can you take me to her? Me and my friend in the car over there?"

Mitchell looked over at the battered and dinged-up Caddy. "That's one of those new Cadillacs isn't it?"

"Yes, it is. Can you help us?"

He studied her. "She ain't going to want to see you."

"She might."

"And pigs might fly."

"Mr. Bewick."

"You're wasting your time."

"It's real important."

"You can't get to her place by car. Boat's the only way."

"That's okay. My friend and I will buy a boat if we have to."

"Simon leave Camille a lot of money?"

Narice didn't respond.

"None of my business, huh? Well, that's okay. I'll take you but it'll cost you a hundred dollars."

"What?! I thought you said we were family?"

"Ex-family."

Narice shot him a warning look.

He shrugged. "Either you want me to take you or find somebody else. Makes me no never mind."

Narice wondered what ever happened to Southern hospitality. "Let me talk to my friend."

She went back to the Caddy and filled Saint in. Afterwards, he fished around in his coat and handed her a crumpled fifty-dollar bill. "Tell him, half now and the rest after we get to your aunt's place."

"He ought to be arrested for extortion."

"True, but we don't really have the time to be choosy. Sooner we get to the swamp the better."

Narice knew he was right, but she wasn't pleased.

Mr. Bewick took the money and agreed to the payment terms. "I get off work in an hour. We can go then."

"We were hoping to go as soon as we could."

"Well, the soonest I can go is when I get off work."

"Okay. Thanks."

"Never could resist a pretty woman."

She rolled her eyes. "We'll be back. Shall we meet you here?"

"Yep. Now, let me get back to my sweeping. Don't want to lose my job."

Narice nodded and hurried back to the Caddy.

Narice and Saint used the free time to head to a fast-food place. They picked up some bags of breakfast, then drove to a city park, turned off Lily's motor, and ate in the early morning quiet. Narice took a sip from the plastic cup holding her orange juice. "Do you think Mr. Bewick's really going to be there when we get back?"

"Maybe, but if he isn't, we'll find somebody else."

Through the window, she watched a man jog by with a beautiful Irish Setter. The temp outside was already eighty-two and it wasn't even eight A.M. yet. It was going to be a scorcher of a day.

Once he was done eating, Saint got out to assess the damage to the Caddy. It was the first time he'd had the time to really check her out. The once mirror-finish paint was scarred by scratches, dings, and dents, and there were a few burn spots the size of dinner plates on her roof. The bumper was blackened from the heat of the deployed missiles. The wire grate over the left taillamp was gone, probably lost when Narice rammed the glass at the convenience store, but the headlights were intact, and the tires felt sound.

Narice said from behind him, "Miss Lily has taken quite a beating."

He turned to watch her walk towards him and loved each and every sway of her hips in the snug black capris. "Yeah, she has, but I think she's okay."

"How about you?" she asked softy, stepping closer.

Saint looked down into the concerned dark eyes of the woman whose presence in his life had altered the way he'd always looked at his life. "Head still hurts, but it's no big deal. How about you?"

"I'm okay. The ice seemed to work." Her cheek was puffy but not as much as she feared.

She reached up and ran her hand down his bearded cheek. "Should we be finding you a doctor?"

He backed up. "Naw. I'll be fine. I've had worse heads."

He could see she wasn't convinced, but to her credit she didn't force the issue.

Narice looked out over the green of the park and asked him instead, "What are you going to do once this is all over?"

He shrugged. "Maybe take some time off—hang out with Portia and the dogs, then head off to the next job."

Narice thought back on the dead bodies that had been left in their wake. "Are all of your jobs this dangerous?"

"Truthfully, this one hasn't been that bad. I'm not sleeping on the ground, eating bad food, or keeping an eye out for stuff that might eat me, like big cats or Great Whites." He walked over to her and stood close enough behind her to smell the faint notes of her perfume. He then reached out and turned her chin so he could drown in her eyes. "My sidekick ain't half bad either."

Her answering grin soon faded beneath the sweetness of the soul-stirring kiss he placed on her lips. He brushed his mouth over hers, hating the idea that these might be some of the last kisses they'd ever share. That distressing thought made him pull her closer so he could show her just how much she'd come to mean to him and how much he was going to ache for her when she was gone.

He held her against his chest and Narice could hear the sure, steady beat of his heart. Before now it had never occurred to her that being held this way could make her feel so good. Leaving him was going to be one of the hardest things she'd ever had to do in life, but leave him she would; she had no choice.

He whispered, "I meant what I said about being there for you if you ever need help."

She nodded. "I know you did. I don't envision any cockroach encounters in the future, however."

He kissed the top of her hair. "Hey, you never know."

She leaned back a bit so she could look into his shaded eyes. "Lord, I hope not."

Saint forced away thoughts of where Ridley and the others might show up next, because all he wanted to concentrate on at the moment was Narice.

He picked up her hand and led her over to a nearby park bench. They sat. He said, "I need to talk to you about something."

Narice noted how serious he seemed. "Go ahead," she said softly.

"Sometimes in my line of work, folks get terminated."

"I know."

He studied her eyes. "This might get real ugly before it's all over, and I want you to be prepared."

She replied honestly, "Do whatever you need to do to keep us alive. If it comes down to them or us, I want us to be the ones walking away."

He stroked her slightly red cheek, then leaned over and kissed her softly. "Thanks."

"Don't worry about me. I'll be fine."

And deep down inside, Saint knew she would be.

To their delight Mr. Bewick was waiting for them on a bench in front of the hospital. When Narice pulled up, he got up and walked over. Narice hit the button for the window and it rolled down silently.

He said, "Now, if the rangers catch us, you and your friend pay the fine."

"We will."

So, he got in. "We have to go by my place first. I need my boat."

Saint turned his shaded eyes on the old man. "We have a four-man inflatable on board. Anything else we need?"

Mr. Bewick squirmed visibly under Saint's pointed stare. "No."

As if Saint were deaf, Bewick whispered to Narice, "Is he from the government?"

She held back her smile. "Sometimes."

Mr. Bewick looked wary. "Boat and some food maybe is all we need."

Saint said, "Then we're straight. Which way?"

Bewick gave him directions and they were once again underway.

Thirty minutes later, they were in the middle of nowhere as far as Narice could tell. They'd taken a series of dirt roads around the park's outer perimeter that seemed to take them farther and farther away from civilization. They saw no other cars or people, just miles and miles of undeveloped land harboring grass, tall pine trees, and the occasional abandoned and decaying house. They were now parked near a tranquil body of water that snaked off into the distance.

Mr. Bewick said, "This here's the spot."

Narice cut the engine and they all got out. Saint looked around at the towering trees and grass filling the surroundings like a landscape painting. "Where are we?"

"Near the Suwannee River."

Saint took out his handheld. After punching in a few codes the GPS screen came on. He fed it some coordinates and a map of the area appeared. That done, he reached in his coat and pulled out a small phone.

Mr. Bewick said, "Pretty fancy phone you got there fella."

"It's a Sat phone."

Mr. Bewick looked confused.

Saint said, "Satellite phone."

Mr. Bewick appeared impressed. Narice knew she was. She'd heard of satellite phones, but had never seen one or knew anyone who had one. Of course, he would have one. Narice listened as he said, "Portia we're going in at . . ."

The series of numbers he reeled off made no sense to Narice, so she assumed they were part of a code.

He closed by saying, "I'll check in in a couple hours."

He clicked off, then said to Narice. "Portia's not there, so I left a message. She's probably on her way to us since I didn't contact her after we left the hotel. That's good, though, because we may need her."

Narice noticed that Mr. Bewick seemed to be watching Saint's every move. Her ex in-law looked very wary of her sunglasses-wearing companion.

Saint sensed the old man's curious eyes but was more concerned with unloading the supplies they'd need on the journey to find Camille Jordan. With that in mind, he opened the back hatch and went to work.

Narice watched him shift some of the boxes and duffels tossed in the back by Green and Jacobs, then unearth what appeared to be a large deflated beach ball the color of camouflage clothing. He tossed it on the ground, then rummaged around some more until he found a small box holding a black pump similar to the one Narice had at home for the inflatable guest bed she'd purchased a few months back from one of the television shopping channels.

A curious Narice and an even more curious Mr. Bewick watched silently.

Mr. Bewick asked in another whisper, "He some kind of army man?"

Narice gave him her standard, "Sometimes."

Mr. Bewick shook his head in what looked to be wonder.

With the pump now attached, the rubberized material slowly took shape. A few minutes later it was ready to rock and roll.

Narice said, "Not bad, Cyclops."

"Anything to impress the lady."

They shared a grin, then while he went back to rummaging around she asked Mr. Bewick, "How far away does my aunt live?"

"Couple hours or so—if you know where you're going. If not, could take all day."

Narice didn't like the sound of that. "But you know where we're going, right?"

"Sure do."

The next item to be unloaded was the rocket launcher. Saint set the long tube on the ground next to the boat.

Narice was glad to see it was going with them. Mr. Bewick asked warily, "What's that?"

Saint opened up another small box packed with small brown rockets. "Shoulder-mount rocket launcher," he answered truthfully.

Eyes wide, Bewick looked to Narice then back to

Saint, then down at the rocket launcher. He then reached into the pocket of his faded black pants and dug out the fifty-dollar bill Saint had given him earlier as down payment. He forced the bill into Narice's hand. "Here. I don't want no parts of whatever this is. You all are on your own."

To her surprise he stalked back to the road and set off on foot. "Mr. Bewick?"

He didn't break stride.

"Saint, do something."

Saint paused in his unpacking to watch the old man progress, then called to him. "At least tell us how to get there."

Bewick stopped and looked back. "Once you see the old turpentine plantation, she lives ten miles east."

And that was it. He walked on.

Narice said, "What kind of directions were those supposed to be? He's going to have a stroke walking in all this heat."

And it was hot. It was Georgia in late July hot, and it was only going to get worse. Narice called out, "At least let us take you back to the main road."

Saint gave her a sharp look.

Narice ignored it.

Bewick yelled back, "No thanks. Got a cousin lives up the way. He'll see me home."

A few steps later he rounded a bend in the dusty road and disappeared from sight.

Saint said, "Guess that's that."

"Why did you look at me like that when I offered him a ride?"

"Because we don't have time to play good Samaritan to an old man who just screwed us."

She supposed he was right.

"Here," he said, "take these shovels. We need to get moving."

Narice put Bewick out of her mind and helped Saint load the boat.

Seventeen

Traveling the channel turned out to be slow, hard work. Narice had always thought of herself as being in good physical shape but after the first hour of paddling her arms were ready to drop off. The surroundings were eerily beautiful though. With Saint paddling from the front and Narice from the back, they steered the camouflaged boat past towering forests of moss-draped cypress growing on thick moving islands of peat, and across open water-logged plains that were in reality marshes. They were crossing once such marsh now, and no matter how hard they paddled they didn't seem to be making much progress.

"Water's getting too shallow," Saint determined grimly. "We're going to have to get out and push."

Narice could think of a hundred things she'd rather

do, but Saint had already gone into the water so she followed suit. She was glad she'd had the good sense to change into jeans and hikers before they left the parked and locked Lily behind. The heavy clothing made her hot as hell, but the protection it offered outweighed the discomfort. She'd brought along her capris just in case she needed a change of clothing. Saint had shed his coat too, and it lay at the ready on the boat's recessed rubber deck

The water she stepped into was barely ankle high. He went to one side of the boat and she the other and together they tried to push the stuck boat ahead. It was weighed down with all the supplies and tools. Attempting to move it over rocks, tree roots, and dead vegetation wasn't easy.

Saint waded to the front of the inflatable and told her, "You push, I'll pull."

Narice leaned on the inflated rubber and braced her legs to push, only to loose her footing on the wet moss covered rocks and go down. The shallowness of the water kept it from being too ugly but she got up wet and covered with muck just the same.

Saint thought she looked like Swamp Thing, but knew if he said that she'd kill him on the spot. "You okay?"

"No," she said, wiping at her face and clothing. The front of her yellow T-shirt and jeans was covered with mud and gunk, and there was wet black plant material in her hair. "And if you laugh, I will kill you."

"Who me?"

Narice could only imagine how she must look. The water was the color of dark tea due to the tannic acid released by all the decaying vegetation, and now, thanks to her fall, so was everything she had on. "Let's go."

So, he pulled and she, making sure her footing was sound, pushed. Ten minutes later the water levels were once again high enough to support the boat. An exhausted Narice climbed in and fell out on the deck with her arms outstretched. "Can we go home now?" she asked wearily, mockingly.

Saint leaned down and placed a kiss on her very dirty forehead. "Hang in there." Were it up to him they'd call this off because it was obvious she was beat, but circumstances were beyond their combined control. The only choice was to go on.

Back in the boat, they continued to paddle. It was just past noon and temperatures were in the blistering high eighties. Narice could smell herself beginning to stink as her clothing began to dry. The oppressive humid heat made sweat pour down their backs and faces with each push of the oars, but they pressed on.

They still hadn't seen another soul, but there were many wading birds, like egrets and herons, feeding amongst multicolored lily pads. At the approach of the humans and their fat rubber boat, the birds took flight. The vast silent openness of the swamp could easily make a person believe herself the only person in the world.

Narice told him, "According to one of the websites, there are alligators out here somewhere, and maybe even a Bigfoot or two."

Saint laughed softly. "Bigfoot?"

"Yep. There's been a few sightings over the years. The Cherokee have legends of giant men being in this area."

"Really?"

"The site also mentioned UFO sightings, and a park ranger supposedly abducted by aliens."

"Yeah, right."

"Now wait, listen. When the ranger first went missing the park service did a massive search. Nothing. A few days after the search was called off, he was found wandering and disoriented in the swamp days. The aliens turned him loose, I guess. This place has a lot of spooky legends tied to it."

Saint wasn't worried about running into Bigfoot or aliens, but he did keep a sharp eye out for alligators.

It was three in the afternoon before they saw the old turpentine plantation. Had it not been for the battered sign dangling from the front of one of the ramshackle buildings that read PETERSON'S TURPENTINE, they might have floated on past thinking it just another of the many abandoned farms they'd seen.

Narice looked around. Many of the buildings were underwater. She thought it odd to base a business in the middle of the swamp, then remembered reading that weather, time, and people had changed the flow and levels of the waters here, thus placing some areas below water that previously hadn't been, and vice versa. She hoped her daddy's homestead hadn't been affected this way, otherwise they were going to need diving equipment to find the Eye's hiding place.

Saint checked out their surroundings, too. So far he hadn't seen anything remotely related to an occupied living space. "Did Bewick say east?"

Narice nodded.

Saint checked the compass he'd brought along, then pointed. "East is that way."

Heading east took them off the main waterway and into a series of vegetation-choked channels. Once again there was no evidence of human life, but the warning calls of birds seemed to be everywhere. There were large ferns and moss trailing from trees. Beautiful lily pads floated like ballerinas on the brownish red water. A fish jumped out of the water after an insect and scared Narice half to death. Once she realized what it was she regrouped.

To Narice, it seemed like the journey through the plant-choked water was taking forever. She was sure she couldn't paddle an inch more when Saint said, "You think that's it?"

A house or what was left of it stood on a large open piece of land near the shoreline. It and the tumble-down barn close by were in terrible disrepair. The wood on the house had faded so much the building was a weathered silver. There was no glass in the two windows that she could see, and the doorway had no door. Rusted farm equipment lay piled on one side of the listing barn. Narice was convinced they'd come to the wrong place because surely no one lived there, but changed her mind when she saw the garden. It was to the right of the house and fenced off with tall green wire. Unlike the house the fencing looked new.

Saint turned to look her way and asked, "Well?"

Narice had no idea. As they maneuvered the boat toward the shoreline, she was able to see that there were clothes, woman's clothes, hanging on a line strung between the house and a large cypress. Apparently someone did live in the place, but would it turn out to be Aunt Camille was the question. Narice hoped so, because she was too tired to go anywhere else today.

Saint hopped out of the boat and tied the mooring line to the fat trunk of a tree. Narice splashed over to the shore, then stood there for a moment to look at the house. She slapped at a deerfly trying to make her arm lunch when a short old woman came from around back. Just as Mr. Bewick predicted, she was toting a shotgun. "Hold it right there," she demanded.

Neither Narice nor Saint moved.

"If you lost, there's a ranger station about six miles east. Head out now and you can make it back before gator time."

Narice noted how much Aunt Camille's eyes favored Simon's. "When's gator time?"

"Dark."

"Oh. Well, I'm—"

"Don't care who you are, missy. Get off my land." Aunt Camille was dressed in an old once-white, now gray, Run-DMC Adidas sweat suit. Her salt-and-pepper hair was thin and pulled back, and on her feet were beat up combat boots with no laces. One would expect a woman her age to be wearing glasses as well, but she wasn't. Her eyes looked sharp and bright over the raised gun. "Giving you ten seconds to get back in that boat."

Saint tried a more direct approach, "Are you Camille Jordan, sister of Simon Jordan?"

She eyed him for a moment before confessing in a hard voice. "I am."

"Then this is your niece, Narice, Simon's daughter."

She didn't blink. "Means nothing to me."

"Daddy's dead, Aunt Camille. I thought you might want to know."

"You came all this way just to tell me that?"

"Yes and to ask you some questions about something he might have hidden away after he came back from the War."

"Don't know nothing about it, so go on back to your boat."

"Please, we only need a few moments of your time."

Aunt Camille's lips tightened. "You've already used it."

That said, she lowered the gun, turned and walked back to the house. She disappeared inside.

Saint cracked, "At least we know it's her."

"Short of truth serum, that's probably all we'll know."

He chuckled and walked with her up to the house.

Up close the house was in even worse condition. The roof had a hole large enough for a UFO to land in and the sitting porch that had at one time encircled the front looked to have collapsed a long time ago. It pained Narice knowing her aunt was living in such poverty, especially since Narice had the means to make life easier and more secure. Getting Camille to accept such an offer, however, was going to be harder than crossing the Sahara in a swimsuit, so Narice set that issue aside for the time being. Right now there were other fish to fry. Narice knocked on the door-jamb.

"Go away," Camille called out from somewhere in the dark interior.

Peering into the gloom Narice could see a dirt floor and a few pieces of furniture. "We need to talk to you."

"You gave me the news. Now git!"

Narice sighed with frustration. "I need your help so the police can get the man who killed my father. The fire was arson."

"I don't care. The po-lice can't bring Simon back. Neither can you."

"But if you would just let me—"

"GO AWAY!!!"

Jaws tight, Narice looked to Saint. He shrugged.

Narice had had it, so she hollered, "I'm not leaving. If I have to sit out here until Christmas, this is where I'll be."

That said, Narice sat down on the porch to wait; it

was all she had. Saint found himself a spot under one of the immense moss-draped cypress trees and settled in with his back against the trunk. The way he figured, neither Jordan women had ever run into anyone as stubborn as themselves, so this was a new experience for both. He made himself comfortable; this was going to take a while.

He was right. Aunt Camille spent the next hour going about her business: she took down her wash, tended her garden for a bit, then took a trip out into the swamp to collect the grasses she used in the baskets she took to the Fargo market once a month. Through it all, she ignored the stubborn-faced woman seated on her porch.

Saint grew hungry as time passed. Since he and Narice had had a long, hard day and it didn't look to be getting any easier anytime soon, he decided to go fishing. He couldn't make Narice's aunt speak but he could keep Narice from starving. He stood, then walked over to where his sidekick was sitting. "How you doing, babe?"

"I'm hot, I stink, and I'm about to be real pissed at that old woman."

"Well, hold off on that last part. She might come around. How about I get us something to eat?"

Narice wanted to kiss him for being so thoughtful. "That would be wonderful, but from where?"

"Place called, Mother McNature's."

She smiled; he was her ever-resourceful Cyclops.

He gave her a soft kiss. "Be back soon as I can."

Narice smiled and watched him go.

Down at the shoreline, Saint took a moment to pull the boat out of the water and to push it up the bank as far as he could. Next, he opened the big waterproof bag holding his odds and ends and extracted his fishing trident. He'd learned to fish with a spear in Madagascar many years ago from some local brothers he met while working on a mission there. Upon his return to the states he'd had a stainless-steel trident custom made. For him, the three laser-sharp prongs were far more efficient than the single point of a spear. Having used it worldwide, Saint knew that no matter the circumstances, as long as he had the trident and a body of water holding fish, he could eat.

From her seat on the porch Narice could hear her aunt moving around inside the house. Until meeting Mr. Bewick, the thought that Camille Jordan might not be interested in a family reunion had never crossed Narice's mind; she'd been so sure she'd be greeted with open arms, but now here she sat waiting for her father's sister to part her lips and give up the information only Camille had. Without the location of the old homestead, the Eye would remain hidden forever; The Majesty's kingdom would fall into the hands of the thug generals; and Ridley would get whatever reward he was after instead of being locked up for murder. Realizing Ridley might get off scot-free only solidified Narice's determination to sit there until hell froze over if she had to; the memories of her father and her mother demanded she do no less.

"How long you planning on squatting on my porch?"

The cross-sounding voice of her aunt made Narice turn around. "Until you let me tell you why I've come."

Camille had been beautiful at one time in her life, and looking at her now, Narice realized Camille was the striking woman standing next to Simon in the picture that Narice had seen in Toledo at Uncle Willie's.

"But I don't want you here. How many times I got to say that?"

"As soon as you and I talk, my friend and I will leave. I promise." Narice prayed the woman would relent; if just for five minutes.

She folded her arms. "Usually folks scat when I tell them to."

"I'm sure they do, but my daddy died in an arson fire and I need your help putting the man who did it in jail, so, if I have to sit here until it snows, I will."

"You got his stubbornness, you know."

Narice smiled. "Thanks."

Camille drew up as if offended. "That wasn't a compliment."

"I'll take it as one because Simon Jordan was a good man who didn't deserve to be burnt to death in his own bed."

The old woman shook visibly under the force of Narice's words. "You don't pull your punches, do you?"

"If this happened to your daddy, would you?"

Camille studied Narice as if seeing her in a different light. "I remember your mother. Died young."

"Yes, she did."

Then she said to Narice's surprise. "Simon raised you well."

"Thank you."

"Now, go on back to where you come from," Camille told her, then went back inside the house. Narice was so outdone, and then angry, she wanted to punch something.

Saint returned with what old folks called, a mess of fish. Not bothering to ask Aunt Camille's permission, he used one of the shovels from the boat to dig a small pit in her hard-packed front yard, started a fire, then cooked the fish on a spit he made out of sticks and twigs. The aroma was heavenly.

"Smells good," Narice told him.

Saint looked up from tending the meal. The tiredness on her dirty face tugged at his heart. "Be ready in a bit." He then asked, "Any headway?"

"No. She did tell me where the outhouse was though."

"That's progress."

"I suppose."

Saint poked at the fire. "It'll be dark in a few hours. There's a two-man tent in with the supplies on the boat. I'll pitch it, and after you eat we'll get you washed up, and you can crawl inside and crash."

Narice stretched her weary bones. "Best plan I've heard all day, but I wouldn't put it past her to duck out on us after gator time."

"I'll keep an eye on the Wicked Witch of the Okefenokee, don't worry."

Their eyes held and all the wonderful and special feelings Narice had for him welled up inside and made her go still. Where would she be if he hadn't stolen her away from Ridley that first night? Since then he'd protected her, fed her, made love to her. It was entirely possible that Narice might have been able to find Aunt Camille on her own, but it wouldn't have been as much fun. "Thank you, Galen Anthony St. Martin."

"For what?"

"For having my back throughout this whole craziness."

He answered softly, "You're welcome. Thanks for saving my bacon, too. Like I said, helluva sidekick."

Mutual affection shone in their eyes, even if he did have on his shades.

The fish was hot. Narice had to juggle the smoking pieces of delicate white meat in her fingers to cool them off before she could put them in her mouth. Then came the taste. It was so good, she groaned, "Oh, baby you can cook for me anytime."

Saint chuckled. Only he knew that hearing her call him baby had his heart grinning like the village idiot. He'd take the sound and its affect to his grave. "Glad I could help a sista out."

Narice had been so hungry but, now, she was in swamp heaven. "Oh, this is good."

Saint was glad he'd brought back a full catch because the fish were small and the curvy, and obviously starving Ms. Jordan had already eaten three.

When Camille came out and stood on the porch, Narice and Saint went still. The woman looked over at them and they back at her.

Narice said, "You're welcome to join us."

Silence.

Then Camille asked, "If I show you where the Eye is will you leave me in peace?"

Narice felt like she'd been hit in the chest with a Louisville Slugger. She stared in amazement at Saint, then stammered to her aunt, "Uh-uh, yes. Yes, ma'am. We'll leave."

"Good. I'll see you in the morning. Sleep in the barn. Storm's coming tonight."

She went back into the house, leaving Saint and Narice to stare at the now-empty space where she'd stood.

In the silence that followed, a still-awed Narice cracked, "I guess we won't be needing that truth serum after all."

"Guess not." Saint was stunned. "Man."

"She blew me away, too." Narice rubbed her arms. "I've got goose bumps."

They eventually went back to eating but neither had much to say.

After they finished the fish, Saint was kicking down

the fire with the toe and soles of his boots and Narice was wondering how and where she could bathe when Camille stepped out onto the porch dragging a big wooden barrel. Both Narice and Saint stopped to stare.

The old woman called out. "There's a pump behind the barn. Wash that stink off you."

Saint cracked. "I think she means you, Ms. Jordan."

Narice laughed and punched his arm in one motion. "Shut up."

Camille went back inside. Saint went to retrieve the barrel.

The water was cold but Narice didn't care. The fat bar of soap she found lying in the tub smelled like spearmint and lathered up real well. Narice had never seen or smelled spearmint-scented soap before and wondered where Camille had purchased it. In the end, the soap's provenance didn't matter; she was clean.

Because her small stash of clothes were in her suitcase inside Lily, Narice was forced to put her capris back on, and the extra black T-shirt Saint had brought along. Unfortunately her open-toed sandals would be useless in the days ahead, so she stuck her bare feet back into her still-damp hikers.

With Saint's help, she dumped out her bath water and he pumped more water for his turn in the barrel. While he washed Narice used the pump's water and the spearmint soap to try and wash the stink out of her jeans and halter blouse. When she was done she laid the garments over a nearby bush and hoped they'd be dry come morning.

Now, they were ready to explore the barn. On the heels of Camille's storm warning, Saint thought the barn might be a wiser choice than the tent he'd proposed they sleep in earlier, but once inside the dark and gloomy building they could see the evening sky through the massive hole in the roof. Evidently the place hadn't been used in quite sometime because all manner of small animals scurried for cover when the humans ventured farther in. Narice had put up with a lot of scary stuff since this little adventure began, but she was drawing the line at sleeping with rodentia. Spider webs thick as 400-count sheets were everywhere. They were so large Narice had no desire to see their arachnid owners. "I think outside may be better."

Saint saw a river rat as big as his foot slide out of the barn between a large gap in the wallboards. "I think you may be right."

Saint pitched the tent and after securing the ground stakes as well as he could, he spread the sleeping bag that had been bundled with the tent on the ground and bowed to Narice. "Your suite is ready, madam."

She grinned. "Thank you kind, sir." She gave him a kiss on the cheek, then crawled in. He took up a seat nearby to keep an eye on Camille, then pulled out his handheld; he needed to find Portia.

The storm blew in later that night with the force of something brewed up by Hollywood; the wind screamed, the trees bowed, the rain poured, and the lightning and thunder went at it. Inside the tent, Narice was jolted awake by Saint's hasty entrance.

"Damn it's bad out there."

She scooted over to give him room while he fought to close the zipper on the wind-whipped flap. Once that was done, he slid in behind her and pulled her close. The sounds of the storm were loud and Narice was certain the canvas would be torn from them but the stakes held and so did the little tent. He pulled a tarp over them, and although she could feel the dampness of his clothes and body, having him near made her content, so she drifted back to sleep.

Eighteen

One minute Narice was dreaming of making love to Saint on a black sand moonlit beach and the next a sound loud as a hotel fire alarm bolted her awake. Saint shot up, gun in hand. They saw Aunt Camille's face staring back at them from the opening in the tent flat; she had a hammer and an iron skillet in her hand. "You two coming with me, or not?"

A stern-faced Saint drew his gun down and let out the breath he'd been holding. "Lady, you almost got your head blown off."

She responded by rolling her eyes and leaving.

Saint, seeing the angry look on Narice's face said in ghettoese, "That's *yo* auntie."

She laughed then punched him in the arm.

Narice's auntie was waiting for them when they exited the tent. She told them, "If you got business to do before we leave, hurry up. Ain't got all day."

They headed towards the outhouse. Narice stopped to check on the jeans and blouse she'd set out yesterday; they were soaking wet from the storm. She sighed with disappointment.

When they returned to Camille, she said, "You won't need the boat. Bring some shovels. You got digging to do."

Saint asked, "How far away are we going?" Her answer would impact how much stuff he'd be able to bring along.

"Mile or two."

Saint and Narice went to the boat to get what was needed. Twin backpacks holding survival items like water, first-aid kits, and dried food had been packed back at the Caddy so they each grabbed one and strapped them on. Narice picked up a shovel and a hoe. Saint grabbed up a shovel and the rocket launcher.

When they hooked back up with Aunt Camille, she took a long look at the launcher Saint was carrying on his shoulder. "That necessary?"

He nodded. "Yes, ma'am."

She eyed it for another second or two. "Then don't miss."

Saint hid his smile. "I won't."

Camille led the way. Holding a tall, whittled walkingstick, she set a pretty good pace for a woman of her years. She didn't talk, so they didn't either.

Narice felt good after her sleep last night and her muscles were no longer tired. Even though the pack was heavy she didn't notice it because she was too busy being wowed by her surroundings; the trees, the birds, the sounds, all added up to a breathtaking experience. There were signs of the storm, however. The ground was muddy, there were trees down, and limbs littered the narrow trail. There were also a lot of mosquitoes. Them Narice could have done without.

The trek ended a while later in a clearing of sorts. The vegetation was waist-high but in the center stood the remnants of an old stone fireplace and chimney. The stones had been bleached white by time and weather. Narice wondered if it was the old Jordan homestead. Across the field she could see crude markers and wooden crosses stuck in amongst the weeds. *A cemetery?*

Camille said to them, "See that chimney? The Eye's buried about three feet down."

Saint wasn't looking forward to all that digging. "Three feet."

"Or four. When my brother brought that thing back from overseas, I told him it was going to bring trouble. Now he's dead." She asked Narice, "Did he tell you it was here?"

"No. He left me a quilt, and Saint and I sort of figured it out."

Camille nodded knowingly. "My quilt."

Narice cocked her head. "Your quilt? You made the quilt?"

"Yes, in case we got too old to remember."

Narice was speechless.

Camille cackled, "Oh, you assumed your daddy made the quilt."

"I did."

"Just like you assume I'm a crazy old woman living this way 'cause I can't do no better."

Narice didn't lie. "Yes."

Her bright eyes hardened. "Park Service wanted me to leave this land twenty years ago. Said I had no right to it. When I showed them my great gran's deed signed by General Sherman himself, they backed off for a little while, then sent some goons around to scare me out. Cowards waited until I was gone reed hunting and tore up the place. Punched holes in the roof, ran off all my livestock, set fire to the barn. I stayed. Told them they'd get the land only after I died and that I'd shoot anybody that came around wanting to prove me wrong. They left me alone after that."

Narice understood now. "I see why you don't like company."

"Thought you might," she tossed back emotionlessly.

"Why do you stay?"

"I was born here, and I'll die here. Most folks are scared of the swamp, but if you respect it, it'll respect you. Seen a lot of strange things living in here."

"Like what?"

"Ghosts of the slaves that died in these waters. Sometimes at night you can hear the chains rattling and children crying on the wind."

"Slave ghosts," Narice echoed skeptically.

Camille nodded. "Back when importing slaves became illegal, the slave owners would sneak their African captives into the south by way of these blackwater channels. Sometimes the boats made it, sometimes they didn't."

"And these ghosts are the slaves who died in the swamp?" Narice believed there was a spiritual world and that what Aunt Camille described was possible, but the analytical side of herself was real skeptical.

"Seen ships from outer space carrying men that wasn't men. Got one set that visits me quite regular."

Now that was a bit too out there for Narice to swallow. She wondered if her aunt was suffering from a mild form of dementia. *Men from outer space?*

Aunt Camille read her mind. "You're still assuming, aren't you?"

Narice jumped like a child caught wrist-deep in the cookie jar.

Camille smiled. "That's okay. Believe what you want. After today, I'll never see you again, anyway." She then turned to Saint. "Start digging beneath the chimney."

That said, she turned and set out walking back the way they'd come.

Narice, feeling properly chastised, said, "Now in the movies, cranky old women like her turn out to have hearts of gold."

Saint wasn't buying it. "I don't think your auntie's ever been to the movies."

An amused Narice shook her head and slipped off her pack.

They dug for the better part of the morning. Beneath the rain-softened topsoil the ground was hard as rock, and made for slow, back-breaking going. For what felt like the hundredth time, Narice used her foot to push the blade of the shovel into the unyielding earth. The force necessary for the movement set off a burn in her knee and the ball of her foot that because of all the digging was constant. "I'm sending Ridley my bill for the knee replacement I'm going to need."

"Me too," Saint said, tossing out dirt beside her. They'd dug about two and a half feet down. Now they were digging through clay.

Narice set the shovel again. "This stuff hasn't been soft since the dinosaurs walked."

"You got that right."

An hour later they hit pay dirt. A small bundle wrapped in a piece of tarp was unearthed by Narice's shovel. Her eyes shining, she looked at Saint.

He said, "You do the honors."

An overwhelmed Narice dug it free then pulled it out of the hole. While he looked on, she very carefully unfolded the frayed tarp and revealed the small tin box hidden inside. Borrowing his knife, she cut away the rope holding it closed and opened the top. Inside, wrapped in another piece of tarp was the Eye of Sheba. Even after being buried for over six decades it glistened like a star in the night. "Do you think the story about King Solomon getting this from the Queen of Sheba is true?"

Saint had no idea.

"It's certainly beautiful."

They marveled over it for a few moments longer, then Narice put it back in the tin box and tied it closed again. Saint picked up his coat and stuck the box in an inner pocket, then he and Narice began throwing all the displaced dirt back into the hole.

They were almost done when Narice looked up to see Aunt Camille enter the clearing. She was waving her rifle and walking fast. "Now what?"

Saint saw her too, and cracked, "Maybe she's bringing us lunch."

Narice studied the old woman's agitated face. "Something's wrong, Saint."

They dropped their shovels and hurried to intercept her.

She was winded but said clearly, "Those folks you brought that rocket shooter for are here. Eight, nine of them coming up the bank like slavers."

Saint quickly scanned the land behind her. "Did they see you?"

"Probably. I shot two of them. When they scattered I took off."

Saint was impressed. "All right, Miss Camille, you and Narice take cover over in those trees."

Saint waited until the women were safely hunkered

down behind the wide trunk of a tree to his right, then took up his own position behind the chimney. The clearing gave him a panoramic view of the surroundings. While keeping a sharp eye out for cockroaches he fed the launcher some shells, then settled down to wait.

It wasn't a long one. Three men; thin, brown-skinned and wearing bad suits and pointed toe shoes crept into the clearing. Aunt Camille said eight or nine. Minus the two she shot, that left three maybe four unaccounted for. Saint didn't wait, he hit the trigger to see how many more he could flush out. The first volley of shells blew up the clearing like a bomb going off in a war zone. He heard screams and cries but closed his ears and fired again; this time to the left of his initial strike. Once again, he heard cries, then came the sound of returning automatic gunfire. The bullets were strafing the area around him so fiercely Saint had to lie flat to keep his head from being sheared off. Ammo exploded around him like hellish rain keeping him pinned down and unable to fire back. He felt like an extra in the movie *Scarface.*

The nineteenth-century chimney was no match for the twenty-first-century firepower now blasting it to pieces. Another automatic weapon joined the fray and began adding its bullets to Saint's dilemma. He got nicked a few times, which made him mad, and by habit he ignored the familiar burn. Instead he concentrated on crawling as fast as he could to a safer spot. It was time to get out of Dodge.

The bullets peppered the ground on both sides of him, but he made it to one of the trees on the outskirts of the clearing and hoisted the launcher on his shoulder. His returning volley caused mayhem and chaos. He blasted, then blasted again. On the heels of his last blast, a voice aided by a megaphone filled the clearing. "This is the Georgia Highway Patrol, I want everybody, and I do mean everybody to drop their weapons and show themselves."

Saint thought he heard a chopper off in the distance but with all the other noise he wasn't sure if he'd heard it or not. He was sure he'd been nicked by a few bullets, though, and looked down at the blood on his arm and cursed. He scanned nearby for his coat and saw it lying on the ground near the chimney; so much for immediate first-aid.

Narice heard the voice on the megaphone too, but worried that it might just be another Ridley trick she stayed put. During the shooting, she did her best to keep out of harm's way, but Aunt Camille had fired back like Rambo. Narice hoped she'd have half her aunt's courage when she reached her eighties. In the meantime, though, she could see Saint in his spot amongst the trees and that he was holding his arm. She was trying to come up with a way to get over to him and see how badly he'd been hit when she felt something hard placed against the back of her head. She went still instantly. Aunt Camille whirled. Too late. It was Ridley.

"If you move old woman I'll kill her."

In the silence that followed, he said, "Stand please, Ms. Jordan."

Narice stood on shaking legs and took a deep breath to calm herself.

Like Aunt Camille, Saint saw what was playing out too late. By the time he realized what was happening, Narice was standing and Ridley had his gun on her. The megaphone hadn't been a trick; the area was now teeming with uniformed officers and government types in suits and ties. They were lining up the cockroaches for questioning. When they saw Ridley holding Narice hostage they all drew their guns.

Saint called out, "Let her go, Ridley."

"I'll let her go in exchange for the Eye."

"It's still underground," Saint told him. "There's no way you're going to make it out of here alive anyway, so let her go."

Saint could see the officers watching him and Ridley. The desperation in Ridley's eyes was easy to see and Saint knew that a cornered criminal was a dangerous one. One of the Georgia state troopers had maneuvered himself to Saint's side, and asked quietly, "Who is he?"

"Arthur Ridley. Prime Minister of a little country called Nagal."

"Prime Minister?"

"Yeah."

"And you?"

"Name's St. Martin. Special Envoy to the President."

"The President? Of the United States?"

"Yeah."

Saint turned his attention back to Ridley who was now forcing Narice to walk in front of him like a shield. Ridley announced in a loud voice, "Ms. Jordan and I are going to leave now."

Saint had no intention of letting him leave with his sidekick. There were at least fifteen officers and agents circling the clearing and all had their guns drawn on Ridley. "Let her go, Ridley. No way you can get out of here alive."

"Back off, St. Martin, or I'll kill her just like I killed Simon."

Saint shook his head. He wondered if it was a life of privilege or arrogant stupidity that made Ridley announce his role in a murder within earshot of so many lawmen and women.

The trooper next to Saint called out authoritatively, "Sir, drop your weapon and let the lady go."

Ridley's reply was to shoot at the officer, but before anyone could react, the man next to Saint asked in surprise, "What the hell is that?!"

Saint looked where the man was pointing and saw Jesse and James hurtling across the open grass. He yelled to the policemen, "Hold your fire!"

The dogs launched themselves at Ridley. Jesse hit him high while James hit him low. The impact of the

Rottweilers' powerful bodies knocked both Narice and Ridley to the ground. Narice managed to roll clear but Ridley was screaming as the snarling dogs tore into him. Before anyone could move, the sound of helicopter rotors filled everyone's ears and they all looked to the sky. A black chopper with purple piping came in for a landing, sending up dust and whipping the trees. Saint gave the dogs a verbal command. The canines immediately backed off and took seats near the badly bleeding Ridley who now lay moaning on the ground. Saint ran to Narice. She hugged him and Narice stared up at the helicopter. Expecting it to start firing, she prepared to run for safety, but the sight of the woman at the copter's controls made her relax. It was Portia. A relieved Narice smiled. It was over.

Saint's eyes glowed at the sight of the cavalry, and he gave the dogs an affectionate pat on their heads. Confident that the police would take care of Ridley, he went to meet the chopper. First, though, he pulled Narice close and gave her a big fat kiss. She laughed and wrapped her arms around his neck in joy. He kissed her hair and held her as tight as his injured arm would allow.

Portia dressed in a sharp black leather jacket, matching pants, and dark glasses stepped out of the copter. The dogs looked questioningly up at Saint, and he told him, "Go meet her."

They took off like kids running to welcome mama.

Portia knelt down to greet them then turned her attention back to chopper. While Narice and Saint looked on, Portia stuck her hand up as if helping someone out. The someone turned out to be The Majesty. With her purple and black robes flying in the wind of the rotors, she crossed the clearing to where Saint and Narice stood.

The state trooper who'd attached himself to Saint asked, "Who's she?"

Saint still holding Narice against his side, said, "A queen."

The trooper's eyes widened. Saint went to get his coat.

When he returned he handed the box to her. "Your Majesty, the Eye."

She untied the rope, then opened the box slowly and reverently. When she held up the big blue diamond, it caught the light and the attention of everyone looking on.

The Majesty had tears in her eyes. "Thank you, St. Martin. Thank you."

One of the FBI agents walked up and said, "I'll take that."

The Majesty looked at him as if he were an insect. He turned beet red. Ignoring him, she then said, "Ms. Jordan, my country and I are forever in your debt. If you ever need anything, just call. Oh, and you both will be pleased to know that Farouk and Fulani are already on their way back home to stand trial for treason and conspiracy to kill their queen. Portia told me about your run-in with them."

She placed the diamond back in the box.

The agent tried again. "Madam, as a representative of the U.S. government I must insist—"

"And I insist you talk with Mr. St. Martin about whatever you need to know. Portia, I am ready to go whenever you are."

The Majesty inclined her head royally, then swept up her robes and strode regally back to the waiting chopper.

Portia said, "She's something else."

Saint said, "That she is."

The police were carrying the mauled Ridley away on a stretcher.

Portia said, "We should have let the dogs finish him."

"I know but I've a feeling he won't escape jail this time. All this mayhem has to add up to some kind of charges."

"He also confessed to killing my father," Narice said. "That alone should put him away for a long time."

Saint put an arm around Narice and they walked Portia back to the chopper. The dogs trailed behind them silently. "Thanks for your help. Portia. I knew you and the dogs were coming, but I didn't know you were that close."

"I set them down at that house on the other side of the clearing. I figured you'd want them on the ground as opposed to in the air with me."

"You figured right."

Narice said, "Thanks, Portia."

"You're welcome. Oh, and according to The Majesty

you have a tiny plastique bug in one of your earrings."

Narice's fingers went to her gold hoops. "Is that how they kept finding us?"

"Yep. Fulani and Farouk gave up that info during their interrogation by The Majesty's security people."

Saint said, "But I scanned everything Narice had."

"A new kind of plastic. If you can find it bring it home. We'll take a look at it and see why it didn't set off your detector."

"Okay."

The FBI agent had had enough. "You all are under arrest for destruction of federal property, illegal possession of military weaponry, jewel trafficking, and anything else I can think of."

By now his buddies had joined him and they didn't look real happy about him being dissed.

A tired Saint asked, "You got a phone?"

"Of course."

"Hand it here. I'll give you all the facts you need to know."

He gave the phone to Saint who dialed, then waited for the call to go through. Then he said into the phone, "This is St. Martin. Is he there?"

Narice watched curiously and so did the police and federal agents. Saint spoke to the person on the line saying, "Got a bunch of Hoovers here who want to talk to you."

He handed the phone to the agent and the man immediately barked, "Who is this?"

Where earlier he'd been beet red, he was now pale as the moon in January. "Yes, Mr. President," he croaked. "Yes, sir. We will certainly give Mr. St. Martin whatever assistance he requires."

The stunned-looking agent gave the phone back to Saint. Grinning, Saint said into the phone, "Thank you, sir. I think everyone's on board now." Then his face lost its grin. "Right now?"

Saint looked to Narice. "But sir. I have plans, I— Yes, sir. I will be in L.A. by midnight."

Narice sighed. She knew what that meant.

A grim Saint clicked off, handed the phone to the agent, then he and Narice walked with Portia to the chopper.

While they walked, Narice asked, "Another pressing engagement?"

He nodded. "I have to be in L.A. by midnight. He's doing a fundraiser there but wants to congratulate me personally. He and The Majesty went to undergrad together. When she needed help, he sent me."

Narice tried real hard not to let her disappointment show.

"You can grab a ride with Portia. I'll have one of the cops get me back to Lily. I'll mail you your stuff."

"Thanks."

He pulled her into his arms and while holding her tight against his heart, whispered, "I didn't want us to end like this."

Fighting tears, she lied, "It's okay."

He looked down into her face, "I'll come to Baltimore to see you as soon as I can."

She nodded.

He hugged her close again, "We'll talk when I see you."

"Stay safe."

"You too"

Portia cleared her throat. "The Majesty's getting impatient. Narice, if you're ready?"

She wasn't, but she had no choice. She looked around for her aunt. Camille was standing out of the way of the rotors, watching silently. Beside her was Mr. Bewick. Now Narice knew who'd alerted law enforcement. When her eyes met her aunt's, Camille inclined her head almost imperceptibly, then walked back towards her house.

Narice wanted to talk to her but Portia was waiting. Narice touched Saint's bearded cheek one last time in farewell, then got on board. The dogs moved over so she could find a place to sit, and then the chopper was lifting off. With her face pressed to the window, and her heart aching, Narice watched Saint until he turned into a dot on the ground.

Nineteen

Portia took Narice to the Atlanta airport. From there, Narice caught a plane home to Baltimore. After a costly cab ride from BWI, she walked into her well-furnished condo around eleven P.M. and fell exhausted onto her blue sofa. She thanked the Lord for getting her home in one piece. Saint's face flashed across her mind's eye and she let herself linger on his memory for a long melancholy moment, then set him aside. The first thing she wanted was a long hot soak in a bubble-filled tub, followed by a cool glass of her finest merlot. Taking off her hikers, she stripped as she walked and by the time she made it up the stairs to the second floor she was naked. Turning on the spigots and jets in the tub, she'd just padded over to the linen closet to get a towel when the phone rang. It seemed like an eternity since she'd heard a phone ring and it took her a moment to recognize it and to answer, "Hello."

"Hey, angel."

The sound of his soft voice made her melt down the wall until she reached the carpeted floor of her bedroom. "Hey, yourself. Did you get your arm taken care of?"

"Yeah."

"Are you on the way to L.A.?"

"No, still in Georgia waiting for the plane that's picking me up. You get home okay?"

Narice couldn't believe how much she missed him. "Yes."

"Miss you."

Her heart swelled in response to his soft declaration. "I miss you, too."

"Just wanted to tell you that."

"Thanks."

Silence.

Then he said, "Plane's here. I have to go."

"Okay."

"I'll call you soon."

"Okay."

"Bye, angel."

"Bye, Cyclops."

He chuckled, and was gone.

Her belongings came a few days later. Included was the quilt, which he'd had framed. The note inside said simply: *For you. S.* Tears in her eyes, she hung the beautiful black-framed piece on her bedroom wall.

On Monday, she returned to school and welcomed the staff and students back from the holiday break. No one knew anything about her activities during her time off other than she'd gone to Detroit to handle her father's funeral, and she kept it that way. No one needed to know that she'd fallen in love, too.

Narice spent the rest of that first week wondering about him. More than a few times she found herself staring at the phone on the desk in her office willing it to ring, but it didn't. She told herself to stop tripping and get on with her life.

But she couldn't. Watching the news a week later, she saw a story on Nagal. There was The Majesty in her flowing purple and black robes holding the Eye. Narice smiled. The election was underway and according to the CNN reporter, The Majesty's block of candidates were being projected as the winners.

Narice spent the rest of the evening working on school paperwork, then went to bed. As always, after she said her prayers, Saint came to mind. She wondered where he was, what he might be doing, and if he planned to be in Nagal for the post election celebrations. She still hadn't heard from him and for a woman who'd always been in control of her world, she didn't know what to do with a broken heart.

That night around two A.M., Saint was in a chair in the corner of Narice's bedroom watching her sleep.

The alarm on her door had been easy to bypass, and he made a note to himself to get her a better one. He'd been thinking about her so much, he had to see her, thus this late-night visit. Not calling her was tearing him up because what they had had been special. However, he was having trouble figuring out what to do. On the one hand, there was his job. Saint liked flitting around the world saving the day, but on the other hand, not having Narice in his life was killing him. He'd been so sure that once he became accustomed to her being gone the pain of missing her would ease; it hadn't. In fact, it was worse than ever. As time passed and his days without her turned into one week and then two, he began to dream about her, waking up hard and ready to play *Make the Principal Hot.* He couldn't cook, eat, or do anything without thinking about her.

He stood then. It was time to go. He forced himself to stay where he was and not approach the bed, because if he moved any closer he wouldn't be able to resist the intense urge to wake up her and kiss her until the were both old and gray. Instead he reached into his coat and withdrew the rose he'd brought with him. Placing it and the picture he'd brought along too down on the chair, a tight-lipped Saint left the room and exited the house the way he'd come.

Narice awakened that next morning and swore she smelled Saint's cologne. Deciding that was nothing more than wishful thinking, she got up to get ready for church. The sight of the dark red rose on the chair made her stop. Unable to believe her eyes, she approached it slowly. Her hands shaking she picked it up. On the chair was a color photo of a cheetah. Narice brought the rose to her lips and let the tears run freely down her cheeks.

By the third week, Portia had had enough. At breakfast that morning, she asked Saint, "Are you going to call Narice or not? Your moping is upsetting the dogs."

Saint looked down at Jesse lying on the floor. The dog looked back at him with such a sad face, he reached down and rubbed her neck.

Portia said, "Call her."

"What if she doesn't want to talk to me?"

"What if she does? For an international super spy you're acting awfully indecisive. She must be really getting to you."

Saint didn't lie, Narice had turned his world upside down.

Portia passed him the bowl of scrambled eggs. "Your sister called this morning while you were out with the dogs. She's worried about you, too. She says you haven't called her in weeks and your brother is waiting on your report on the SUV to send to GM."

He ran his hands over his hair. "I'll call them later in the week." He got up from the table.

Portia looked confused. "Aren't you going to eat?"

"Nope." He headed towards the door.

"Where are you going?"

"To see the President and then to Baltimore."

A smiling Portia spread her homemade strawberry

jam on her toast and began humming the Wedding March.

Saint stood in the Oval Office. Even for someone as jaded as he, the room and the history always overwhelmed and humbled him.

The President, a former five-star army general and the first African American to hold the job, finished his phone call and looked up. "That was The Majesty. She and her cabinet are settling in. She sends her regards." The President studied him for a moment. "You look grimmer than usual, St. Martin. What can I do for you?"

"I need to resign, sir."

"Excuse me? Why? You're one of the best in the business."

Saint was silent for a moment, then said, "I think—no change that. I *know,* I'm in love, sir."

The President's brown eyes widened. "With whom?"

"Narice Jordan. The Keeper's daughter."

The President surveyed Saint for another few moments. "You know, the First Lady had her niece all picked out for you."

Saint allowed a small smile to peek through. "I know, sir. Please send your wife my regrets."

The President smiled. "Are you sure about resigning, son?"

"Yes, sir. I am. I can't live without her, and to have her I have to step away from my covert life."

"Can I still call on you for jobs like the one you handled in Belize?"

Saint nodded. "No more coups or assassinations, though."

"I understand. Okay, soldier. I accept the resignation. I'm not happy about it, but I understand love. If I had to choose between love for my wife and love for the country, she'd win hands down."

"Thank you, sir."

"Go with God, St. Martin."

Saint nodded and headed for the door.

"Oh, St. Martin."

Saint turned.

"I expect you to bring Ms. Jordan to see me sometime soon. I want to meet this Wonder Woman."

Saint smiled. "Yes, sir."

Narice was seated in her office going over some budget items when her secretary Juanita stuck her head in the door and said, "There's a piece of eye candy out here asking to see you."

Narice looked up from the figures. "Eye candy?"

"Yep. Says he's here to take you to Tahiti."

Narice's heart began to race and she had to catch her breath before she could regroup and say calmly, "Send him in."

Juanita gave her a sly smile then disappeared.

In the two seconds she had while waiting, Narice debated whether to meet him standing or sitting behind her desk. She opted to stand and was in front of the windows with her back to the room when Juanita came back.

Narice turned and said, "Thank you, Juanita."

Juanita closed the door softly after her exit and Narice's eyes met Saint's. The sight of him made her jaw drop. He had on a suit! "Where are you on your way to? You look good."

He checked himself out. "I do clean up pretty good, don't I?"

"Yes, you do." Narice couldn't believe he was here. She also couldn't believe how seeing him filled her heart, even if she hadn't heard from him in almost a month, but she kept that to herself, for now.

"So," she said, "have a seat. How are Portia and the dogs?"

He sat and they spent a few moments chit-chatting about the dogs, then Narice said, "The police in Detroit called me. Ridley's been charged with first-degree murder. He'll go to trial sometime this summer."

"That's good news. Heard anything from your aunt?"

"No, but I'm going back down there when school's out and see if I can't help her get her place fixed up. I know she's not going to move." Narice smiled looking at him in the suit. "I can't get over you in that suit."

He met her eyes. "I wore it so you'll know I'm serious."

"About what?"

"Loving you."

Narice went stock-still, then her hands went to her mouth.

"Before I talk to you about the other reason I'm here, I want to say two things. First. I apologize for not calling. I had some issues to deal with, but once I figured I can't live without you, the issues were resolved."

Narice was so outdone she couldn't speak.

He chuckled. "Whoa, you speechless. That's different."

She wanted to sock him. "Go on," she told him with a smile in her eyes.

"Secondly. I quit my job. Well, the gun-carrying parts of it anyway."

Narice couldn't believe her ears. "Why?"

"Because I want to marry you, sidekick."

Narice was really speechless now.

"She's still speechless, folks."

"Serve you right if I say yes."

"Then say it."

She looked into his shade-covered eyes and whispered, "Oh yes, Saint. Yes, I'll marry you."

His grin filled the room. He stood, "So, do I get a kiss now?" He held out his arms and she went to him.

The kiss left her breathless and him wanting so much more, he asked, "Do you get recess?"

She looked up at him and chuckled. "Recess? Why?"

He nibbled her ear. "Thought we'd get in a quick round of *Make the Principal Hot* before I kidnap you and take you to Tahiti."

She laughed, then reached around him and hit the button on her intercom. "Juanita. If anybody asks, I'm unavailable until after recess."

"Yes, ma'am," Juanita responded, sounding amused.

Narice's smile met Saint's and he pulled her into his arms, saying, "I love you, angel."

She could hear his heart beating against her cheek. She said the only thing that could be said, "And I love you too, Cyclops."

Author's Note

I hope you enjoyed Saint and Narice's story. Underground Railroad quilts and the fascinating part they played in the path to freedom are finally being recognized for their unique history and value. One of the best books I've found on the topic is *Hidden in Plain View: A Secret Story of Quilts and the Underground Railroad,* by Jacqueline L. Tobin and Raymond G. Dobard, PhD. For readers who want to share the story of these quilts with the youngsters in their lives, please check out: *Sweet Clara and the Freedom Quilt,* by Deborah Hopkinson.

In closing, I'd like to give special thanks to Ava and Gloria for organizing another slam-dunk PJ Party, and to *Black Issues Book Review* for their support of this wonderful event. Keep reading everybody, and I'll see you next time.

Blackboard bestselling author

BEVERLY JENKINS

THE EDGE OF DAWN

0-06-054067-2/$6.99 US/$9.99 Can

Before federal agents can interrogate her about her father's brutal murder and a stolen diamond, Narice Jordan is wrested from their grasp by a shadowy figure. Narice isn't sure if this dark, handsome stranger is her kidnapper . . . or her savior.

THE EDGE OF MIDNIGHT

0-06-054066-4/$6.99 US/$9.99 Can

Sarita Grayson is desperate, that's the only explanation for her late night rendezvous with a bag of stolen diamonds. But now a covert government agent stands between her and a clean getaway . . .

And don't miss these Romances—

A CHANCE AT LOVE
0-06-05229-0/$6.99 US/$9.99 Can

BEFORE THE DAWN
0-380-81375-0/$6.99 US/$9.99 Can

ALWAYS AND FOREVER
0-380-81374-2/$6.99 US/$9.99 Can

THE TAMING OF JESSI ROSE
0-380-79865-4/$6.99 US/$9.99 Can

THROUGH THE STORM
0-380-79864-6/$6.99 US/$9.99 Can

TOPAZ
0-380-78660-5/$6.99 US/$9.99 Can

NIGHT SONG
0-380-77658-8/$6.99 US/$9.99 Can

Available wherever books are sold
or please call 1-800-331-3761 to order.

AuthorTracker
www.AuthorTracker.com

JEN 0804

Brown Skin

Dr. Susan Taylor's Prescription for Flawless Skin, Hair, and Nails

SUSAN C. TAYLOR, M.D.,

Director, Skin of Color Center, New York City

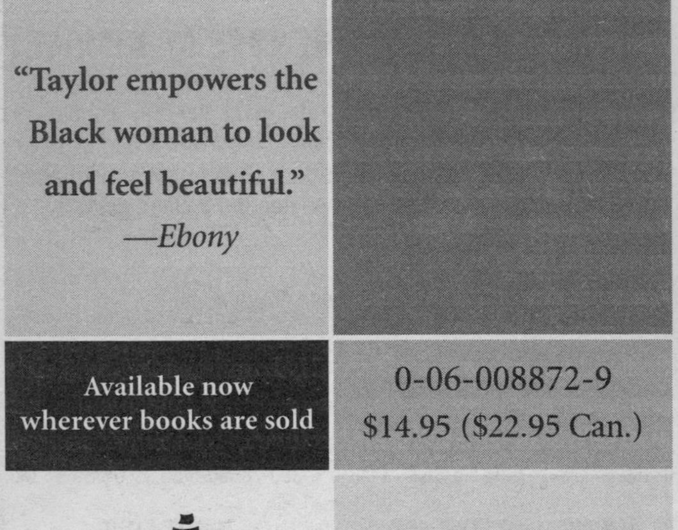

AuthorTracker

Don't miss the next book by your favorite author. Sign up now for AuthorTracker by visiting www.AuthorTracker.com

www.drsusantaylor.net

BSK 0504